She didn't want to stay alone.

But the thought of Matt in the tiny bed alongside her aroused a much more elemental fear than the one she had just been experiencing.

He felt her stiffen, and chuckled softly. "Don't worry. The thought of making love with you isn't exactly repugnant—you're a beautiful, desirable woman. But I don't shoot sitting ducks."

She jerked erect and withdrew her hand quickly. What a typically male way to express it! As though she were the prey and he the hunter! "Don't be too sure you would have had the opportunity," she said stiffly. "I'm grateful for your concern, but it's nearly morning. I'll be all right alone now."

"Probably," he agreed, rising from the bench and looking down at her, a half smile on his lips. "But I'll stick around just to make sure."

Dear Reader,

Once again we have a lineup of compelling, passionate and impossible-to-put-down books for you. If excitement is the hallmark of Silhouette Intimate Moments, you'll find lots of it this month.

Lee Magner's *Sutter's Wife* was especially well-received when it was published last spring. Now Grant Macklin, introduced to readers in that book, has a story—and a romance—of his own. In *The Dragon's Lair*, he meets a woman who is his perfect complement, but neither one of them may live long enough to achieve "happily ever after" unless they can catch the killer stalking them. Jeanne Stephens's *Hiding Places* proves once again why its author is so highly regarded by those who like a little suspense mixed with their romance. The lush island setting of St. Thomas is deceptive, for it is against this seemingly peaceful background that a life-and-death drama is played out for Darrin Boyle and the woman he knows as Cathy Prentiss. Round out the month with Marilyn Cunningham's *Enchanted Circle*, a tale of centuries-old rituals with the power to threaten today, and Linda Turner's *Moonlight and Lace*, a story of two people who are given a second chance to find the love they missed the first time around.

In months to come, look for new books by Emilie Richards, Linda Shaw, Barbara Faith and all the other authors who make Silhouette Intimate Moments so special.

Leslie J. Wainger
Senior Editor and Editorial Coordinator

MARILYN CUNNINGHAM

Enchanted Circle

SILHOUETTE·INTIMATE·MOMENTS®

Published by Silhouette Books New York

America's Publisher of Contemporary Romance

SILHOUETTE BOOKS
300 East 42nd St., New York, N.Y. 10017

ISBN: 0-373-07355-0

First Silhouette Books printing October 1990

Printed in the U.S.A.

Books by Marilyn Cunningham

Silhouette Intimate Moments

Someone To Turn To #334
Enchanted Circle #355

MARILYN CUNNINGHAM

lives in the high country of Idaho, which she often uses for the settings of her books. She lives twelve miles from the nearest habitation, and interruptions to her writing include the herd of elk that parade by her front window, the coyotes that pad down her driveway and the Canada geese that stop by the pond behind her cabin on their yearly migrations. When not writing, she hikes unmarked mountain trails, works in the garden with her own hero, John, or rides her quarter horse accompanied by her two poodles, Andre and Denali.

When nature palls—which it can, with snow drifting up around the cabin eaves and the gravel road blocked with drifts—she travels to visit her daughter in California, or explores Alaska with her two sons. She has used both places as settings for her novels.

ENCHANTED CIRCLE

Drifting through the cool green world of shadow,
through shifting fragments of ancient dreams
that undulate and cling, then disappear
into the fathomless depths
like fronds of seaweed, barely glimpsed,
her body is aware of warmth and light.
Shattering the surface of time,
she emerges,
beginning the endless cycle.

Chapter 1

She pulled the battered camper off the gravel road onto a wide spot by the edge of the lake, braked and took a deep breath. Relaxing for almost the first time since she'd left Boise more than eighty miles back she stretched luxuriously, deliberately loosening each tense muscle. If getting here was half the fun, she didn't have much to look forward to.

On the road map, which she had consulted before leaving California, eighty miles had seemed a reasonable distance, but the cartographer must have measured "as the crow flies." She hadn't counted on a narrow twisting road that wound endlessly through deep canyons, then climbed the sides of granite cliffs that a mountain goat would have had difficulty traversing.

She swung her long legs out of the vehicle and steadied herself as the heels of her sandals sank into the soft moss. Standing quite still, she raised her hand to lift her heavy golden hair off her neck and took a deep breath. The breeze from the lake held a subtle excitement, carrying the scent of spring-flowering syringa and crisp pine, and she turned her head toward it, lifting her face and closing her eyes. Her pulse quickened with an answering excitement. She was here, and she would soon know whether the trip was a colossal waste of time or the key to her future.

Opening her eyes, Brianna Royce looked around at her bucolic surroundings, frowning slightly. Her first instinctive excitement was followed by a faint uneasiness, but there was nothing she could see to account for it. To her right, the lake stretched away into the blue distance, its surface shimmering slightly in the breeze, but still serene enough to reflect the snow cone of a mountain on the far side. To her left, the forest rose abruptly against a mountain, a dark fortress of pine and fir with an occasional birch punctuating the shadows with a blaze of green light. Set back among the trees was a scattering of weathered frame houses, blending almost imperceptibly with the forest.

A slight tremor ran down her spine, and she tightened her lips. This place seemed somehow familiar, an obvious impossibility since she'd lived most of her life in California, leaving the state only to accompany her father on his summer photography trips. His commissions by institutions such as the National Geographic Society had necessitated trips to a bewildering variety of places—New Zealand to photograph the Maori, the Philippines to photograph the Stone Age Tasaday, the Kalahari desert where the primitive peoples of the region made that barren wasteland their home. But Idaho? Never.

Perhaps the uneasy feeling was caused by her sense of isolation. She seemed to be at the end of nowhere.

She scrutinized the line of frame houses, aware of a slight feeling of disappointment. When her father had told her of a little known tribe of Indians who lived in the vastness of the Idaho mountain country she had envisioned more primitive surroundings. These houses looked just about like any other rural dwellings. The huge mounted disk ahead even appeared to be a satellite dish situated on a slight knoll!

Then she smiled briefly at her naïveté. Here she was, firmly rooted in the twentieth century, approximately eighty miles from a cosmopolitan capitol city. She shouldn't expect Stone Age savages.

For an instant, she wished she had gone with her parents to Europe, but that had hardly been feasible. Her father, having spent much of his married life away from home in out-of-the-way places, had agreed with her mother that taking a real vacation together had been long overdue. She couldn't blame her mother for wanting to tour the castles and cathedrals of Europe, instead of camping in the isolated Idahoan outback. She had also sensed that her parents had longed for the opportunity to renew the romance in their lives, and the presence of an adult daughter, even a beloved adult daughter, wasn't required.

She couldn't afford the time anyway. It was important to put the summer to maximum use. She needed the best possible source of material for her Ph.D., which she was obtaining in anthropology—right now, that was the focus of her life. She had decided to collect the myths and folklore of primitive tribes, but so much work had been done in the field that it was hard not to cover old ground. To make the impact she wanted to, she had to adopt an unusual approach and find unique material.

Her dad had suggested the Daynew Indians. She had never heard of them, but he had picked up an old journal at an estate sale many years ago in which the tribe was mentioned and he had been intrigued. He had nearly forgotten it, until she had mentioned she wished to study and research a little-known tribe for her thesis. As far as he knew, there had been very little written about the tribe's history, and it could be her big chance to make a name for herself.

Brianna's introductory investigation of the tribe hadn't seemed terribly exciting. Articles in history texts and anthropology journals were not very detailed, but the Daynew were apparently a small branch of the Shoshoni. The last mention of them she could locate was an article written more than twenty years ago. The author had found them extremely primitive with a low level of culture.

When she brought this to her father's attention, he shook his head. "Maybe," he said doubtfully. "But there is something unusual about them. This journal was written by an old mountain man who apparently lived with them a while. He made only a few references—but he described their facial characteristics. They didn't sound like Shoshoni to me."

She had read the journal and had been intrigued, although entries about the Daynew were tantalizingly brief. Mostly the writer chronicled his own hunting and trapping, but the few references to the tribe indicated they were more advanced than the other articles implied. Whatever the case, she was in luck. Most tribes even verging on the primitive had been studied to death, and there was surprisingly little written about the Daynew. Could the anthropologists have been wrong in classifying them? She'd felt a surge of excitement.

She'd had no trouble formulating her main proposition for her thesis—it was the resolution that was difficult, and for that she needed a large body of data. Always fascinated by myths, she had begun to wonder long ago if there was a common thread in them all over the world. Were the myths similar because the human race evolved in one spot, and then dispersed all over the world, taking their myths with them? Or did facing the elemental mysteries of life and death trigger a similar response in the human brain? And, of course, there was the theory of racial memory.

Brianna shook her head, laughing at herself for the excitement that always engulfed her when she thought of her subject. Maybe this summer would enable her to contribute a little to the controversy—she certainly had her own ideas!

Reaching back into the vehicle, Brianna picked up the journal her father had given her, turned it in her hand and gazed curiously at the faded lettering. Caleb Stuart was a mountain man who had thought the Daynew unusual, and he should know—he was familiar with many of the intermountain tribes. The Daynew were such a small group and had been so isolated when all the other American tribes were being identified and conquered that they might have escaped the main brunt of "progress." She didn't know how westernized they had become, but since very little, if anything, had been documented about their myths or oral traditions, it was possible she had found virgin territory.

Her pulse quickened. She was here, and she would soon know.

She glanced at the hand drawn map she had been given when she stopped at the forest service office in Boise, and then walked across the gravel road toward a little frame house. There was no number but she recognized the signs she had been told to look for. Dark green paint, a cedar shingled roof, uneven rock foundation. Carved on a rough log to one side of the door was an odd looking cross upon which a series of linear marks had been scratched. This had to be the home of Tom West, the man she'd been referred to as leading elder of the Daynew.

For an instant she hesitated, wondering if she should take a more oblique approach, obtain an introduction, perhaps. Then she squared her chin. There should be no problem. She had to start sometime, and there was no time like the present.

She took a deep breath, unconsciously smoothing her oversize white cotton shirt along her hip, then pushed her long hair back from her face. The first thing to do was establish rapport. Gain his confidence. She walked up the dirt path, stepped onto the small wooden porch, raised her hand and knocked.

She heard the sound of heavy footsteps and then the door swung inward, revealing a tall, imposing man of about sixty dressed in jeans and a blue denim shirt. His hair was dark brown and cut haphazardly to clear his collar; the old leader's large features appeared to have been carved from rock, and his wide set, light brown eyes met hers squarely.

He waited, his expression neutral. Not obviously hostile, but certainly not welcoming.

"Tom West?"

"Yes."

Not much of a conversationalist, either. He appeared ready to wait as long as it took. She gave him her brightest, most ingratiating smile, the one her father said was guaranteed to melt granite. "I'm Brianna Royce. I wonder if I could talk to you."

He hesitated before moving back a step and motioning her inside, then waved her to a chair, his face revealing nothing. "Please sit down."

She glanced quickly around the small room; it was neat and clean and disappointingly like any other rural American household. Crisp green curtains hung at the two windows, a brown hooked rug lay on the plank floor, and the furniture looked comfortable. The couch and matching chair were of serviceable tweed, the coffee table might have been found in any department store, and yes, there was a TV in the far corner of the room.

"Will you have something to drink?" he asked courteously. "Some tea? Coffee?"

"Thank you. I'd enjoy some tea." She watched him walk through a door into what was apparently the kitchen, and she used the time to reevaluate her approach. He was so westernized she wasn't exactly sure how to bring up the subject of interviews. When he returned she accepted the tea, took a sip of the fragrant, steaming brew, and made up her mind. She might as well be direct.

As he sat down across from her, she swallowed nervously, somewhat taken aback by his apparent lack of interest in the purpose of her visit. "I do appreciate your seeing me," she finally said. "I'm told you may be able to help me."

He nodded gravely. "How may I do that?"

"They told me in Boise that you are an elder in the Daynew tribe...."

Still he was silent, and she became a little flustered. "I came here because I'm interested in the Daynew...."

Had she imagined his sudden closed expression?

"In what way?" he asked gently.

"I think you must have a very interesting history," she said, "and there has really been very little written about you."

"There has been enough," he replied. "And I'm afraid we're really not very interesting."

"Oh, but you are!"

"Are you just curious, Miss Royce?"

She didn't imagine it—there was steel in his voice. "No, it's not just idle curiosity." She took a deep breath. "I'm working on a Ph.D. in anthropology. I'd like to talk to you about the history of your people, their stories, myths—"

She broke off as he raised a silencing hand. "We don't talk about our history." His tone was quiet, polite—and very firm.

"But why not!" She had thought she might have to take a few minutes to persuade him, but she hadn't expected to be cut off so abruptly. "Surely you realize how important it is to have a written record of your past. For your children, for—"

He half smiled. "So we have been told."

"Oh." Disappointment colored her voice. Apparently she was too late—he had already been approached by anthropologists, and might have had unfortunate experiences with them. But if so, very little had been published. She had researched well, and had found only one or two articles about the Daynew, and those were surprisingly succinct.

"You mean it's already been done," she said slowly. "Your oral history has already been recorded?"

He shook his head, his eyes as hard as obsidian. "No. It hasn't been done, and it won't be done. We consider our beliefs private, Miss Royce, and our history concerns no one but us." His voice was not unkind, but the tone sounded very final.

"But it *should* be recorded! Even if you are a branch of the Shoshoni, there are bound to be differences..."

He raised a dark eyebrow. "You think we're Shoshoni?"

"Well, from what I've read..."

Now he smiled, as though to soften his words. "Don't believe everything you read, Miss Royce." He stood, obviously dismissing her.

His words only piqued her curiosity. Why was he so reticent if there was nothing to tell? "But I wouldn't be any trouble at all!" she implored. "If I could just talk to you for a few minutes!" She continued to babble as he escorted her through the door and out onto the porch. The click of the door echoed as it closed very firmly behind her.

Brianna's shoulders slumped as she walked back down the path. She had handled that meeting as if she were a complete amateur. Perhaps she should have written first, done something to prepare him for her request. But she had never expected any opposition; the other groups she had talked to had been flattered by her interest, eager to tell her everything she wanted to know. She'd supposed the Daynew would be the same. Obviously she was wrong. If Tom West was an example, he and his brethren were so civilized that they had probably been the target of all types of observers, and might even feel exploited.

Were they even what she wanted? The frame houses, the articulate Native American, all pointed to the fact that these people were very much a part of the modern world.

But they had been primitive at one time. There was the article written by Phillip Jones, the anthropologist who had visited them only twenty years ago. He ha[illegible]sidered them backward. Centuries before, they had lived a simple hunting and gathering life, later developing into a more sophisticated society—Caleb Stuart's journal proved it.

Her cheeks flushed with anger at her ineptness as she opened the door to the camper and swung up into the seat. She slammed the door in frustration, but it didn't help. She had mishandled the entire interview. She was a twenty-six-year-old scientist who had charged in with the unprofessionalism of a schoolgirl. What was needed here was a little diplomacy, a subtler approach. She'd take her time, get to know someone, then broach the subject of their legends and folklore. As she should have done in the first place.

She made a three-point turn on the shoulder of the road and started driving toward the little town of Hope that she'd noticed a few miles back. At least, she thought, a wry smile curving her full lips, it was marked on the map as a town. When she had driven through it she had noticed only two or three buildings. But she could get information there, and decide on her next move.

She could also ask about a place to stay. Even though she was prepared to live in the camper if nothing convenient was available, the cramped quarters wouldn't be her first choice. If she was going to be here awhile, she'd try to seek more comfortable accommodations. It looked as though she were—she certainly wasn't going to give up. If the only thing written about the Daynew was the sparse material she had managed to locate, their story held promise for a real coup, and her thesis would make her a household name in anthropological circles. That would certainly be a help in job hunting.

Brianna pulled up outside a low frame building whose weathered wooden sign proclaimed it was Hope Mercantile. She wondered idly who had named such a forlorn-looking place Hope. There were several pickups parked in a haphazard manner by the door, two gas pumps, and a brown dog. Two signs flashed in the window—OPEN and BEER. The town social center, she decided. She stepped from the van, walked a few short steps and opened the door.

Inside she stood quite still, holding her breath as she surveyed the small room. There was quite a crowd, and it consisted entirely of men; some sprawled at the scattered tables, others leaned against a short counter, and almost everyone held a frosty bottle of beer. Similarly dressed in work shirts, jeans, and heavy boots, they all looked dusty and sweaty. Their shouts and raucous laughter seemed to bounce off the walls, doubling the din.

As she hesitated in the doorway the noise gradually abated, as one man after another turned to look at the door. Finally there was a moment of absolute silence as they all became aware of her presence. Under their intense scrutiny, she had an unreasonable impulse to turn and run.

Then she relaxed as she saw that the person behind the counter was a woman. A comfortable-looking woman, probably in her mid-thirties, with dark hair pulled back from a pleasant face. She wore a blue cotton, short-sleeved blouse tucked into tight jeans and appeared relaxed and competent.

Brianna felt ridiculously overdressed in her narrow trousers of light beige cotton, open sandals, and oversize shirt. Her outfit had seemed fine for travel when she left Boise—it was light and comfortable, and didn't wrinkle easily. Now she felt as though she had arrived at a party and was the only one in costume.

The woman gave her a cheery smile. "Can I help you, miss?"

"Yes, I think so." Straightening her shoulders and taking a deep breath, Brianna moved over to the counter and slid onto a stool.

The tall, powerfully built man sitting at the end of the bar didn't appear to notice her arrival, but anyone who knew Matt Stuart wouldn't have been fooled for a minute. Although his posture was indolent, his lean body relaxed in the high-backed bar stool, and his bronzed hand curved loosely around the light beer, his deep blue eyes were completely alert and aware. But not even someone who knew him well would have guessed that the sight of the woman hesitating in the doorway, the sunlight outlining her slender form in a soft halo, had very nearly riveted him to his stool.

From under thick black lashes, partially lowered now to hide his reaction, he surveyed her carefully as she sank onto the stool. Her beauty had gone straight to his chest like the shock of a sledgehammer, and it left him momentarily unsure of himself. What was a woman like her doing here? She was definitely a stranger, and very few strangers ever made their way to Hope. It wasn't exactly on the beaten track.

Slowly he started his thorough appraisal with the top of her well-shaped head, approving of the way her heavy golden hair fell in waves around her slender shoulders. Sun-streaked hair, he saw, immediately knowing it would feel heavy and silken in his hand. Her body was slender and well proportioned, and her breasts, under her gauzy white shirt, appeared high and firm. A silk scarf of royal blue accentuated her narrow waist, and her hips, covered by the thin material of her slacks, had just enough of a sweet curve to leave him in no doubt that she was a desirable woman.

He drew his gaze away, aware of a definite tightening in his groin. Better take a good look at her face; it might be safer.

He saw now that she wasn't classically beautiful, as he had thought at first glance. Her features were too strongly sculpted, with a straight nose and a generous, coral mouth a little too wide to be perfectly proportioned. Her lightly tanned skin was flawless, glowing with health. A broad Nordic face with high cheekbones, wide-spaced, intelligent eyes.

Those eyes. His throat felt suddenly dry. Tiger eyes. As her gaze swept around the room, he saw that they were a pale gold color, and that the irises were rimmed with black. He'd never seen anything like them.

He took a long, slow swig from his beer, grinning inwardly at his unexpected reaction. It had been a long time since just the sight of a woman affected him like this. Obviously he needed to get to town more often!

He saw Margie shrug, realized the woman had been asking a question, and eavesdropped unashamedly.

"Gosh, I dunno." Margie shook her head as she expertly uncapped a bottle of beer and handed it across the bar to a waiting masculine hand. "There aren't any motels I know of within twenty or thirty miles. But maybe Matt can tell you." She turned to the tall man and gave him an inquiring look.

Matt slid from his stool and sauntered toward the two women, a heavy dark eyebrow raised inquiringly. "Problems?"

Margie waved a plump hand toward Brianna. "Matt, perhaps you can help this lady—you know the area better than I do. She's looking for a place to stay." Apparently feeling she had done her duty, Margie moved off to the end of the bar and began chatting with one of the men.

"You won't find much around Hope," Matt said, regarding her with open curiosity. He stuck one booted foot on the rail and hooked one thumb in the band of his worn jeans. "By the way, I'm Matt Stuart. But you can call me Matt." He gave her a grin that flashed strong white teeth.

He watched wariness grow in her eyes, and knew his frank interest must have shown in his expression. He tried to make his grin as boyish and innocent as several women had told him it was. They had also told him it was criminally misleading.

"Let's get a table, and I'll see if I can help you."

Brianna threw a perturbed glance at Margie, and he knew he had been right—she felt his awareness of her.

Margie gave her a reassuring grin. "Don't worry about Matt, honey. If he lays a hand on you, I'll hit him over the head." She brandished a bottle, and the roomful of men guffawed. Not looking particularly reassured, Brianna let herself be led to a table near the far side of the room.

He seated her, then pulled out a chair and hooked the heels of his western boots over the rungs. Propping his elbows on the oilcloth-covered table and cradling his beer in his hands, he gave her another wide boyish grin, guaranteed to disarm.

"Now, how about telling me why you're here, and then we'll figure out how to help you."

Brianna hesitated, then gave him a facsimile of a warm, open smile. Nothing he did or said implied his interest was any more than casual, so why did she feel he was coming on strong? When he had stood by her at the bar she had been acutely aware of him and had seen in his eyes that he was assessing her. She had only wanted to ask a question, but he had smoothly taken charge, maneuvering her to a table, and seeming to take it for granted that she would follow his lead. She had to admit he had been perfectly polite, though; perhaps it was her own unexpected response to him that was making her unreasonable. Still, he did have that irritating masculine way of expecting her to put her problem in his capable hands.

She blushed faintly, a little unnerved at the thought. His hands did look capable. Strong, square, well formed, bronzed by sun and weather, they looked completely competent to do most anything.

The rest of him was equally impressive. Even sitting down, he looked powerful, exuding restless energy. His wide shoulders and broad chest pushed against the confines of his blue plaid shirt. The sleeves were rolled and his muscular forearms were deeply tanned with dark crisp hair shining through a coating of dust and perspiration. She wondered about that; his face, with the determined jaw and strong nose, was also covered with dust. Didn't Idahoans own showers?

As though reading her mind, he widened his grin. She saw that it was slightly crooked, and noticed for the first time the cleft in his square chin.

"I just got off work—besides, it's good Idaho soil." His eyes crinkled at the corners, and she saw that he was amused by her discomfiture. "You didn't tell me your name."

She had to get information from someone if she were ever going to accomplish her goal of ingratiating herself with the Daynew. She might have preferred to interrogate someone else, someone less threatening, but she was stuck. She twisted slightly on her chair. The force of this man's personality was keeping her on edge. Sexy was the word for him. If you cared for untamed, raw sex, she amended, which she definitely did not.

"Brianna Royce," she said finally.

He gave her a lazy smile. "Do you want a drink, Brianna Royce?'

"Uh—not right now, thanks." She liked the sound of his voice. It was deep and rich, resonating from deep within his chest. A quick prickle of something very like fear rippled through her, some intuition that she tried to suppress. She had come here to study primitive people and compared to the men she had known, this man certainly qualified.

"Okay. So you want a place to stay." His blue eyes were lit with interest, and he leaned toward her. "Why would anyone like you want to stay in Hope? Aren't you a long way from California?"

She jerked erect and gave him a surprised glance. "How do you know I'm from California?"

His grin was cheerful and a little mocking. "Easy. You could pose as the typical California golden girl. A sixties rock band recorded a song about women who look as you do."

"That makes me sound rather like a stereotype," she said slowly.

"Maybe. But a very attractive stereotype. Beautiful complexion, lightly tanned by the sun reflecting off the ocean. Sun-streaked hair from running on beaches. Clothes that look so casual, but weren't bought in any department store around here."

At the expression of astonishment on her face, his grin broadened. "Besides, I saw your California license plate."

"You certainly are articulate, Mr. Stuart," she said thinly. "And observant."

"Because I noticed you were beautiful?"

"No, of course not!" She was getting a little flustered. "Because you noticed my California plates."

"That's not all," he said cheerfully. "I have other great qualities. But back to you. If you are looking for a place to stay, you won't find it in Hope. Unless, of course," he said, his eyes dancing, "you'd like to stay at my place."

Her eyes narrowed. She had been right all along; he was making a play for her, and subtlety apparently wasn't one of those strong points he'd mentioned.

"No, thank you—I wouldn't dream of troubling you," she said dryly. "If there's no motel I can stay in my camper."

"You still haven't told me why you're here."

"'I'm not sure you'll understand. I study myths, folklore. I'm an anthropologist—" She stopped, embarrassed as she realized how patronizing she had sounded.

"An anthropologist! Is that anything like an astrologer?"

She raised her eyes quickly to see if he were serious. She couldn't tell. He had an innocent expression, but that might be a deceptive ploy.

"Not quite. I personally think there is very little validity to astrology, while an anthropologist—"

"Deals in fairy tales?"

"Not at all," she said stiffly. "I believe myths may be based on actual happenings, garbled a bit in the telling."

He smiled and shook his head. "It just doesn't seem like the kind of work a grown person would get involved in."

"Mr. Stuart—"

"Matt."

"Matt, are you one of those people who don't believe in anything you can't see or feel?"

"Probably. I prefer to use the word realist."

"I'm not sure reality is the completely known quality you think it is."

She met his gaze squarely, surprising a glint in his blue eyes. What were they arguing about? It was as though he had issued a challenge of some kind and she had blindly accepted it. She didn't even know him, and there was no reason she should try to change his philosophy.

She shrugged, turning her hands palms up in a gesture of conciliation, and smiled. "Perhaps we just come from two different cultures." Her voice was teasing. "Idaho macho—"

"And California kook?"

His intimation that she was a lightweight stung. "I nearly have my Ph.D. in anthropology, Mr. Stuart—"

"Matt. You keep forgetting."

"Matt. Believe me, I didn't get it by daydreaming."

"So what is a folklorist doing here?" His smile was lazy as he watched her closely across the narrow table.

"I want to study the Daynew Indians." She leaned toward him eagerly, her voice quickening as it always did when she discussed her pet subject. "I believe that myths are a key to understanding the past, and also the present! If I can show the similarities in cultural legends in this particular Native Idaho tribe and those in New Zealand, for example—"

She broke off as a shadow darkened his face. His expression, so open a moment before, had taken on a closed, wary look.

"What's the matter?' she asked.

"Nothing." His voice was carefully neutral. "I just can't imagine anyone coming all this way to study the fairy tales of the Daynew."

She started to protest his choice of words, then sighed. He probably had a closed mind. "I'm not having much luck. I s[illegible]Tom West, but he refused to talk to me. I thought if I could just get to know some of the others, gain their trust, I still might succeed."

His blue eyes were hard and wary. "So why don't you talk to them?"

She looked at him in confusion. What had happened to change him so quickly? He almost seemed to dislike her. "I was hoping you—or someone—would tell me where to find them and who would be best to talk to."

He turned and gestured to a group of men sitting at the nearest tab[illegible] might start with Joe," he said dryly. "Or Chad."

Startled, her gaze followed his pointing finger. The four men certainly would never have impressed her as being Native Americans. They looked about as esoteric as Matt did. Although, she saw, looking more closely, there was a certain similarity in their strong, well-defined features. Their hair varied from light brown to black, their eyes were hazel or brown—one man's eyes were a light gray—and their skin was no darker than Matt's.

"Don't they look like the noble Redman you expected to see?"

"Well, no. That is, I realize all Native Americans don't look alike. East Coast Iroquois don't look much like Navajo. But these—these men look just like anybody else."

"They are very nearly like anybody else," he said tersely. "Joe and I were on the same football team in high school. Oh, they still have problems—jobs are a little harder for them to get, and they stick to themselves a lot. But things are changing, getting better. And they don't need anybody patronizing them."

She ignored the last comment. "You seem to know a lot about them."

"I should. My family has lived here on the lake, side by side with the Daynew, since my great-grandfather made it over the mountains from Denver. Several of the men work for me."

"Work for you! What do you do?" She had assumed he was a laborer, perhaps a ranch hand or logger, and she dropped her eyes as she realized how condescending the thought was.

"I own Stuart Logging," he said, enjoying her confusion. "It's the only job in town, and most of the men in here belong to my crew. We'd just gotten off work, and were having a quick one when you came in."

She turned her face to his, excitement glowing in her golden eyes. "Then you can help me! You must have influence. You can talk to them, and convince them it would be okay for me to interview them!"

"I hardly think I can do that."

"Why not!" Disappointment made her voice sharper than she had intended.

"Because I don't think it's a good idea." His lips tightened and his eyes darkened to near indigo.

"But that's silly! What harm could there be in talking to people about their past?"

"You might ask Joe." He jerked his thumb toward one of the men at the table. "He was a teenager when that other anthropologist came through about twenty years ago."

Twenty years ago. He must be referring to the work Phil Jones had done here. "I think I read the work you're referring to," she said slowly. "It wasn't very thorough."

"Of course not, he only stayed two days. Hard to know how he came up with all his interesting conclusions," he said dryly.

"So it was brief. What harm could it do?"

"The stay? Not much. The article he wrote about it and sent to the local paper? Quite a lot."

"But that's unethical."

He raised a dark eyebrow. "So he was an unethical anthropologist."

So he had been teasing her all along, pretending he knew nothing about anthropologists. She met his eyes firmly. "Whatever happened before may have been unfortunate, but it has nothing to do with me. All I want to do is record some of their folklore. How could that hurt anything?"

He sighed. "I don't know. It just doesn't seem like a good idea. These people are a long way from being primitive. That article was wrong. They've had a hard time of it, but they are finally being assimilated into the mainstream. They don't need reminders of their past."

"Everyone should know about their roots."

"I'm not sure theirs aren't best forgotten. Most of them work for me but I can't really say I know them. They are still clannish, and there have been rumors about some of their former practices. Oh, nothing definite, but my grandfather used to hint about some rather peculiar things going on—"

"Your grandfather! That was years ago."

"Yes, it was. And the Daynew have become steadily more westernized. Live in western-type houses, wear western clothes, have telephones, TV." He frowned and glanced down at his hands lying motionless on the table, then raised his head and gave her a challenging stare. "I just think it's to their advantage to keep on the way they're going, not get hung up on the past."

"And you think my merely talking to them will cause that?"

He was silent and she watched his face, looking for some hint of what to say to convince him. This meant such a lot to her—how could she get him on her side? Should she flirt? She knew that her femininity had occasionally smoothed her way, although she had never knowingly used it. But no, that could never be her way. She was uncomfortably aware that there was some kind of current sizzling between her and Matt, a current of pure animal attraction, but she had never knowingly traded on her sex appeal, and she never would.

He must have seen the struggle going on in her face, because he gave her a surprisingly sweet smile. "But then, the decision isn't mine, is it? The Daynew have to decide."

She gave him a helpless look. "They already have. Tom West wouldn't even consider it, and he's the leader."

"Where did you hear that? The forest service in Boise, I suppose. They never did know much about the Daynew. The Daynew operate on consensus. The entire tribe makes the decision."

He paused, rubbing his hand thoughtfully across his jaw. "I will do one thing for you. I won't try to persuade them, but I'll set up a meeting, and you can plead your own case."

"Oh, thank you!" In her exuberance, she barely restrained herself from reaching out and squeezing his hands. Recovering her poise, she pushed back her chair and rose from the table. "You have been very helpful—Matt. And if there really is no motel near here, I'll just go find a place to camp for the night. Any suggestions?"

He told her where to drive to a forest service campground, only a couple of miles down the road, and then watched her gravely as she left the restaurant. He couldn't shake a faintly uneasy feeling as he saw her get into her camper and drive away. Somehow her arrival was going to cause problems.

The best thing to do was to set up the meeting and let the Daynew refuse to cooperate, as he was sure they would. He wouldn't even have gone that far, but there was something in the set of her jaw that convinced him she would barge ahead, with or without his help. This way, he would get it over with quickly, and she would be on her way.

That thought should have made him feel good, but somehow it didn't.

Chapter 2

Brianna sat bolt upright on the narrow bed and clutched the blanket to her constricted chest, her eyes staring sightlessly and wildly into darkness. Her heart thudded with painful intensity and her breath was coming in short gasps.

For a moment she was completely disoriented. The dream was still with her, intense and frightening, and she struggled to escape; then it was already receding into the depths of her unconscious. The details were gone, but what remained was familiar—alarmingly familiar. She'd had the dream recurrently when she was a child, and although it faded as she grew older, finally vanishing entirely, she had never forgotten the sheer terror of the experience.

It was always the same, she remembered, shuddering. The forest, dark and mysterious, alive somehow, pressed in on her, seeming to reach out to her with hungry, greedy hands. She was aware of people moving around her, and saw that a ritual of some kind was being performed. Somehow she knew that the ritual concerned her.

Faces, ghostly and anonymous, floated around her, but she was chillingly aware of one particular face. Half veiled, the eyes of the tall, commanding woman seemed to reach right inside her. The face was one she saw again and again, in every dream, although she was never sure who it was. Yet something told her she should have known.

Now, she pushed back the blanket and put her bare feet on the carpeted floor of the camper. Stepping softly to a window, she pushed aside a curtain and stared out into the night, gradually becoming aware of where she was.

In darkness, the place was unfamiliar, even scary. She had driven to the campground last night and found a space in which to park, but everything had looked different in the daylight. There was life: a few dogs, a child or two, some bustle and activity. Now the forest service campground was quiet, her parking place screened from other campsites by a wall of evergreens. In the faint light of the stars, the trees shone silver and ghostlike, immensely forbidding as they encircled her vehicle.

She relaxed a little, her pulse slowing as she sat back down on the narrow bed. Undoubtedly the strange surroundings were the reason the dream had reoccurred after all this time. Nevertheless, she was isolated in the forest, and although she knew there were a few campers somewhere nearby, she couldn't see them. She was alone. Vulnerable. A perfect stage for the old, frightening dreams.

She hadn't thought of them for so long, but at one time they had been a regular, frightening part of her life. Perhaps they had left her with a sense of mystery and awe that was at least partially responsible for her decision to study myths.

Shivering, she glanced at the luminous dial on her watch. It was still an hour or two before dawn. She should try to sleep. She had a long day to get through before she could see Matt and find out whether he had been able to schedule a meeting with the Daynew. Pulling the blanket over her head, she resolutely shut her eyes, but she was still wide-awake when dawn finally came.

* * *

Hours later Brianna sat on the bench by the picnic table, drumming her fingers on its worn plank surface as she debated whether it was time to leave the campground to try to find Matt. She had no idea when the meeting with the Daynew would be scheduled; he had said only that he would try to set one up. Presumably he had worked today, and she might find him at the Hope Mercantile if he and his crew made a habit of stopping off there every afternoon after work.

But maybe not—somehow, he didn't seem the type that required his daily beer, or always went along with the crowd. She'd had the definite impression that he liked to be in control at all times, and that didn't go with alcohol.

She herself had spent the day familiarizing herself with the country. She knew from reading her map that the Daynew village, a cluster of frame houses, was situated at the end of the county road. One could drive as far as the lake; the mountainous terrain beyond was traversed only by trails and logging roads.

She knew it—but actually driving to the end of the gravel and having to turn around made it much more immediate. Although her map might show she wasn't even a hundred miles from Boise, it didn't begin to convey the actual isolation she felt.

It was easy to see why the Daynew had remained relatively undisturbed. They were protected by nearly impassable terrain, and in addition there was nothing here that would motivate anyone to seek them out—or force them out. The land was too mountainous for anything except the most minimal farming, too elevated for any but an occasional cattle ranch. She supposed there were no minerals worth mining. Stuart Logging apparently provided their only means of economic survival since the days of hunting and gathering were over.

Matt Stuart. The name brought the image of the man forcefully to her mind, and she rested her chin in her hand and gazed unseeingly out across the lake. Away from the magnetism of his presence, she was able to assess him more coolly, and she was beginning to wonder if he weren't a little more complicated than his "good ol' boy" image indicated. She'd had the impression that he'd only gone as far as high school, but his manner of speaking was that of an educated man, and his blue eyes sparkled with a keen intelligence.

"Hi, there."

At the sound of the rich masculine voice Brianna jumped and swung partially around to see the visitor. She relaxed and eased into a smile as she recognized Matt standing about ten feet away, thumbs hooked in the band of his jeans, a broad smile on his bronzed face. He was, she thought, an incredibly sexy looking specimen, if you were interested only in the physical aspects of a man. Which, of course, she wasn't.

"I hope I didn't scare you."

She turned the rest of the way to face him fully, waiting for her pu[illegible] slow and her heart to get back where it belonged after his unexpected appearance.

"Of course not," she lied. "But you do have a way of sneaking up on a person."

He moved toward her with all the grace of a mountain animal completely at home in his environment. He was a physical type of person, she decided, vibrantly alive, his body toned and shaped by work and hard exercise. Watching him approach, she was aware of how snugly his jeans fit over his powerful thighs. His shirt was rolled at the sleeves, open at the neck, revealing deeply tanned skin. His dark hair was neatly combed, and looked slightly wet. She guessed he'd stopped by the house for a shower instead of going to the Hope Mercantile, and felt a little thrill of pure feminine pleasure. He'd been looking forward to seeing her.

She was glad she'd had time to change to fresh jeans—her only pair—and an emerald-green tailored shirt. She didn't feel so overdressed.

"I wasn't sneaking," he said cheerfully, answering her earlier comment. "I made enough noise crashing through the brush to wake up a cemetery, but you were in another world. What were you thinking about?" He stood looking down at her, a half smile on his face.

She was glad he hadn't been able to read her thoughts. It was almost as though thinking about him had conjured him up!

"I was wondering how to find you," she said evenly. "And whether you'd been able to set up a meeting with the Daynew." It wasn't a lie—that was certainly part of what she'd been thinking.

"No problem." He eased himself down on the bench beside her. Instinctively she shrunk back a little. She hadn't imagined the pure sensual force of his presence. Even with her retreat, he was still sitting so close she caught the aroma of his fresh, sun-warmed skin mingled with a crisp aftershave. But the feeling that coursed through her wasn't dependent on the sexy aroma, or the sight of powerful, bulging muscles. Something intrinsic in his personality was vibrantly, confidently masculine. And somehow threatening. She'd never experienced this unreasonable response to a man who was practically a stranger before.

From the glint in his blue eyes she suspected that he had noticed her involuntary withdrawal and enjoyed the impact he made on her, but his voice was perfectly matter-of-fact.

"I talked to some of the boys today, and they agreed to put the matter of the meeting before the rest of the tribe as soon as they get off work. We'll meet with a group of them tonight around seven to see how successful they were."

He saw her glance at her watch and his grin broadened. "Several hours from now. I thought you might like to have a little something to eat before then."

The mention of food brought an unexpected hunger pang. She'd had a hamburger at Hope Mercantile around noon and hadn't been looking forward to returning there, nor was she enthusiastic about opening a can of something here at the campground.

She hadn't seen any other restaurant around here, either. Just what did Matt have in mind? Perhaps she shouldn't accept any more favors from him, or lead him to believe she had any interest in him other than obtaining his help with the Daynew. It was obvious that something about him attracted her on a physical basis, and she certainly didn't want that to interfere with her study here. They had nothing in common, and even assuming they had, all she wanted from him was an introduction to the Daynew. She'd complete her investigation and be on her way, leaving no unfinished business.

"I appreciate it, but I really don't want you to go to any trouble, Matt. You're doing enough for me. I can whip up something—"

He gave her a quick, amused look from under heavy dark lashes. "Don't they do things like this in California? Can't a man invite a woman out for dinner? Just for a little conversation?"

"Well, yes, of course..." She probably was overreacting to a simple dinner invitation. It was really only a friendly thing to do, considering the circumstances. "But I haven't seen any restaurants around here," she added dryly.

His blue eyes widened in mock astonishment. "I'm surprised at your lack of creativity. And you a mythologist. The entire world doesn't eat in restaurants, you know."

She bit her lip in vexation. How had she managed to come across as naive and superficial? She'd been on enough trips into isolated areas with her father to think of herself as quite at home away from civilization. No, she thought. It wasn't the lack of civilized amenities that caused her to be unsure of herself. She just wasn't sure of the depth of civilization in this particular man.

Without waiting for her reply, Matt came lightly to his feet and reached out to pull her up beside him. She felt the warmth and strength of his hand closing firmly around hers, and a slight anticipatory shiver went down her spine. His muscles tensed briefly, and she became a little more confident. At least the unexpected attraction wasn't completely one-sided.

"Where are we going?" she asked as he propelled her along the trail that led out of the campsite.

"I thought you might like a change of scene. Dinner's in my pickup."

They didn't speak again as he handed her up into his diesel four-wheel-drive truck, then walked around and jumped up into the seat beside her. As usual, he was taking over, she thought, feeling a tiny prickle of irritation. He'd had everything prepared, sure of her agreement.

But why wouldn't he be sure? He undoubtedly knew the limitations of dining places in and around Hope better than she did!

She had thought the campground was nearly at the end of the line, and was surprised and a little uneasy when he drove beyond it, turning off onto a narrow dirt road that climbed steeply around the side of the mountain.

She looked out the window to a sheer drop down the mountainside. "Where does this road go?"

"No place," he said, turning his eyes toward her with a quick grin, then looking hastily back at the road. "That is, if you're talking about a destination. It's an old logging road, but we're not using it this season. It does have a nice view."

After that they were silent. She sat well over on her side of the seat, wondering again if this had been a good idea. She had thought she was isolated before, but she had at least been in a campground with people close by. Here, there appeared to be no one for miles.

Half an hour later he pulled to a stop and switched off the engine.

"Shouldn't you get off the road?" She glanced behind them; his pickup was parked squarely in the middle, taking up nearly the entire width of the narrow road.

"No reason to. No one comes this way." He swung down from the cab, reached into the pickup bed for a backpack and walked around to her side of the vehicle. "Come on," he ordered.

She hesitated, a little uneasy over the way things were going. Then she shrugged and jumped down beside him. She was here and she would make the best of it.

Puffs of dust rose around her feet as her shoes hit the dry soil of the road. She admitted to herself she was still nervous. Dinner with Matt had sounded fine, but she hadn't bargained on being alone with him so far back in the mountains.

Instinctively she felt she had nothing to fear from Matt, but was instinct always reliable? At least instinct that has been dulled by civilization? She had told her father and several colleagues that she would be in Hope studying the Daynew, but she hadn't realized at the time exactly how remote the place was. What if something happened to her?

Or was her uneasiness based on something else entirely? She was no stranger to remote areas, though she had never been [illegible]e before. Was it simply that she felt she could handle her own reactions better in a restaurant, with other people close by?

Oblivious to her hesitation, Matt moved swiftly ahead, parting low-hanging branches of Douglas fir and an occasional ponderosa pine, and she hurried after him. There was no trail that she could see, but he seemed to know exactly where he was going.

Suddenly they burst out into an open space, and Brianna gasped with delight. They had climbed higher than she realized and were now on an open, grassy spot at the edge of a granite cliff. Thank heaven she wasn't afraid of heights! The pristine country stretched endlessly out in front of them, and for a moment she couldn't say a word.

Matt grinned smugly at her rapturous face, as though he were personally responsible for the breathtaking vista.

"On a clear day, you can see almost as far as Boise from here."

She turned slowly, taking in everything: south, the mountains receded in an ever decreasing line, finally becoming just a blue haze; to the northeast, she could see the entire shoreline of the lake beside which she had camped; it was larger than she had dreamed. Behind the turquoise water, rising steeply into the cloudless sky was the snow-capped mountain she had seen mirrored in the lake. From this vantage point it seemed larger, even more impressive, than before, with its reflection shimmering in the deep water. Nowhere, in whichever direction she looked, did she see a sign of human habitation.

She hadn't realized places like this were still left in the country. Awestruck, she turned to meet Matt's eyes. They were watching her face with lively interest.

"Like it?"

"It's incredible. I knew we were a long way from anyplace, but this looks just as it must have looked a hundred years ago!"

"Probably longer than that." He slipped the backpack from his shoulder and carried it to a relatively flat boulder, where he began pulling out vario[illegible]ms. His back was to her, and she noticed the play of muscles under his flannel shirt, the way the material of his Levi's stretched tautly across his hips as he bent, and she looked hastily away.

"Not much happens around here to change things," he continued, oblivious to the effect he was having on her. "Nobody knows how long the Daynew have lived here, but it could be hundreds, maybe even thousands, of years. They didn't change the land much. Mostly they just coexisted with nature. And the white man never found much here that he wanted. There weren't any minerals discovered to bring in the hordes."

He stepped back and surveyed the impromptu table, then beckoned to her. "About the only thing going on is logging—and we don't cut it any faster than it grows. It will last a long time. Yes," he said, satisfaction evident in his voice, "I imagine things look just as they always have."

"You like it that way?"

He shrugged, frowning slightly. "Sometimes people use the word progress when they mean destruction. My family has lived here a long time, too. Stuart Logging is the only thing that stands between most of the community and poverty."

He shot her a quick glance. "You might say we have a symbiotic relationship."

She couldn't help a little jolt of surprise at his use of the word. "Symbiotic?" she said before she could stop herself, then flushed.

He knew exactly what she meant. "Sometimes I use words that have more than two syllables," he said, his eyes mocking.

She decided not to reply to his reproof; she had merited it.

"And you don't want anything changed," she said slowly. "You like your life as it is."

"Sure. Oh, I wouldn't mind making a little more money but I really can't complain about anything."

"Living here gives you a sense of freedom?"

"It's not really freedom," he said slowly. "There's too much responsibility for that. It may sound silly, but I feel I'm needed. Or at least Stuart Logging is needed."

"El Patron?" she said dryly. Maybe that was why Matt didn't want her talking to the Daynew. He had a proprietary interest in keeping them dependent.

"I'd hardly say that. But I look after them." There was a touch of steel in his voice.

"Like children?"

"Of course not children! But I won't see them exploited."

"Would that be easy to do? From what I've seen, they can take care of themselves."

He glared at her. "They probably can. They've come a long way since their last setback."

"You mentioned an unethical anthropologist. Just what happened?"

"I was just a kid when he came here, and I'm not too sure about exactly what went on. He stayed a few days, and from what I heard the questions he asked were all slanted to confirm his own theory. They were primitive, lacked any culture."

"But surely he knew better by talking to them. They can't have changed that much in twenty years."

"Oh, the Daynew contributed to the misunderstanding. When they got the gist of his questions I think it amused them to mislead him. Then, the article was published, and they were in the limelight. Joe quit the football team after a few jibes about dirty Indians, and others were singled out, too. But that wasn't the worst."

She looked at his angry face and asked quietly. "What was the worst?"

"The way they seemed to regress," he said slowly, "turn inward. They were outgrowing their clannishness, but it was as though all the furor reminded them of something. Some even quit their jobs."

"And you think it's very important for them to keep working for you," she said dryly.

"If they want to eat," he said, just as dryly. "Besides, you can't turn back time. They have to learn how to make it in the real world."

"You seem very protective of them...."

They stared at each other, both astonished at how heated the discussion had become. Deciding not to pursue the subject now, she strolled toward the boulder where he stood, then leaned back against a dried pine branch that had fallen from the parent tree during a heavy snow. The bark felt rough through the thin material of her shirt and a light breeze played across her warm face. She searched for something to say.

"That mountain." She gestured toward the snowcapped peak directly across the lake from them. "I suppose I saw it on the map, but I never realized it was so high. And so symmetrical. It looks just like an ice-cream cone."

"The name you saw on the map wouldn't be recognized around here. The Daynew just call it 'The Old One.' It's symmetrical because it's an extinct volcano."

"How extinct?" She realized there was a hint of nervousness in her voice.

"Very extinct." He gave her a sidelong glance. "There is no history of an eruption even close to modern times. Geologists say we're talking thousands of years since it last blew its top." He gestured toward the array of food enticingly displayed on the rough surface of the granite boulder. "Ready?"

"I'll say. I didn't realize how hungry I am." She moved to stand beside him, looking down hungrily at the food.

"Try one of these." He handed her a giant roast beef sandwich made of crusty whole-wheat bread. His hand brushed hers fleetingly, and she had to exercise all her control to keep from pulling sharply back from the voltage that seemed to spark between them. Whether in anger or physical awareness, she certainly reacted strongly to this man.

As she bit down on mustard, onions and sharp dill pickles, her eyes went to his face. There was an intent, speculative look in his eyes that made her slightly uneasy. She recognized it for what it was, frank sexual interest, and realized once more that she was a long way from her own world. Had it been wise to come here with a man who was nearly a stranger? His eyes, she saw, were now nearly the color of indigo, and they held her for an endless moment until she was finally able to look away.

"Did you make these sandwiches?" She said the first thing she could think of. "They're delicious."

"Nope." He threw her a mocking glance, the intensity of the moment broken. "Cooking is woman's work."

She glanced at him sharply, and saw the teasing look in his eyes. He was baiting her, and she wouldn't reply.

"My housekeeper put a few things together for us," he said when she remained silent.

"Housekeeper?" She realized she hadn't thought much about where and how he lived.

"Yep. When Mom and Dad turned over the logging and the homeplace to me, Mom asked Mrs. Clayton to take care of me." His grin dared her to comment, so she did.

"A typical helpless man? Where are your folks?"

"On an extended trip to Ireland and Scotland. Dad wanted to check out his roots." He shrugged. "Maybe I'll feel that way when I'm older, but I doubt it. The present is enough for me. Making every day a good one has priority."

"How do you go about that?" she asked lazily. "There really doesn't seem to be that much to do in Hope. What do you do besides work?"

"You'd be surprised at my resources," he said dryly.

"A girlfriend?" Now why had she asked that? It really wasn't any of her business.

"Not at the moment." His grin widened. "How about you? A boyfriend at home?"

She certainly wasn't going to admit that right now there was no one special. Briefly she thought of Roy, a fellow anthropology student whom she'd thought she loved. It soon became clear that he thought her place was typing up notes on his digs, and that he hadn't cared at all about her concerns. She couldn't settle for a man who didn't value her and treat her as an equal.

"Several," she replied.

"Then there's no one special," he said, raising a heavy eyebrow. "I'm surprised."

"You needn't be," she retorted, suddenly defensive. "Right now, my work comes first." That was certainly true. It was also true that she hadn't met anyone she was interested in since her disillusionment with Roy. She seemed to have a problem that way, she thought ruefully. Most of the men she knew seemed rather weak, ineffectual. Or, if they were strong, they were too strong, insisting that she accept a subordinate role.

He turned from her and reached for a sandwich, then took a bottle of beer from a six-pack. "Want one?" He raised an incredibly sexy eyebrow. "I didn't bring any white wine."

"As it happens, I like an occasional beer," she said coldly. "But not right now. I want a clear head for tonight."

A shadow seemed to pass over his face, and she gave him a questioning look. "You still don't approve of my talking to the Daynew, do you?"

He sighed, moving from the boulder and squatting on his heels beside her. "It just seems a little silly, that's all. Why would anyone care about recording a bunch of old superstitions? Superstitions they don't even believe themselves anymore?"

"Then why are you helping me?"

He didn't answer, refusing to meet her eyes, and suddenly she knew. He was hoping she wouldn't get anyplace with them, and she'd have to leave.

She sat down beside him on the soft grass. It seemed silly now to have worried about being here alone with Matt. Now that he wasn't looking directly into her eyes, his interest seemed hardly more than friendly. If that.

"Myths are more than superstitions," she retorted. "Many of them are based on actual ancient occurrences. How can we understand the present if we don't know the past?"

"You mean you believe that stuff actually happened? Like the Greek gods overcoming the giant race of Titans? Or old Zeus's wife turning maidens into cows or swans?"

"Not literally, of course," she snapped. "But if you trace the symbolism—" She broke off and gave him a suspicious look. "You seem to know a lot about myths."

He shrugged, then stretched out on the grass beside her, propping himself on one elbow to look up into her face. "You can't get through high school without being exposed to a few fairy tales. I always figured myths were something people outgrew as they evolved, became more rational, more scientifically oriented."

"You think the Stealth bomber, or Star Wars, is more rational than Pluto stealing Persephone and hiding her underground?"

"Well, the Stealth bomber is sure more relevant. Kids who will go to the moon can't be expected to be interested in symbols formulated before gunpowder was invented!"

"Those symbols aren't irrelevant. They aren't irrational, either. I believe they're deep in our subconscious, racial archetypes if you will, and that they still touch and release the deepest center of all. They are completely relevant to the present!" She raised her chin and glared at him.

He raised an incredulous eyebrow, then threw back his head and laughed. "I'll admit one thing. I don't have much of a rational basis for wishing you'd leave the Daynew alone—but I sure wish you would. Maybe I listened to my grandfather too much. He got a lot of stories about the tribe from his father, old Caleb Stuart. The old man left a journal of some kind, but it's disappeared. Anyway, I understand he didn't write down a lot of detail. Just hints."

"What kind of stories?" This was indeed a happy coincidence. Matt was a descendant of the mountain man who had written the journal which had somehow found its way to her father. She made a mental note to tell him about it and give it back just as soon as she had the opportunity.

Matt shrugged, took a huge bite of his sandwich, then leaned back flat on the carpet of grass. "He was pretty evasive—just hinted about a lot of things. Weird things, spooky, but he would never come right out and say exactly what they were."

She smiled at the frown on his face as she finished the sandwich, and reached for a paper napkin. "Then you don't think my interest is merely silly?" she teased. "Maybe more like dangerous?"

He snorted. "Dangerous? Of course not. What could harm you? No, it's just that I don't see the necessity of digging around in the past," he said stubbornly. "It's over—let it lie."

She started to reply, then relaxed. They obviously disagreed about this, and arguing wasn't going to change him. She would just be grateful for the help he was giving her, however unwillingly.

For several minutes they said nothing, and she became increasingly aware of the great stillness of the place. A strange feeling crept over her; it was as though she wasn't merely out of the ordinary world, but out of ordinary time as well.

She looked over at him, about to comment on the feeling, but something in his expression stopped her. He was staring at her intently. The pupils of his eyes widened, darkened, as his gaze moved slowly over her face. She felt the force of his attention almost like a physical touch, and when he looked again into her eyes, she stared solemnly back.

"Brianna...that's a lovely name." His voice was a husky whisper that she felt down to her toes. She knew she should move away, break the contact, and in just a moment, she would....

"You said you didn't have a girlfriend at the moment," she said hastily, sitting up very straight. "What happened?"

"Nothing much," he said. "I guess it just wasn't the right time or the right woman."

He raised himself on one elbow, leaned slightly toward her and touched her cheek with a gentle, questing finger. He was so close she felt his breath warm and moist against her skin.

Slowly, as though examining a rare work of art, he traced the delicate curve of her jaw, then ran his finger across her full, slightly parted lips. She caught her breath sharply as he moved his hand gently over her cheek, then to the back of her head where his fingers dug softly into the wealth of her hair as he pulled her gently toward him.

She knew she should pull away.

His kiss was like the touch of a feather in flight, and almost as ephemeral. Certainly it wasn't enough to justify the confusion she felt. It was just a kiss, and a tentative one at that. She had been kissed before, and kissed with considerably more determination. Yet when he drew back, she could still feel his lips against hers and felt an unaccountable desire to feel them again.

Suddenly he released her, and rose quickly to his feet. She dropped her gaze to the ground, embarrassed by the rush of feeling that seemed all out of proportion to what had actually happened. She hardly knew the man, and it had undoubtedly been a mistake to come here alone with him. Perhaps it gave him the wrong idea. Anyway, she should have been the one to pull away. In fact, she shouldn't have let things develop as they had in the first place.

She was angry with herself. She'd had experiences with men, and even one or two rather intense relationships. She knew the kind of man she liked. He was thoughtful, sensitive, the kind of man who treated her as an equal. Not someone so—so intensely masculine. She knew that a physical relationship developed out of mutual ideals and values, shared interests. Friendship and respect became love.

Matt Stuart had a compelling primitive sexuality, and on a purely physical level, it was understandable that she might notice it. It wasn't understandable that she would respond to it.

Keeping her eyes averted, she rose to her feet, dusting off her jeans with exaggerated care.

He gave her a rueful smile. "I'm sorry. I shouldn't have done that."

She merely looked at him, unable at that moment to think of a reply.

"You have every reason to be angry with me," he said. "I shouldn't have taken advantage of you."

"Forget it. Nothing really happened."

His blue eyes smoldered. "That wasn't my impression."

She managed a smile that she hoped was cool and composed. "Aren't you making quite a fuss over a little kiss? Or an almost kiss?"

He scowled. "I certainly try never to take advantage of a woman." His eyes narrowed to slits as he scrutinized her face. "You're a real temptation, though. It was lucky I stopped."

Now he was implying that she would have let him do anything he wanted! It had been a mistake to come here!

"Don't you think we should be getting back?" she said coldly, brushing by him and heading for the pickup.

* * *

Matt watched the scattering of people file into the room and seat themselves at the larger desks or along the wooden benches that lined the walls. A schoolhouse during the day, the one-room frame building was often utilized at night as a meeting room.

He knew them all, of course, and he nodded and smiled at each. He should know them; he had lived with the Daynew, played with the Daynew, since childhood. He employed many of the men. Usually he didn't think of them as a bit different from himself. Now he tried to look at them with new eyes, wanting to see how they would appear to Brianna.

There was nothi[illegible]out of the ordinary about them, he decided. They could have been a gathering of people nearly anywhere in Idaho, except there wasn't quite as much variance in their appearance as there would have been in another, unrelated crowd. Tonight the men all wore jeans and work shirts, the women were either in jeans or colorful cotton dresses. They had cleaned up after work, eaten supper, and were now here to listen to the lady.

A smile quirked his lips. Not a feather among them! Brianna would be disappointed.

He narrowed his eyes as the Daynew continued to straggle in. They might be a little taller than normal, he decided; most of the men were over six feet, the women only slightly shorter. Their hair was predominately black or dark brown, but here and there he saw a thatch of light brown that was nearly blond, an occasional hint of auburn. Their features were strong—deep-set eyes, well-defined lines to cheeks and jaws. He wondered briefly how they came to be so uniformly attractive, and then shrugged. Good genetic make-up to begin with, and eons of isolation.

He saw Chad, his jammer operator, a lithe, bronzed man of about thirty, coming through the door, and raised his hand in a half salute. "Glad you could make it, Chad."

The man grinned widely. "Did I have a choice, boss?"

Matt gave him a rueful look. "Did I come on that strong?"

"Only to somebody who knows you. It sounded like we'd better listen to the lady, or pack up!" Still chuckling, Chad made his way to a bench and said something to his friends. There was an appreciative laugh.

Matt looked over at Brianna who was standing rather nervously at the far end of the room. It was true he'd had to twist a few arms to arrange this meeting; none of the men on his crew were even slightly interested in talking to an anthropologist. In fact, if he hadn't known better, he might have thought they were even a little uneasy at the prospect. He'd caught several oblique glances when his men didn't realize he was watching, had seen groups murmuring together, falling silent as he approached. He knew they were genuinely reluctant.

Well, he thought, it won't hurt them to hear what she has to say. Then they could politely tell her to get lost.

He wasn't much used to introspection, but he wondered a little uneasily if his own motivation was really to speed her on her way. She was certainly attractive, and he'd been surprised at the depth of the reaction he'd felt when he kissed her.

Out of the corner of his eye, he watched her shuffle some papers, lose one, and bend quickly to pick it up. He had a little trouble with his breathing, as her jeans tightened enticingly around the sweet curves of her buttocks, and he felt the heat rise to his face. Almost angrily, he jerked his eyes away. With this kind of reaction, it would be better for both of them when she was gone.

His flush deepened as the remembrance of their tentative kiss this afternoon flashed through his mind. She was right; it had been only a kiss, and he hadn't intended to do even that. It wasn't like him to be so impulsive, but the sight of her leaning above him, golden hair falling across one flawless cheek, her coral mouth soft and moist and inviting, her shirt falling open to reveal a glimpse of the valley between her luscious breasts, had triggered something that had been dormant for a long time.

He really needed a woman, he thought. Needed one in the elemental, physical sense. That must be why he had reacted so strongly to Brianna. Yet the thought of a one-night stand wasn't at all appealing. He needed more than the quick easing of sexual desire. He remembered the sensual pull of her body, the way she had leaned toward him before she turned away. She'd responded, too, he knew she had, and it had taken every ounce of willpower he possessed to pull away from her. A few more minutes, and he might have taken her right there on the fragrant grass, like the savage he suspected she thought he was.

He clenched his jaw in frustration. No, he wouldn't have. He knew himself too well for that. He knew that seduction wasn't the way, knew what would follow. There would be regret that he had betrayed her trust, anger at his own selfishness. She had come with him willingly to that isolated spot, believing him to be an honorable man—as he usually was. Physically he might have sated his passion—but he would have only created a larger problem.

His mouth tightened. He had never lacked for women, had even thought himself in love a couple of times. Mostly he'd wanted, needed, relationships, but occasionally there had been one-night stands. They left him frustrated and unsatisfied; he didn't plan on anymore, and that was the extent of what he could have with Brianna. Then she would be on her way back to lotusland.

He felt the roomful of expectant eyes on him and, shaking off the thoughts, strode to the middle of the room; everyone that was coming must be here by now. He waited until the buzz of conversation quieted, shoved his thumbs under the band of his Levis, and spoke quietly.

"Thanks for coming. I appreciate it."

There was a murmured response, and he continued, nodding his head toward Brianna. "This is Brianna Royce. She's asked to talk to you about recording your legends, your history."

A little buzz ran through the room, and he saw the men glance sideways at each other and shuffle their feet. Was he imagining the hint of anxiety in those glances? The women merely regarded him with impassive eyes and waited.

"There's not much use in my saying anything more," he concluded, stepping away from the center of the room. "I'll let Ms. Royce speak for herself."

She gave him a confident smile and faced the crowd, and he grinned back, inwardly amused. She seemed much more sure of herself now than she had been an hour or so ago, up on the mountain! Arms crossed over his chest, he leaned against a wall and watched her as impassively as the women.

He listened as she briefly outlined the reason for her visit, the procedures she would use, and explained why it was important to her to be able to talk to them individually. No one knew anything at all about the history of the Daynew; they would be advancing science by cooperating. She leaned forward, eager to convince the group, and he felt a flash of sympathy. This certainly was important to her.

Near the back of the room, Joe West stood quietly. Tom West's oldest son, Matt knew. Tall and solid, with brown hair and a broad face, the young man had an air of quiet dignity that effectively stopped Brianna's flow of words.

"You say our cooperating would help you," he said slowly. "It would help science. What would it do for us?"

There was a murmur of agreement, and Brianna gave him a blinding smile. "Everyone wants to know about their roots. Think of your children. Their history won't be lost."

Another hand was raised. "Our children hear the old stories. Why should they have to read them?"

"Because things change," Brianna said firmly. "What will happen to the stories when the old people aren't around to tell them anymore?"

The group murmured together, and Brianna sought Matt's eyes. He knew she recognized the mood of the gathering, just as he did. The Daynew were polite, they seemed to be discussing her request, but from the set look on their faces, Matt suspected a decision had already been made, and her project rejected.

He frowned thoughtfully, sensing something in the atmosphere. Something was strange. Then he got it; it was the men who were murmuring together, the men who spoke up. The women were silent, and that wasn't like the Daynew. The women were usually every bit as vocal as the men. Now they merely watched, faces impassive, eyes blank.

He didn't listen to her words as Brianna made another impassioned speech, content to float in the soft, low tones of her voice. What was there about her that affected him like a blow to the solar plexus? He could hardly breathe when he looked at her. It was ridiculous; he knew other attractive women and they didn't affect him as she did. True, she was as slender and well formed as a tender spring willow, and her full, moist lips were made for kissing, but could that account entirely for his reaction?

He felt a stirring in his groin, and suddenly wished he weren't leaning back against the wall, the length of his lean body almost totally exposed. True, she was sexy as hell, but that couldn't be all of it, could it?

A wry grin twisted his strong features. Maybe that was all, and in his experience, it was rare enough. Why knock it?

His thoughts were interrupted as the door swung open. A tall, elderly woman entered the room like a proud frigate in full sail. Her brown hair, streaked with gray, flowed over her shoulders nearly to her waist and her strongly etched features gave evidence of faded beauty. She wore a long dress of some soft gray material, belted at the waist with a braided rope. Compared to the other women, she was a real anachronism.

He raised an eyebrow in surprise. What was Alta Thompson doing here? He knew she hadn't been to the Daynew public meetings for the last few years, and he had thought she might be letting the younger people manage things. And why had she come late?

He watched, still puzzled, as one by one the group of people looked hastily at the woman, then quickly away. She didn't acknowledge them, didn't say a word as she made her way along the wall and sat down on a vacant bench, but her imposing presence had somehow changed the nature of the meeting. He noticed that her eyes, as fierce and predatory as an eagle's, were fastened to Brianna's face. The look never wavered as the young woman, after an instant's hesitation to acknowledge the older woman's entrance, continued her plea.

When she had finished Chad rose abruptly, casting a nervous glance over his shoulder at Alta Thompson; she returned his gaze with single-minded intensity.

"We'll think about it, Miss Royce," he said shortly, walking toward the door.

One by one, like children released from school, the others rose and followed, some smiling and speaking to Alta, some merely glancing at her as they passed, others studiously ignoring the elderly woman.

He wondered what it was all about. He could ask Chad or Joe tomorrow, but his experience with the Daynew told him it would probably be futile. For all their apparent openness, their surface friendliness, he knew that even after all these years he was still an outsider.

At the sound of a deep sigh, he took his eyes from the retreating Indians, and looked at Brianna. Her slender shoulders were slumped, and there was a look of defeat on her lovely face; she looked as though she might burst into tears at any moment.

"They're not going to talk to me, are they?"

For a moment he forgot that this was exactly what he had hoped would happen.

"Don't worry," he said softly. "It's not over yet."

Chapter 3

They stood staring at each other, both surprised by the depth of feeling in Matt's words. Then Brianna gave him a shaky grin, retrieved her hands, and made a big business of turning and shuffling some notes she had placed on the desk behind her. She didn't want him to see the confusion on her face. She didn't understand; he had helped her under duress, and she knew he had a motivation of his own for doing so, but he had sounded so sympathetic.

"It's okay," she finally said, still looking down sightlessly at the papers as she chewed her underlip. "But I appreciate your support."

He leaned back against a desk, his weight on one hip, and crossed one booted leg over the other. "Don't tell me you're giving up."

"I thought that was what you wanted me to do." She still wouldn't look at him.

"Well, it is. I mean—anyway," he floundered, "they didn't actually turn you down. Just said they'd think about it."

She turned and gave him a tremulous smile. "No, but I think they would have turned me down right then if they hadn't been so polite." She hesitated, then took a deep breath as she realized she had come to a decision. "But no, I'm not giving up. Not yet."

"Somehow I knew you wouldn't. You're too stubborn. Like most women, you have to be hit over the head to get your attention."

She began an angry retort, but he came to his feet in a lithe, catlike motion, took her firmly by the arm, and moved her toward the door. "There's nothing more you can do here tonight. I'll take you back to your camp."

They left the little building and stood for a moment on the low porch, looking out into the night. The Daynew had all gone and they were alone in the warm night. She was still seething over Matt's remark, but confused also. One minute he was helpful, the next almost insulting. She wished he would pick one attitude and stick to it.

Still, she made no move to draw away, and she was secretly glad that he didn't let go of her arm. It wasn't that she needed the support, she told herself. His touch was comforting, even if he did disapprove of what she was doing. When she'd had this idea to go by herself to interview a primitive people, she hadn't realized she'd feel so alone.

And how did Matt feel? She sensed his ambivalence, alerted by his firmly set jaw. His remarks certainly confirmed it. Had he hoped the Daynew would turn her down firmly instead of saying they would think about it? That was certainly a reasonable surmise, given that he was so adamant about protecting their privacy.

She raised her head to catch the light evening breeze, sniffing the fresh scent of pine, and lifted her hair from her neck with her free hand. Hearing the rustle of small animals in the bushes, the sharp cry of a nighthawk, she relaxed a little and gave herself over to the evening. Nothing had to be decided now; there was still a faint possibility that the Daynew would decide to cooperate. Tomorrow she would think of a plan, decide on her next step, but tonight she would just drift.

Suddenly she stiffened as she caught sight of a furtive movement several yards to the right. The bushes parted for a second, revealing a dark form, then closed. She had only a glimpse, but the features of the person lurking in the shadows were clearly revealed by the moon; the image was etched on her brain. She felt a sudden chill, and her fingers unconsciously dug into Matt's arm. The elderly woman who had come in late to the meeting had been watching them from behind the bushes that screened the schoolhouse yard.

"What's the matter?" Matt, feeling her stiffen, pulled her closer and looked at her sharply.

"I thought I saw someone over there behind the hedge," she whispered, gesturing into the darkness.

Matt turned his head sharply, following her gaze. Something moved again. The moon was already high in the sky, casting silver light over the landscape, and the outline of a woman's gaunt form was clearly revealed as she peered out between the branches....

As Matt made out the woman's face, he relaxed slightly. "Oh, yes. I see her. Alta Thompson."

Brianna swallowed nervously. She hadn't been mistaken; she had recognized the watcher. The fact that Matt took it so calmly didn't quell her uneasiness. "You don't sound concerned," she murmured. "Is she spying on us?"

"Probably." He chuckled, a rich sound deep in his chest. "She likes to know what's going on, and not much escapes her. But don't worry. She's a little eccentric—but certainly not dangerous."

"Who *is* Alta Thompson?" Brianna continued to whisper. The woman was several yards away, as motionless as a rock, and she probably couldn't hear a word they said, but her presence was eerie enough to make Brianna keep her voice down. "I saw her come late to the meeting and she made quite a stir."

"She's one of the older generation Daynew. Used to be a pretty important one, I understand. Deferred to, had an opinion on most everything. Since she's gotten older she's pretty much retired from the tribal affairs."

The woman, perhaps realizing she had been discovered, slipped back farther into the shadows. Brianna could no longer see her, but from the prickly feeling that ran down her spine, she suspected the woman hadn't gone very far.

She bit her lip thoughtfully, deciding how to phrase what was only a nebulous feeling. "From the way the others reacted to her when she came to the meeting," she said slowly, "I'm not sure she's completely on the sidelines."

"What do you mean?" He sounded a little as though he were hedging; she had a quick flash that he knew exactly what she meant. The moonlight played across his hard face, and Brianna saw he was frowning slightly.

"It was a little strange, that's all, the way some of them ignored her. If it didn't sound so ridiculous, I'd say some of the men were afraid of her."

"Afraid?"

"Well, I noticed that several of the men wouldn't meet her eyes as they left. They kept looking at the floor."

He thought about it a second, then replied cautiously. "I had that feeling, too, but it doesn't make sense. She's just an old woman . . . and she didn't act threatening. . . ."

"Maybe not. But she sure looked peeved about something!"

"Well," he replied. "Probably nothing to it. Maybe they forgot to tell her about the meeting, which would have been a blow to her ego; she ran things for quite a while. Then when she showed up anyway they may have felt guilty about neglecting her and thought she'd give them hell. She probably will. You know how some older people can be—they hate to turn over the reins to the younger generation."

"I suppose that was it. But there was something else . . ." Her voice trailed away.

"What?"

"Oh, nothing, really. . ."

Matt didn't pursue the subject, although he gave her a keen look, and she was glad to let it drop. She wouldn't know how to explain the feelings the old woman had aroused in her. From the minute Alta Thompson strode imperiously into the room, Brianna had been acutely aware of the woman's scrutiny and had felt ill at ease. Alta Thompson's sharp gray eyes had seemed to look right inside her.

For just an instant Brianna had thought she knew the old woman. There was a haunting familiarity about her, a niggling awareness hovering around the edges of Brianna's consciousness. Annoyed with herself, she thrust the intuition aside; there was no way she could have known Alta Thompson. It was merely that the older woman reminded her of someone.

But who? She shook her head impatiently, trying to clear it of the perplexing question. It was just one of all the other weird things that had been happening to her since she arrived in Hope; the sudden sense of familiarity when she had arrived at the lake, the recurrence of the old, frightening dreams, now this nagging feeling that she should know the old woman.

Suddenly she felt the plank floor move under her and a spasm of terror drove all thought from her mind. The porch shifted beneath her feet. She lurched forward. She was aware of a rolling, undulating motion, as though solid ground had turned to liquid waves. She clutched desperately at Matt, fighting to keep her balance. A scream rose soundlessly in her throat as she was pitched backward again, then helplessly toward him. At some level she was aware of the anguished creaking of the frame structure behind her, and of a sound like wind swooshing through the tops of pines.

Then, as suddenly as the motion began, it was over. She was clinging desperately, mindlessly, to Matt.

He held her tightly against his chest and patted her shoulder softly, waiting for her shudders to subside. Her breath was coming in harsh gasps, and only his strong arms kept her from collapsing.

"There, there," he soothed. "It wasn't anything. Just an earth tremor."

"*Just* an earth tremor!" As scared as she was, she still felt somewhat indignant at his casual assessment of the earthquake. Saying that what she had felt was *just* an earth tremor was like saying that a hurricane was *just* a big wind.

She didn't move away, although now that everything was quiet she felt a little embarrassed by the way she had panicked. Crushed against Matt's chest, encircled by his arms, his dark head bent protectively over hers, she felt momentarily secure.

As her fright lessened, she felt something else, too. His heart was beating strongly against her cheek through the material of his shirt, and she was enveloped in the heady, sexy aroma rising from his warm skin. She was pressed so closely against the lean length of his body that she was acutely aware of the exact instant when his protective feeling turned to active desire. Without conscious thought, almost as though this moment had been ordained, she raised her lips to his kiss.

They stood there, molded together, lost in the desperate need of the moment, until she realized what was happening and moved shakily away. This was another weird thing to add to what was happening to her in Hope, she thought, summoning as much detachment as she could muster. Her physical response to this man, this man she hardly knew, this man who epitomized everything she disliked in a male, was the weirdest of all.

When they finally pulled apart, both shaken as much by their bodies' obvious affinity as by the tremor, she waited until she was sure her voice was under control. She would ignore what had just happened; it had been an overreaction to her fright.

"You said, just a tremor, as though you were familiar with them," she said quietly. "Does it happen often?"

He took a deep breath, and she suspected he was fighting for control just as she was. "Fairly often," he finally replied, his voice suspiciously husky. "We're used to them—

a geologist told us tremors are normal around extinct volcanoes. The ground may be slightly unstable, but it doesn't necessarily mean anything is going to happen."

"That seemed like more than a tremor to me."

"It was a fairly large one, all right," he admitted. "They've come that strong before." He gave her a keen glance, but made no move to touch her. "Scared? Maybe you shouldn't be alone tonight."

She shivered slightly, but shook her head. She was getting over her fright, and suspected she had overreacted. She had felt earth tremors, as most Californians had. It was probably a combination of all the strange things that had been happening to her that had caused her panic. She would be all right alone.

Anyway, the only alternative to her present quarters was to stay at Matt's house and she didn't want to get in any deeper than she was. He'd mentioned a housekeeper, but she had no idea whether the woman lived in or out. Right now, considering the way Matt affected her, she thought she'd be much safer in her camper, even though she would be alone.

"I'm fine," she assured him. "It was just that it was so unexpected. I'd appreciate it if you would drive me back to the campground."

He nodded, and they walked toward his pickup. Matt's kiss had left her emotions so turbulent that she was having a hard time pretending to be in control of them, and her legs were still trembling from the aftermath of the tremor. Or from the aftermath of the kiss.

That must have been why she completely forgot her concern about Alta Thompson. She didn't even look toward the bushes where the woman crouched, her fierce eyes blazing with excitement. She didn't know that the woman waited, motionless, until the pickup disappeared and not even the sound of the engine lingered on the night breeze before she slipped off into the night.

As they drove through the darkness, Matt and Brianna were equally silent. The entire evening had been so full of stress that she couldn't wait to get to her camp and assimilate what was happening. She didn't know what Matt was thinking, but she was well aware of her own chaotic thoughts. Hope no longer seemed a peaceful, sleepy little community; there were undercurrents everywhere. Worse, this unexpected response to Matt was getting completely out of hand, and she had to stop it immediately.

It wasn't really a response to Matt as a person, she decided. As a person, she didn't approve of him. She had met his type before, take-charge, forceful men, although admittedly not quite so elementally sexy. She was beginning to question her initial idea that he was just a handsome male with more muscle than brainpower, but nothing had made her change her perception of him as a controlling, overpowering male. For instance, his concern for the Daynew was definitely overprotective, even patronizing. It was as though he carried the entire weight of everyone's destiny on his own shoulders, a rather arrogant idea, she thought. In a relationship, overprotectiveness translated into pure possessiveness.

They pulled into the campsite and she jumped from the pickup before he could come around to open the door.

"Thanks, Matt. I'll be all right now."

He didn't reply as he stepped from the pickup, moved to her side, took her arm, and walked beside her along the dark trail.

"Really, you don't need to—"

"Yes, I need to," he said calmly.

They reached her campsite and she pulled away from his arm. "Really, I appreciate everything you've done. I'll be fine." She knew she sounded a little nervous.

Still he didn't move, his narrowed eyes assessing her thoughtfully. Was he expecting to come right on in and tuck her into bed!

Suddenly she was acutely aware of the isolation of the campground. Presumably there were a few other campers around, but she wouldn't swear to it. No phone, no electricity, not even a radio jarred the silence. Her vehicle, parked at the back of the site, looked abandoned and forlorn. The pines that screened her from the other campsites were dark shadows looming around her, and even the moonlight was partially blocked by their branches. She knew suddenly—felt it down to her toes—that when Matt left she would be frighteningly alone.

Her words came without conscious thought. "Would you like some tea? It would only take a minute to heat some water."

"I hate tea," he replied. "But the thought's a good one. How about coffee?"

The thought of Matt's large hand curved incongruously around a delicate teacup flashed through her mind, and she grinned. "Instant?"

"Fine."

She moved toward the camper door, then stopped as he made a move to follow. The thought of Matt's vibrant masculinity in the confines of the little dwelling was almost claustrophobic. She wouldn't be able to breathe. It was hard enough now.

"Why don't you sit over at the picnic table? I'll bring it right out."

He grinned knowingly, his teeth flashing white in the moonlight, but he didn't reply. Instead he went docilely to the table. From inside the camper she watched him through the window as he leaned against the rough planks and propped one boot up on the bench. His thumbs were stuck in the band of his jeans and she could hear him whistling softly.

When she brought the coffee they sat down across from each other at the table, eyeing each other cautiously. In the silence she heard the far-off howl of an animal and shivered.

"Just a coyote," Matt said.

"Are there any other wild animals around?" She forced herself not to look over her shoulder.

"Nothing that will hurt you. I thought you said you were used to camping."

"I am—but this is a little different. When I went with my father, there were always a lot of other people around."

He frowned. "I really wish you'd reconsider. I don't like to think of you out here alone and scared. You're welcome to stay at my place."

That thought was even more disconcerting. "I appreciate it, but as you said, there's nothing here that will harm me."

He smiled slightly. She liked the way his lips curved into a crooked grin, alleviating the sternness of his strong features. Even with the space between them, Brianna felt the force of his presence like a physical touch, and hastily tried for a neutral subject.

"Matt, what did you really think of the meeting tonight? What are my real chances of getting the Daynew to cooperate?"

She knew by the slight surprise in his eyes that her change of subject had been too abrupt. He looked at her soberly, then shrugged.

"I don't know. I would have said you didn't have a prayer, but now I'm not sure."

"Why not?"

He looked thoughtfully into his cup, then raised his eyes. "I got the feeling that they were all prepared to give you a big no. Then Alta came in, and they seemed in a big hurry to get out of there, told you they'd consider. Almost as though they were wavering..."

"We both thought they were just being polite."

"I wonder..."

She tensed at his tone. "And you don't like that, do you? The thought that they might actually talk to me?"

He took his cup in both hands, drank and then set it down carefully. His mouth was a thin line. "Like I said—the decision isn't mine—it's the Daynew's."

"You don't believe that. I *know* you have influence over them. I saw the way the men reacted to you tonight."

He smiled. "I doubt I have as much influence as you seem to think."

His lazy smile was somehow infuriating. Who did he think he was kidding? He considered himself their patron, and he certainly controlled the economic strings. He could make everything easy for her if he wanted to.

"You haven't given me one good, logical reason why you are opposed to my study," she said stiffly.

In the moonlight she could see him raise a heavy eyebrow. "No? You don't consider what happened when the other anthropologist was here a good reason? One of the boys—the first one to go—dropped out of college because he couldn't take the disgrace of seeing his people described in the media as backward, primitive Indians."

"You can't think I'm that type of person! Besides, people were much more intolerant then. No one would speak derogatorily of them today."

"No? Well, I don't want to find out."

"Why are you so protective of them? It's insulting to them."

"Why are you running around here so sure you're right? Don't pretend you want to help the Native Americans. Or science. You're only concerned about making a name for yourself."

She hesitated. There was a kernel of truth in what he said. Naturally she wanted a good dissertation; she had never pretended she wasn't ambitious. But if she really thought she was hurting anyone she would stop. And by no stretch of the imagination could she see that collecting oral histories was hurting anyone.

"You're so adamant about everything," she accused. "If you feel that strongly, why did you help me at all?"

He was silent, and suddenly her earlier suspicion returned with full force. "When you got them to listen to me, you were sure they would turn me down, weren't you. And that I'd give up and run on home."

He smiled, taking another sip of coffee. "Something like that," he murmured.

She jumped up from the bench and faced him across the table. "Well, forget it. I don't quit that easily. They haven't actually turned me down—and if they do, I'll try another approach."

He rose, too, and put his cup down softly on the table. His eyes glinted like agates, but he spoke softly. "I've about come to that conclusion. You're a stubborn woman."

"Stubborn! Just because I don't do what you tell me to do?"

"Because you won't listen to reason."

"If you came up with a reason, I'd listen!"

His lips were pressed firmly together, and she saw he was controlling himself with difficulty. She decided he wasn't used to opposition. Wasn't that just like him! Challenged by a woman, and he didn't like it one little bit!

"You're determined to keep digging into this, no matter what the Daynew tell you?"

"I don't see that it is really your concern."

He spread his hands out on the table, unclenching each finger, and took a deep breath. "No, you're right. It isn't my concern. I'll let you handle things on your own. Good night, Brianna."

She watched him turn on his heel and disappear into the darkness, her throat suddenly tight. He'd said good-night, but he'd meant goodbye. It was in his tone, the set of his shoulders, the length of his stride.

She listened until she heard the engine of his pickup roar to life, then walked inside her camper and slumped down on the bed. Now that he was gone, everything seemed so anticlimactic. Why on earth had she provoked the fight?

Because she had definitely provoked it. She knew they disagreed on her project, and there had been no reason to rehash it tonight. The truth was that she had been compelled to put up a barrier between them.

She never lied to herself, and no sooner had the thought come to her than she recognized the reason. It was a defense. She had wanted Matt tonight, wanted him as a woman wants a man, and that was completely unacceptable. True, the longing was entirely physical, but it was intense.

There might be excuses for her feeling the way she did, but never justification. The disappointment of the meeting, the shock of the earthquake, all contributed to her need for closeness. She had been so vulnerable that she might have welcomed intimacy.

But only for tonight. Tomorrow she would have had to face remorse, the knowledge that she was weak enough to accept comfort from a man who wasn't her kind at all.

The only thing Matt could offer her was momentary passion. He was opinionated, blatantly physical, and thought the work she did—the work she loved—ridiculous. They lived in two different worlds, were two different types of people. Unconsciously she had instigated an argument to drive him away. He had picked it up so quickly that perhaps he felt the same way.

Well, it had worked. He was gone tonight. She hoped he was gone for good.

She sighed and slid farther down onto the bed. From the scowl on his face when he turned and walked away from her, she suspected she had succeeded.

Matt took the turn at a speed that rattled his pickup, but he didn't notice the jolt. The headlights picked out the familiar steep grade ahead, and he angrily shifted gears, swearing softly. His attention was still on Brianna and the defiant look on her face when she told him she planned to go on with her project and she didn't care what he thought about it.

Which was probably just as well, he thought, steering expertly but subconsciously around a pothole. He didn't need a stubborn, opinionated female causing him problems, even for the short time she would be here. Oh, he'd thought how nice it would be to take her in his arms, bury his face in her soft, fragrant hair, touch her delicate skin—but that was absolutely all the interest he had in her.

But he could get that from any number of more pliant females, females who were gentler, sweeter, amenable to guidance. It angered him that she didn't think of him as an honorable man. Look at the things she had accused him of tonight!

Mostly true, of course. He *had* tried to manipulate events to get her out of town. He wasn't even sure that concern for the Daynew was his real motive. Still, he didn't need her messing up his head. For the short time she would be in Hope, he would stay completely away from her.

Chapter 4

Matt sat in his pickup, which he had pulled off onto the shoulder of the road, his hands gripping the steering wheel as though it were someone's neck, as he tried to control his frustration and anger. He was still seething from last night's encounter with Brianna; he mustn't let it color his reaction to what was going on with his crew.

But it certainly didn't help his disposition to look out at the scene in front of him. The logs were decked alongside the logging road as they should have been. The jammer, the huge log-loading machine that picked up the logs, was positioned perfectly to pick them up and load them on the trucks; the trucks were backed up waiting, the drivers either sitting in their cabs or lounging alongside the trucks joking with one another. The two hookers, chain saws propped up beside them, leaned against the log deck, occasionally casting a glance in Matt's direction. Almost everything was ready to go.

Almost everything. The only thing missing was Chad Gardner, the jammer operator, without whom the entire operation ground to a halt.

Matt glanced at his watch. Three other crew members were late, too, a skidder operator and two log hookers, but the operation could go without them. Chad was essential. He was nearly an hour late, and it wasn't like him. Matt had tried calling his house on his radio phone, but there had been no answer. He'd have to decide soon what to do—wait for Chad, which meant more lost wages, or run the log loader himself, which meant he would have to forgo driving over to check on the sawyers. He didn't like either alternative.

At the sound of an engine, he glanced in the rearview mirror and saw a battered blue pickup coming around the curve. Relief combined with irritation put a slight flush under the deep bronze of his skin. At least Chad was here, but he had taken his time about it, and it wasn't like him.

He jumped from his pickup just as Chad pulled up opposite him and cut the engine of his truck and stepped out. Matt felt some of his irritation evaporate as he looked at the familiar face of his employee and friend. Chad was a big man, over six feet tall and strongly built. His dark hair glinted with an auburn light under the morning sun, and he had the wide-set eyes and square face that was characteristic of the Daynew. That face now wore an expression of sheepishness combined with bravado.

"Sorry I'm late, Boss."

Matt quelled a sharp retort. Chad was usually punctual and responsible; he realized how much depended on his presence. He should at least find out what happened before chewing him out.

"Problems?"

"Uh—not really. Some things came up." Chad looked everyplace but at Matt.

Matt glanced at his waiting crew and then back to Chad, frowning. "Like what?"

Chad studied his heavy boots, then brought his eyes back to Matt, a placating grin on his face. "Ah, nothing serious. I'm just on Indian time, Boss."

Matt started to retort, then grinned in spite of himself. He and Chad went back a long way, and their friendship had survived more than an hour's tardiness. Chad's reply reminded him of when they had played football together. Chad was often late for practice, and it had become a running joke that he was on Indian time. Matt knew he had picked up the phrase from the article the anthropologist wrote about the Daynew—they were backward, primitive, had no concept of time.

"Okay," he said abruptly. "Just get over there and start loading."

Chad hurried over to the jammer and swung up into the cab. Matt watched until the first truck had been loaded and was on its way back down the side of the mountain. Although an hour's tardiness wasn't earthshaking, he couldn't get over his feeling that something was amiss.

Chad's phrase also reminded him, if he had needed a reminder, of Brianna; she was set on seeing the Daynew as a backward tribe instead of modern individuals. He was glad he had finally made up his mind to stay away from her. He had never known himself to be so ambivalent about anything, and he didn't like it. In his opinion, a man should think a situation through, make up his mind and then follow his decision to its logical course. He didn't sway with every breeze, the way he had been doing with Brianna.

He frowned, his thoughts returning to Chad's tardiness. It was really a minor thing—the first time the man had been late all season. Yet the timing made him uneasy. And Chad's use of the phrase "Indian time" was troubling. Somehow, it had set him apart from Matt, warned him there were barriers in spite of their friendship.

The other men who were late were Daynew, too, he suddenly realized. But it was ridiculous to connect that in any way with Brianna's presence. Most of the Native Americans on his crew were present and working.

Satisfied that this group was now working well, he started his pickup and inched by the deck of logs. Sawyers were waiting up the line for morning instructions.

As he pulled to a stop on the narrow road Joe West swung down off the hillside, boot heels digging into the dark forest soil of the cut bank, chain saw in hand. His hair was darker than Chad's and his body, clad in the usual heavy jeans and red flannel shirt, was somewhat sturdier, but he had the same direct gaze and square jaw. He, also, had been in school with Matt, and he approached him with an easy familiarity.

"You're late. I was just about to get started on the new sale, but I wasn't sure that was what you wanted."

Matt swung easily to the ground, his booted feet stirring up puffs of dust. "That will be fine. You've been around here about as long as I have, Joe. Start wherever you think you should."

Joe rested his chain saw on a nearby stump and stuck his thumbs through the blue suspenders that held up his denim jeans. His dark brown eyes were full of amusement. "Figured you might even be a little later."

"Why would you think that?"

"I doubt if I'd have been on time if I was in your place. That's a good-looking woman, that anthropologist, or mythologist, or whatever she is. Don't tell me you didn't take her back to her campsite—or someplace."

"Her campsite, Joe," Matt retorted dryly. "And speaking of Brianna Royce—what did you think of her?"

"She's a good-looking woman."

"I agree," Matt said, "but you know that's not what I meant. What do you think of her project?"

A look of wariness came into Joe's wide-set eyes. "Oh, I think she's wasting her time. Not much reason to study us. But it's her time."

Matt wasn't really satisfied with the answer, but he realized from Joe's bland look that he wasn't going to get anything else. He tried another tack.

"Anything go on last night? Chad and a few of the boys came dragging into work late this morning."

Joe hesitated, then faced Matt with a cool, closed look. It was a look Matt didn't see often, but when he did he knew he'd get no more information from the Daynew.

"Oh, some of us played a few cards last night," Joe said easily. "Got carried away. Didn't break up until around three this morning."

"On a work night?" Matt asked dryly.

"Oh, you know us Indians, boss. No sense of responsibility." Joe stooped and picked up his saw and was striding up the side of the mountain before Matt could question him further.

Matt's lips tightened as he looked thoughtfully after the man's retreating form. Probably a coincidence, and he was reading too much into this episode. Still, a few things bothered him. Both Joe and Chad had made a point that they were Indians and they didn't usually do that. Also, they'd had some kind of a meeting, and he doubted that they had played cards all that time. It was equally clear [illegible] they didn't want to talk to him about it.

He frowned as he stepped back into his pickup. Stuart Logging was a precise, efficient, well-organized company, and it operated on a basis of teamwork and mutual trust that Matt knew was rare. It was profitable, and Matt didn't kid himself that it was all due to his efforts. His men were an integral part of it, and were paid accordingly.

It might be because he was looking for it, was alert to any change brought about in the dynamics by Brianna's presence, but it might equally be true that a tiny crack had opened in the firm foundation of Stuart Logging. He would just have to watch and see.

He spent the rest of the morning driving from site to site, smoothing out problems, giving directions, but his mind was only half on his routine activities. He couldn't stop thinking about Brianna.

Was her presence like a small rock thrown into the middle of a deep pool, making an initial splash and then causing ever-widening ripples in the placid surface? Ripples that continued long after the splash had subsided?

He had told her he planned to wash his hands of the entire affair and let her blunder around as she wished. If his hunch was right, and her project was somehow affecting his men, he might not be able to do that. Still he had very little to go on; he was reaching to assume she was somehow involved with Chad's tardiness. Maybe he was paranoid.

He drove back to the jammer site and parked his pickup a few hundred yards away, not wanting to block the access for the trucks. Pulling a brown paper bag from the cab, he strode lightly up the side of the mountain, intending to go to the tiny spring that he knew gushed from the side of the hill a few hundred feet away in a little grove of trees that he had purposely left standing. He often had lunch with his men. He didn't hear the jammer and suspected they might already be at the spring.

He was only a few feet away when he paused to catch his breath. Turning, he looked down the way he had come and as always, the sight caught at his heart. He stood completely still as he took in the breathtaking vista—the forested mountains, the green fading to a thin blue, the sky so blue it looked unreal. The light breeze carried the cry of a hawk, and the astringent scent of pine. He took a deep breath.

He stiffened as he heard voices behind him and started to move, then hesitated. The spring was in an enclosed glade, screened from his view, but the voices were perfectly audible. Something in the guarded tones held him motionless.

"I don't like it."

He recognized Chad's voice. As he had suspected, the men were already at the spring; apparently they hadn't heard him coming up the hill.

"Well, I don't like it, either." That would be Sam, Chad's younger brother. "But I still don't see what harm she can do."

"I just don't like it," Chad insisted.

"Well, none of us do," another voice chimed in. Matt recognized it as coming from one of the skidder operators who had been late that morning. "But we went all over it last night. She's bound to get discouraged and leave."

"What if she doesn't?"

There was a moment of silence and Matt took that opportunity to move toward the spring, making as much noise as he could. When he stepped into the little enclosure, he was met by a dozen pair of blandly innocent eyes.

"Hi," he said, "looks like things are going good down there. How many loads did you get out this morning?" He moved to where the spring bubbled from a gash in the hill, squatted on a boulder and opened his lunch sack.

The men seemed to relax, and for the rest of the lunch break they discussed the morning's logging with only an occasional burst of horseplay.

When they were all back at work Matt got into his pickup and drove down the mountain toward Hope, his face thoughtful. He might as well call it quits for today, he decided. Everything in the woods was going smoothly and he could use the time to get some records in order for his accountant.

Still abstracted, he drove to his house, a large log structure situated on a wooded knoll, and entered his small office that had its own separate entrance. It was a functional room bare of anything but essentials: file cabinets, a couple of chairs, a small table. Sitting down at a battered rolltop desk, he tried to immerse himself in the accounts. It didn't work. His thoughts kept returning to the Daynew.

Something was going on, but he didn't have the slightest idea what it was. The men with whom he had lived all his life had demonstrated once again that cohesiveness that always made him feel as though he had come up against a stone wall. He could enter their lives only so far.

But they had talked together last night, and he would bet they had talked about Brianna, probably debating her request to interview them. He was positive they had been discussing her today when he had inadvertently overheard them, and they had seemed perturbed.

Had there been a shade of menace in their voices?

He shook his head angrily. Of course not. No, they were reacting normally, resenting some stranger coming along and prying into their affairs.

He thought of Brianna and of the contradictory emotions she aroused in him. If he had been admitted to that men's circle, he would have agreed with them; he didn't like her being here, either. On the other hand, he had only to shut his eyes and he could feel the length of her body pressed against his with such clarity that his nerve ends sizzled.

He didn't intend to change his mind about seeing her, though. Even if she were only a few miles away, and the sight of her face, frightened and bewildered when she heard the howl of the coyote, was etched on his brain.

What he needed was a little diversion. He had been too much of a recluse himself, lately. What had happened to his social life? It was Friday, and no work tomorrow. He would call a friend and have dinner in Boise, laugh a little, relax, and forget about both Brianna and the Daynew.

He reached for the phone.

Brianna tossed her head to get her hair out of her eyes, then raised a hand to lift its weight off her shoulder, glad of the feel of the breeze on the back of her neck. Straightening, she put her hands on her hips and proudly surveyed the results of her morning's work.

Even a campsite could be a little more comfortable, she had decided, and since she was staying here for an indefinite time she might as well get things organized. It was much too cramped inside the van; she needed to stretch out a bit. She had covered the bare planks of the picnic table with a bright plastic cloth weighted down at the corners with smooth pebbles. Her barbecue stood at one end, filled with briquettes and ready to light. A few feet away she had positioned a small card table and a chair with a large beach umbrella to shade it. A kerosene lantern hung in the low branches of a pine tree at the edge of the site—just in case her flashlight batteries failed. If she were going to be here a while—and she was determined that she was—she might as well be comfortable.

She stretched languidly and looked around the peaceful scene. Even at this altitude, the sun of early June was warm and she rubbed her arm across her forehead to wipe off the perspiration brought about by her exertions. Now all she needed were a few supplies and she would be all set.

Set for what? The question kept nagging her and she didn't have an answer. She had slept late this morning, perhaps as an unconscious way of postponing her problem. She had decided last night that today she would think of a plan to gain the trust of the Daynew, and she still hadn't a clue as to how to go about it.

At least she wouldn't have to contend with the conflicting emotions that Matt provoked. Thinking about last night, she bit her bottom lip with chagrin. In the rational light of day, she realized she had been impossible: first she wanted him to stay, then she didn't, then she did, finally even picking a fight. No wonder his final words had convinced her that he intended to wash his hands of her.

That was what she wanted, of course. He obviously wasn't going to help her any more than he had, and she was competent to do the rest herself. Perhaps a meeting of the full tribe wasn't the way to go about gaining their trust, anyway. She should find a way to meet someone alone, relate in a one-on-one manner.

The earth tremor had driven the incident so far from her mind that it was only now that she remembered Alta Thompson lurking in the bushes after the meeting. Had the woman wanted to talk to her? Spy on her? Perhaps she should try to locate the woman and find out what she had wanted.

She was reluctant to start with Alta Thompson, though. Something in the intensity of the older woman's eyes when she looked at her made her hesitate. Alta Thompson had looked like a fanatic, with her stern face and piercing eyes. It would be better to start with someone else.

Now that the campsite was organized, she would see about supplies. She was adequately dressed for the Hope Mercantile, she decided, looking down at her sleeveless white cotton blouse and narrow sea-green slacks. Backing the van out onto the road, she headed toward Hope. The woman she knew only as Margie worked there. Although she wasn't a Daynew, she seemed to know a lot of the people. Maybe she could give her some advice.

A few minutes later she parked her vehicle by the front door and entered the little establishment. No one was in the bar, but she heard the murmur of voices coming from the back and walked on through the bar into the small room that contained the groceries and other sundries.

"Hi. We're open. Come on in," a cheery voice called out.

She turned toward the voice and saw Margie stretching to put some canned goods on a shelf. Although she'd seen her once or twice behind the bar since that first meeting, this was the first time she'd gotten a really good look at her. As usual, the woman was wearing a short-sleeved cotton shirt and jeans that had to stretch a little to accommodate her ample hips. The face she turned to Brianna was unabashedly friendly, though, with plump cheeks and a small rosebud mouth, and Brianna felt more at ease than she had since coming to Hope.

"How are you getting along out there?" Margie asked, brushing her hands on her jeans and walking toward Brianna.

"Oh, just fine. I need a few supplies, though."

Margie's blue eyes sparkled with curiosity. "So you're planning to stay a while? I must say I'm a little surprised. It's pretty lonely out there. Later in the summer there will be quite a few campers, but right now they're pretty scarce. Nothing to harm you, of course," she said hastily as Brianna opened her mouth to respond.

"It is a little lonesome," Brianna said, giving Margie a warm smile. "But maybe I'll meet a few people soon. After all, the Daynew village is quite close."

Margie's eyes darted toward the back of the room and for the first time Brianna noticed they were not alone. Two women were seated at a small, oilcloth covered table, and both looked steadily at Brianna. On a hot plate atop a shelf behind them a kettle burbled, and as Brianna watched, one lifted a teapot and poured some steaming liquid into a cup.

"Well, my goodness, you don't have to go to the village to meet a few people," Margie said sternly. "Truth to tell, I thought Matt was going to monopolize you, or I'd have asked you to stop by." As she spoke, she walked toward the women, gesturing to Brianna to follow.

"Some of the ladies usually drop by during the day for a doughnut and a bit of tea. Breaks up the day, and we can catch up on all the gossip," she said, pulling out a chair and motioning Brianna to sit down. "I'll get you a cup. This is Louise Gardner and Diana Thompson. They know who you are," she said cheerfully.

Brianna looked across at the two women with a tentative smile, but her heart was pounding. What marvelous luck! She recognized them; both had been at the meeting last night. She had stumbled on to a casual, nonthreatening way to meet the Daynew.

As did the men, the women bore a strong resemblance to each other. She thought they were probably in their thirties, but their smooth, tanned, unlined skin gave few clues as to age. Louise Gardner's face was a little rounder, her expression a little softer, than Diana Thompson's stern, angular face, but both had strong, well defined features, definite eyebrows over wide-spaced eyes, full mouths and dark brown hair. Louise, however, flashed a ready smile and conveyed an impression of sturdiness and good humor, while Diana's countenance was much more reserved. Both wore brightly colored blouses, but Louise had on a matching skirt and Diana's long legs were encased in the ubiquitous denim jeans.

There was another difference that struck her forcefully. Louise's eyes were a soft dark brown, while Diana's were a cool, analytical gray.

Her interest was immediately heightened. She had noticed the odd eye coloring before; where she had expected only brown, she had seen gray, blue, hazel. It was probably one of the reasons her dad thought the Daynew weren't a branch of the Shoshoni. There were logical explanations, though. Perhaps there had been intermarriage long ago. Perhaps some trapper years before Caleb Stuart had found the Daynew, and stayed to mix his genes with theirs.

"I'm very glad to meet you," Brianna said, smiling at each of the women. "You were both at the meeting last night, weren't you?"

"Oh, yes," Louise replied, giving Brianna a ready smile. "My husband is the one who spoke up and told you we'd think over your proposal."

Gardner. Brianna connected the names. "Your husband is Chad? He works for Matt Stuart?"

This time Diana replied. "Just about everybody does."

"Your husband, too?"

"Oh, I'm not married."

Brianna studied her face, and wondered how she could have overlooked the similarity so long. The last name, Thompson. And the features were a younger version of Alta Thompson, the older woman who had come late to the meeting and who had waited outside in the dark afterward. Now that she recognized it, Brianna remembered that both Diana and Louise had been among the women who stopped for a friendly word with the old woman.

"Alta Thompson is your mother?"

Diana waited as Margie placed a cup of tea in front of Brianna and sat down beside her. Then she smiled briefly, but her eyes remained unreadable. "Yes. I hope she didn't bother you, coming in late as she did."

Brianna wanted to ask why Alta had been late, but there was a reserve about Diana Thompson that she hesitated to breach. She would learn only what the woman volunteered, she thought.

"Well, I'm really happy that I ran into you two," she said, taking a sip of the fragrant tea. For a minute she wondered what it was, then decided it was some herbal blend. "While I'm waiting for everyone to decide what to do with me—" she grinned ingenuously "—perhaps I could drop by and talk to you sometime."

Louise looked troubled and glanced at Diana, who in turn gave Brianna a long, cool look. "Perhaps," she said.

It wasn't the most welcoming of statements, but it wasn't a clear turndown, either. She decided to drop the subject for now; she didn't want to pressure them, and she would come back to it later.

For a couple of hours Brianna sat in the Hope Mercantile, drinking tea, and talking to the various women that came in for supplies and gossip. She was beginning to get a sense of the Daynew. Although for the most part the women did not work outside the home they were by no means idle. Most kept gardens, made many of their own clothes and those of their children. They were articulate, occasionally witty, and they talked freely on almost any subject.

Except about what she wanted to know. Once or twice again she had brought up the subject of visiting with them in their homes and talking about their history, and each time they had shrugged off her comments, their eyes going almost furtively to each other's face. Were they frightened of their men, she wondered. From their confident manner and breezy conversation, she doubted it.

By early afternoon they had all left; the men would be home soon and most planned to have dinner waiting.

Brianna said goodbye to Margie, promised to stop in real soon, and headed for her campsite. The herbal tea had been invigorating, and she felt more optimistic than she had since she had been here. All in all she thought the day had gone reasonably well. No one had volunteered cooperation, and she hadn't asked any, preferring to go slowly this time, establish friendship and trust. In time, she was confident the women would open up to her.

Which meant she definitely wouldn't need Matt's help. The thought was slightly depressing, but she shrugged off the feeling; she knew it was for the best. She couldn't deny that Matt had affected her strongly. Well, that was an understatement; he had swept her up like a tornado. But now, in the calm after the storm, she'd landed on her feet, shaken but unhurt, and it was just as well he had decided not to see her again. She wasn't the type to think with her hormones, and when she was around Matt they seemed to go completely berserk. He was a complication that she was just as well off without.

As she drove up the road toward the campground, she wondered if there was any possibility that she would see him again. It was a small place; obviously she would run into him, but it could just be a casual meeting. They had no unfinished business....

Of course, she should return his great-grandfather's journal to him, or at least offer to. She had thought of it when he mentioned it was missing, and it was the ethical thing to do. However her father had obtained it, it was rightfully Matt's.

Strangely enough, the thought made her feel much better. She didn't like to end any relationship in angry misunderstanding. She would just pick up the journal from the metal box she had left at her campsite and drive by his place someday. She didn't know exactly where he lived, but she could ask Margie.

She pulled off the main road and onto the narrow track that circled the campground, deciding not to analyze the elation that had speeded up her heartbeat when she thought of taking the journal to Matt. Instead she began wondering about how to approach him. She would explain that she had been under stress last night, and that although she didn't really retract anything she had said, perhaps she had been a little too adamant. Hope was a tiny place, and there was no use having an enemy when, with a little diplomacy, she could have a friend....

She pulled into her campsite and braked sharply. The sun was still high in the sky, and she saw everything in sharp detail. But she didn't believe it.

Her breath caught in her throat and her mouth felt dry. Clutching the steering wheel like a lifeline, she forced herself to look slowly around. The neat, well-organized campsite she had left was now a mass of disorder. The plastic table cover was ripped to shreds, and pieces hung like trapped birds on branches of the encircling trees. Her barbecue was dumped upside down on the grass, the briquettes scattered like ashes in a high wind. The umbrella was torn, the chair and table overturned.

She clutched her stomach, fighting a surge of nausea, a sense of violation; someone or something had done a very thorough job of destruction.

Her heart hammering in her chest, she stepped down from the vehicle and walked unsteadily to the overturned table. It wasn't fear she felt so much as a sense of bewildered outrage. Who could have done this? Or was she jumping to conclusions? Perhaps it was an animal—a bear, perhaps, attracted by the smell of food.

Hurriedly she bent to examine the metal box that she had left under the picnic table, and sighed with relief as she saw it was intact. She should never have left it outdoors, but she felt no harm would come to it here. Opening it with trembling fingers, she took out the journal. Thank heaven it was safe.

As the shock wore off, she examined every inch of the campsite. If an animal had attacked it would surely have left tracks, but she found only a few indefinite impressions in the soft ground—impressions that could have been made by her own footsteps.

A cold feeling ran along her back, finally settling like a chunk of ice in the pit of her stomach. The fact that there were no tracks was ominous; it made it much more likely that the camp had been trashed by humans. Humans who had taken great care not to leave a trace.

She sank onto the bench by the table and put her head in her hands. She had never been the target of hostility before, and it made her slightly sick. She didn't really think she was in danger; the destruction had been done while she was away from camp. But whoever had done this was very definitely leaving her a message. Trying to scare her away? Who wanted her gone?

In spite of her anguish, she almost smiled. Who didn't?

She couldn't stay here now. She looked up and saw that there were still several hours left before dark. Plenty of time to return to Hope and find out where Matt lived. Maybe—just maybe, if he were still speaking to her, she would take him up on the offer to spend the night.

She placed the case containing the journal and some other papers inside the camper and backed hurriedly onto the road without even stopping to straighten any of the mess. As she drove back to Hope, her mind kept racing like a squirrel in a cage, wondering who could want her gone so badly that they would stoop to such measures.

It was only later that she wondered about her own actions. What deep wellspring of need had sent her hurrying to find Matt at the first sign of trouble?

Chapter 5

With a squeal of tires on gravel, Brianna pulled up by the Hope Mercantile and jumped down from the vehicle. Margie was just locking up. Taking the key from the lock, she turned to Brianna with an inquiring look.

"Well, hi there. I didn't expect to see you again so soon."

"I didn't expect to be back so soon." The trip from the campground had enabled Brianna to get a firmer hold on her emotions and although her heart was still racing, her voice was even. "I had a little trouble."

"Oh?" Margie's smooth forehead puckered in concern. Her boot heels aroused protesting creaks from the wooden porch as she stepped down to meet Brianna. "Serious?"

Brianna shrugged. "Serious enough to scare me. Although I wasn't hurt or anything like that." Her full lips thinned to a stern line. "Somebody messed up my campground."

"Are you sure?"

At Brianna's angry glance, Margie stumbled on. "I mean, are you sure it was a person? There are still a few wild animals around . . ."

Brianna's shoulders slumped. She had been thinking the same thing as she drove toward Hope. So she hadn't found animal tracks; perhaps the ground wasn't soft enough to hold the prints. It certainly made more sense to think that a bear had wandered in than to believe that a hostile human had committed such wanton destruction.

"I'm not really sure," she admitted. "Anyway, I thought I'd stop by Matt's and see what he thinks." She wasn't about to tell Margie that she hoped to spend the night there. She'd only been in Hope a short time, but long enough to know that such news would travel with the speed of a grass fire. "I thought perhaps you could tell me how to get to his place."

Margie shook her head slowly. "I could tell you where his place is, but it wouldn't do you any good."

"Why not?" She knew her tone had been too sharp, and she spoke again more softly. "I mean, I just planned to drop by..."

There was obvious sympathy in Margie's face, and just a tiny hint of amused malice, as she replied. "Matt came by here late this afternoon on his way to Boise. All dressed up—must have had a hot date. He said he planned to spend the evening in town."

"Oh..." Brianna felt as deflated as a balloon pricked by a heedless child. It had never occurred to her that Matt might not be available. But why not? He was a handsome, virile male and she should have realized he didn't spend all his time alone in Hope.

Margie's keen eyes took in her crestfallen face. "Look, if you're afraid to go back out there, you're welcome to stay with me. There's not much room, with three kids and the old man, but you can have the couch..."

Brianna shook her head and tried to smile. "Thanks a lot, but I wouldn't want to bother you."

"It's no bother," Margie insisted.

For a moment Brianna hesitated. She really didn't want to go back out to her campsite, but the thought of Margie's couch amid the clutter and clamor of three healthy children wasn't much more appealing. She supposed she wasn't in real danger. It was always possible that the campsite had been ravaged by an animal, as Margie had suggested, but even if the perpetrator had been human that still didn't mean she was in actual danger. She thought of the trashing as more of a warning. But of what? What was she doing to threaten anyone?

Anyway, she could always lock herself in the camper. Just in case. An involuntary shiver went down her back, but she gave Margie a warm smile. "I appreciate your offer, but I'll be all right."

Margie still looked doubtful. "I wish there was a phone out there."

So did Brianna, but she wasn't going to dwell on it. With a final goodbye to Margie she got back into the camper and started toward the campground. In the rearview mirror she saw Margie's troubled face, and she felt a rush of warmth for the woman. At least someone cared about her.

By the time she reached the campsite the first raw flush of fear had been replaced by a grim determination. If the destruction had been meant to frighten her away, it would soon be evident that it hadn't worked. In fact, it strengthened what her dad had always called her stubborn streak.

And it convinced her of something else. This had to be connected somehow to her project about the Daynew. If someone were so anxious for her to leave, there must be something they didn't want her to find out. Perhaps the Daynew weren't quite the simple people they appeared to be.

Driving to her spot, she noticed that the campground was nearly empty—only a couple of tents several campsites away whose occupants were apparently backpacking; she hadn't seen them since she arrived. Maybe the weekend campers would be coming in soon. She hoped so; just the knowledge that other people were near was comforting.

She parked, stepped down on the hard surface of the campsite and started immediately to straighten things. The activity helped relieve the nagging anxiety, and she moved quickly, righting the table, picking up the briquettes and barbecue, retrieving the shreds of plastic tablecloth and placing them in the forest service debris box. Her initial impression had been correct; there was very little broken—mostly things were just strewn around as though they were toys thrown by an angry child.

By the time she had straightened her belongings, heated a can of beans and washed her face and hands in the small washbasin she had warmed over the glowing coals, the sun was down and long shadows lay across the forested valley and the mountains that encircled it. As she watched the purple shadows deepen in the gorges and ravines, saw the sky change from blue to gold to a delicate ivory, then darken to gray, the atavistic fear she had been suppressing by activity strengthened. She had never realized before how artificial light changed things. Here, with the sun down and the stars and moon not yet out, the darkness came down like a heavy blanket, nearly suffocating her.

She thought of lighting her lantern, but rejected it. Its tiny flame would only accentuate the blackness. With the absence of light, sounds were accentuated: the fitful whine of the wind in the tops of the pines like a restless ghost; the rustle of some night rodent in the dry bushes; the harsh scream of a night bird's prey, followed by deafening silence. A cold shiver went down her back and the fine hair along the back of her neck rose in primitive response to the cry. She had understood intellectually the comfort her distant forebears had obtained from the leaping flames of a fire that kept the spirits of the darkness at bay. Now she understood it emotionally, in every cell and nerve.

The scene was eerily familiar, too, reminding her of her frightening dreams. All she needed, she thought, were the disembodied shapes moving around a circle of fire, and she would be right in the middle of a dream.

Hastily she went inside the small dwelling and switched on the little light that ran from the battery. Then she locked the door and checked the windows to be sure they were securely fastened. The light didn't help much, as it fought forlornly against the blackness that surrounded the camper and pressed against the windows.

She tried to read but soon gave it up and switched off the light. Her mind was too occupied with the events of the day to involve itself in vicarious living. She thought over what she had found out about the Daynew—besides the possibility that one of them might like to trash campsites. She must have picked up some clues while she was talking to the women and endlessly drinking tea.

That tea. A special, herbal blend grown in the village, Margie had said. She had enjoyed the full, mellow taste, and she had drunk a lot, having another cup as each new group of women came to the store. She realized now it had a stimulating effect. Perhaps that was part of the reason her heart had been racing so and why sleep was almost impossible. Had she discovered that the Daynew were skilled herbalists? It would certainly make sense. Most native people were well versed in the uses of plants.

The matter of their coloring still bothered her. Their skin was lighter than she would have expected, their hair color varied from nearly black to light brown, with an occasional auburn tint. And the eyes: gray, hazel, even blue. Could it all be explained by an interloping ancestor?

But even if that were not the case, she thought, sighing and turning restlessly in the narrow bed, they were hardly unique. There was the Mandan tribe, those legendary Native Americans whom early explorers said lived someplace in the wilderness at the headwaters of the Missouri River. Tales had filtered back to civilization and fueled a century long quest. They were said to be light skinned, comely, with blue eyes and light hair. Farther advanced than their neighbors. There was endless speculation as to their origin and numerous efforts to reach them, but smallpox outdistanced the advancing white man. By the time the tribe was finally located there were only a few Mandan left alive, lonely survivors living with other tribes, their history and folklore lost forever.

She continued to toss and turn, her anxiety at being alone now mixed with excitement. Could she possibly have stumbled onto a tribe as unusual as the Mandan? But it hardly seemed possible. This was the twentieth century. All Native Americans had been cataloged and recorded long ago.

But if the original researchers erroneously thought them a branch of the Shoshoni and no one had bothered to delve further?

Aware that her hands were clenched at her sides, she loosened each separate finger and forced herself to take deep breaths. She had to get some sleep.

The sound of a diesel engine drifted through the night, and she relaxed slightly. Perhaps the weekend campers were beginning to arrive. There was a moment or two of silence, and then she froze, her straining ears picking up the sound of footsteps on the dried pine needles that covered the path to her vehicle.

Hardly daring to breathe, she listened to the approaching steps. A glance at the luminous dial of her watch told her it was nearly two o'clock; not a usual hour for visitors unless they had a nefarious purpose in mind.

She couldn't move as the steps came closer. Had she been wrong that today's trashing of her campsite was only a warning? Had someone returned to finish the job? Thank heaven the door was locked; it would take a lot to break it down....

There was a sharp tap on the door. Her heart jumped into her throat and she pulled the covers up to her chin, staring through the darkness at the sound.

It came again, followed by a firm voice. "Brianna? Are you in there?"

"Matt!" Relief surged through her in a wild flood, and she jumped from the bed, scrambling for the door. Swinging it open, she saw Matt standing on the little step in front of her camper, and she did the only thing she could have done. She choked out a sob and threw her arms around his neck, nearly knocking him off balance.

He steadied himself and his arms tightened convulsively around her; they felt hard and muscular through the thin material of her nightdress. Pressing mindlessly against his chest, her cheek rubbing against the softness of his flannel shirt, she felt the strong steady beat of his heart and inhaled the warm, musky scent of his skin. She trembled as he stroked her shoulder bones with his sure, competent hands, then moved down to her waist to pull her even more tightly against his body.

Wordlessly he held her until her trembling lessened and she was able to draw back a little and look up into his eyes.

"What are you doing here?" she managed to say.

His eyes were in shadow but glints of starlight accentuated his craggy features, and she was mesmerized by his mouth, which was coming inexorably closer. She opened her own lips slightly, involuntarily, as his warm lips touched hers with a sure, claiming motion. Forcefully, almost desperately, he pressed her tightly all along the hard length of his body as his mouth captured hers.

The force of his kiss called forth a wild abandon as desperate as his. She clung helplessly as the sweet delirium flooded through her, leaving every cell of her body aching and aware. Everything except the two of them was extraneous; need swirled inside of her, voracious desire, as she strove to get even closer. She wanted—needed—more, and her lips opened fully to admit his urgent tongue into the velvet sweetness of her mouth.

Then, slowly, reluctantly, they pulled apart. She wasn't sure who had instigated the retreat; perhaps they both realized together the folly of what they were doing. His breath was coming in short gasps and she knew it matched her own. Shaken, she waited for the wild tremors to die down.

As he loosened his hold she was aware of the thin material of her nightdress; now that she was no longer in his embrace, the breeze felt suddenly chilly.

He put his hand on her back and turned her gently, urging her back toward the camper. "We'll talk in a minute; you'd better get a robe on. It's cold out here this time of night." From the husky timbre of his voice, she knew he was as shaken as she was.

Aware that she was almost naked, she hastily reached inside and took a quilted robe from a hanger in the tiny closet space. Tying it, she followed Matt to the picnic table and sat down beside him. For a long moment they just looked at each other, both apparently deciding to ignore what had just happened between them.

"I don't think you ever answered my question," she said, making a huge effort to smile. "What are you doing here this time of night?"

"I'm sorry if I scared you," he said softly. "I should have called out earlier."

So he was saving her pride, indicating he knew her passionate embrace had been purely a response to fright. Which it was. "That's all right," she protested. "I was relieved to see you. Just tell me how you happened to come by. Margie said you were in Boise."

"I was. But I came home earlier than I expected." His face was faintly illuminated by starlight, and she saw his white teeth flash in a grin. "Margie said you were looking for me, so I decided to stop by."

"But it's two o'clock!"

He took her hand in his warm palm and pulled her a little closer, his touch protective rather than passionate. "She was worried about you. There was a message on my recorder when I got home tonight. She wanted me to call her when I got home, whenever it was. She was quite concerned about what happened at your campsite today."

Brianna looked at him blankly. A message on his recorder. This place never ceased to surprise her with its combination of modern technology and provincial living. Of course he would have a recorder. Why hadn't she thought of that?

"I did want to see you," she admitted, refusing to look into his eyes. "Perhaps I overreacted to what happened today, but I was a little worried about staying alone. I was going to ask if your offer to stay at your place was still good—after our argument the other night."

His face was grave. "Of course. We'll move you there tomorrow. And I'll stay here tonight—it's pretty late to get you out of bed and moved."

She tensed at his words, almost completely ambivalent. She didn't want to stay alone tonight, but the thought of Matt in the tiny bed alongside her aroused a much more elemental fear than the one she had just been experiencing. The wild burst of desire she'd felt just a few moments ago was frightening. She had this nearly overwhelming urge to accept the comfort he offered, but she knew it would be disastrous. She was vulnerable from fright, and although she didn't think Matt was the kind of man to take advantage of vulnerability—after all, he had pulled back when she hadn't been sure she could—she knew that she could never let him stay the night in her bed.

He felt her muscles stiffen and chuckled softly. "Don't worry. The thought of making love with you isn't exactly repugnant—you're a beautiful, desirable woman. But I don't shoot sitting ducks."

She jerked erect and withdrew her hand quickly. What a typically male way to express it! As though she were prey and he the hunter! "Don't be too sure you would have had the opportunity," she said stiffly. "I'm grateful for your concern, but it's nearly morning. I'll be all right alone now."

"Probably," he agreed, rising from the bench and looking down at her, a half smile on his lips. "I'll stick around just to make sure."

Before she could protest again, he strode again down the path toward his pickup. In a minute he was back, a sleeping bag over his shoulder. As she watched, he unrolled it on the picnic table, then turned to her.

"Just in case I forget to be a gentleman, perhaps you had better get on into bed, Brianna. See you in the morning." Without waiting for a reply, he took her shoulders, turned her gently and pushed her back inside her shelter and closed the door.

She leaned back against the wall until her pulse slowed to normal, then slid underneath the covers of her narrow bed. She thought she would lie awake hours, agonizingly aware of Matt just outside her door, but she didn't. In a minute she was fast asleep.

Matt wasn't. He lay on his back, hands pillowing his head, looking up moodily at the stars. Just what was he getting himself into?

After stomping away from Brianna last night, he had fully intended to stay away from her. She was much too disrupting an influence, not only on the Daynew, but on himself. He had thought that if she floundered around a day or two, running into stone walls, she would give up and go home, and things could settle back to normal. He could settle back to normal.

Because, he admitted, things weren't normal right now. He had gone to Boise, fully expecting to enjoy himself. Bettie, as usual, was bright and companionable, as cute as a cricket. The dinner at the Chart House was marvelous, and he had fully expected to go home with Bettie and see what developed. He had surprised them both by telling her an early good-night.

It was true that he was physically attracted to Brianna, he told himself, but that wasn't why he had rushed right home. He was worried about her and she was his responsibility as long as she was in Hope. In spite of her belief that she could handle whatever came along, she was a babe in the woods here. Out of her element. And protection of the weak and helpless was an integral part of his nature, instilled in him by his father. A man takes care of women, protects them, as he does everyone who is dependent upon him. She was stubborn and opinionated, but even so he shouldn't have let her goad him into leaving her to her own devices.

He re-experienced the shock that had gone through him when Margie told him about the trashing of Brianna's campsite and how frightened Brianna had been. He thought of her alone, scared, shrinking from every noise, and he had to come.

Not that he thought she was in any real danger. A marauding animal was the most likely culprit. The Daynew he knew—the Daynew he had known since they were all children together—would never engage in wanton destruction. They were peaceful, friendly—

He remembered the words he had overheard at the spring, and his chest tightened. *I don't like her being here. She'll leave soon. And if she doesn't?*

The ground shook slightly; if he hadn't been awake he probably wouldn't even have noticed the slight tremor. It was nothing like what he had experienced when Brianna came to the door and threw her arms around him, he thought dryly. That had shaken him down to his very toes. He could still feel the imprint of her body burning against his skin. Would anyone ever believe that he had managed to send her back inside her camper—alone? He couldn't believe it himself.

He gave up on sleep and resigned himself to a long night. Tomorrow he would move her to his house, and he wouldn't have to worry about her safety. He refused to think of what he might have to worry about.

Brianna awoke to the smell of coffee drifting through a window, and sat up slowly, still foggy with sleep. She rubbed her eyes with clenched fists, then opened them again. Slowly yesterday's events came back to her, and she slid her long legs from the bed and into her jeans. Slipping into a shirt, she thrust her feet into thongs and peered out the door.

Matt was leaning over a fire pit; he had erected a tripod over the fire and a can was suspended over the flames from a wire bail. It was from this that the tantalizing aroma of coffee floated toward her.

At the sound of the door opening he straightened and turned toward her; his eyes opened wide and for an endless moment he seemed frozen in place, his gaze taking her in like a thirsty man who had just seen water. She was uncomfortably aware that her hair was tumbling around her shoulders, she had no makeup on, and her eyes were still soft with sleep. Yet surely that was admiration in his eyes.

The moment broke and he smiled, white teeth flashing in his bronzed face, and pushed his dark hair back from his forehead. "You're a sleepyhead. I've been up for hours."

"I wouldn't be up even now if I hadn't smelled the coffee," she admitted.

"It's my only claim to culinary fame," he said, moving toward her and handing her a steaming mug.

She accepted it, took a sip and glanced at her watch. "Don't you have to be at work?"

"It's Saturday," he said, taking his cup to the table and sitting down on the bench. "I have a few odds and ends to take care of; then we'll move you to my place. Do you mind being alone that long?"

"Oh, no." She came to sit across from him, and smiled a little sheepishly. "In fact, I'm feeling a little silly. Things look a lot different in the daylight."

He reached across the table and ran his finger along her bare arm, his eyes following the path his fingers took. He seemed to leave a trail of liquid fire.

"You don't look so very different," he mused. "You look just as I imagined you would, all tousled and warm from sleep."

"Tousled is right," she said, keeping her voice as calm as she could. It wasn't reasonable that such a casual touch should send shivers all along her arm. "I'd better wash up and comb my hair. I hope you weren't too uncomfortable last night; I feel a little guilty."

"Don't. I'm used to sleeping out. Dad and Mom always took me camping a lot when I was a kid."

"Camping?" She looked around in amusement. "I'd say just living in Hope is a form of camping."

"You're spoiled by city living. We really have most of the amenities here, and none of the crowds."

"Don't you like people?"

"Not in bunches. I prefer them one-on-one."

His voice was insinuating, and she spoke hastily to cover her nervousness. "Do you like your job? Do you plan on being a logger always?"

He smiled. "With an entire community depending on Stuart Logging, I'm not sure I have a choice. I'd like to expand a little, though, maybe set up a mill..."

"Couldn't the people get other jobs?"

"Not without leaving Hope. And in spite of what you think of the place," he said, grinning, "they don't want to go."

"So you're stuck in Hope, too."

"Oh, I don't consider it stuck," he said cheerfully. "I like it here, too. And as for taking care of the community—everybody needs a purpose in life." He turned his eyes fully toward her. "What's you purpose in life, Brianna?"

"Recording myths, I guess," she said slowly. "Seeing how history repeats itself."

He raised a dark eyebrow. "Is that enough? What about marriage, a family?"

"I suppose that will all come..." She hadn't given that too much thought, either. She had concentrated on her education, making a name for herself, supposing that marriage and family would just normally come along. Sometime. She wasn't in a hurry.

She met Matt's questioning eyes. Matt certainly didn't change the timetable. She desired him; she admitted that, but he wasn't anyone she'd think of for a permanent relationship. They were from different worlds, and while sometimes people could merge different worlds, she knew she and Matt couldn't. It wasn't just the worlds; it was their characters, their values, their temperaments.

And what was she doing even thinking about it, for heaven's sake! She stood abruptly. "I guess I'd better wash up."

He rose, too, and quickly downed his coffee. "And I had better be going. I'll be back in a couple of hours."

She sat very still at the table, watching his retreating back until he disappeared around a bend in the trail. He was definitely attractive, she thought, observing the width of his shoulders taut under his shirt, the play of his hips through the snug denim jeans, the long, confident stride. She definitely responded to him on a physical level. But she knew that now and could guard against it.

After last night, she knew that he wasn't a man to take advantage, either. She would be perfectly safe at his house as long as she remembered the danger and kept things on a level keel between them. It might be a little tense at first, but it was bound to be better than the fear she had experienced last night.

For the next hour she bustled about the campsite, tidying up and stuffing things back into her camper. Then she started on herself, humming slightly as she took a sponge bath, brushed her hair to shining obedience, lightly applied makeup—a touch of mascara, soft coral lipstick.

She wasn't sure just when she became aware that she was not alone.

Chapter 6

Awareness began with a slight prickling at the back of her neck, an uneasy desire to glance back over her shoulder. A quick survey of the campsite convinced her she was imagining things, but she stopped humming, vaguely uneasy.

The feeling didn't go away, although she tried to ignore it and continued putting on her light makeup. Sitting down on the bench, she rested her elbows on the picnic table, noticing that her hand shook a little as she held the mirror and inspected the coating of soft coral lipstick. She felt as though someone were staring a hole in her back.

She turned swiftly, feeling silly but unable to stop the involuntary action, but not even the movement of a leaf indicated there was anyone there.

Then, drawn by something she didn't understand, she slowly raised her head and met the eyes of the woman who was standing as still as a statue in the shadow of a large pine that overspread her camp. Her heart seemed to stop in her chest, then erupt into a frenzy of wild beating, as she recognized the woman. Alta Thompson.

The eyes of the tall woman held her as securely as though she were tethered with ropes. For a long moment she was incapable of movement. Then, released by a spurt of anger, she rose from the bench and managed a cold frown. "How long have you been watching me?"

Disdaining a reply, Alta Thompson stepped out from the shadows and moved imperiously toward her. "You're Brianna Royce, I know. I'm Alta Thompson." She held out her hand.

"I know who you are, Mrs. Thompson. I saw you at the meeting." Although she would have liked to say she had also seen her lurking around outside after the meeting, she didn't. There was something so commanding about the woman that Brianna found herself placing her hand in Alta Thompson's strong grip, although she would have preferred no contact at all.

She did take a good look at her uninvited visitor. At the meeting she'd had only an impression of faded grandeur—a hawklike face, an imperious bearing, and deep, piercing gray eyes. Outside the schoolhouse, of course, she had caught only a glimpse of the woman's face as she hid and spied on her from the bushes. Now she studied her intently.

Alta Thompson's eyes were her most striking feature, but they no longer held the fierce intensity Brianna remembered. They were gray as she recalled, shaded with long black lashes, but the expression was almost mild. Her waist-length hair was in a tight braid and wound around her head, and she wore a flowered housedress that looked like those of the other Daynew women, except that it was somewhat longer. Even her features, though still gaunt and sharply chiseled, were softened by the smile on her face.

She didn't seem to represent a threat now, and Brianna relaxed slightly. Why had she been so upset by this woman? Her faint fear was probably caused by the fact that Alta Thompson was a dramatist: sailing late into a meeting to call attention to her presence; waiting outside in the shadows; now sneaking up to her camp instead of approaching openly. Matt had been right; she was an eccentric old woman, but no one to cause concern.

"Yes, I was at the meeting," Alta Thompson said, answering her earlier comment. "And please call me Alta. We don't go much on ceremony around here."

Brianna waited. Should she ask her to sit down? But this was hardly a social call, was it? She was still upset at being spied on; she didn't know how long the woman had been watching her.

"I understand you met some of the women at the store yesterday," Alta said, moving confidently to the bench and seating herself.

One thing seemed certain; Alta had not been at the store, but she'd gotten reports, probably knew everything that had been said. Brianna smiled blandly. "Yes, it was a pleasant afternoon."

"Diana and Louise said you were anxious to see them in their homes, talk about our history."

Before Brianna could reply the woman continued. "If you'd like to come with me now, that should be possible."

"But—"

Alta rose and nodded abruptly. "We all like to get together a couple of times a week—just talk. Hen parties, I believe the men call them." There was a faint shadow of contempt in her voice, and her lips curved in a smile that did very little to soften the sternness of her features. "You're welcome to join us."

Brianna glanced at the woman, then back down the trail where Matt had vanished. She wasn't sure when he would be coming back, and he would expect her to be here. But this was an unexpected break—she couldn't pass it up. The women must have discussed her request among themselves and decided to talk to her. It was, after all, the reason she had come to Hope; she couldn't miss the opportunity.

She could leave him a note. But he had said he'd be gone several hours. She'd be back by then.

"I'd love to, Mrs.—Alta. Do you have a car or shall we take my camper?"

"It's not that far." Alta turned abruptly and strode from the campsite. Brianna reached hastily for a pen and pad and hurried after her.

Alta walked swiftly, leaving Brianna to follow along as best she could. A trail took off from the campground and the woman followed it for nearly a mile. Then she plunged into unmarked woods, and Brianna began to feel a little uneasy. Should she have followed Alta so willingly? As she made her way through ravines and along thickly forested meadows, she realized that she was completely lost. The knowledge sent a shiver of fear through her. As usual, she had acted too impulsively; she should have left a note for Matt.

The older woman's legs were long and she walked briskly; Brianna's chest was heaving and she was gasping for breath by the time they broke out of the woods onto a gravel road.

Then Brianna saw the neat row of houses that lined the road, and she sighed inwardly, feeling a little foolish; again she had been close to misjudging Alta Thompson's motives. She had obviously brought her by another route to the Daynew village. She doubted it was a shortcut, though. Perhaps the woman took a perverse pleasure in showing up her city visitor.

Alta slowed and walked with her up the path to a neat little cottage. Like most of the others, its frame structure was neatly painted, its roof shingled, and it sported a small roofed porch with peeled pine supports that were decorated with various carvings. Brianna glanced at them, then took a closer look.

The carvings were somewhat like those she had seen at Tom West's house: random markings, geometric figures. She noticed one carving that caught her interest: a deeply engraved spiral.

Before she could take a closer look, Alta opened the door and ushered her into the house. She had a quick impression of a pleasant, well-kept room: a wood-burning stove in the corner, serviceable brown carpeting, cheery curtained windows, but most of her attention focused on the occupants.

About a dozen women clustered in the small space, several sitting on the sofa and the chairs, with two sitting cross-legged on the floor. The buzz of chatter ceased as the door opened and all eyes focused on the newcomers.

A young woman, a warm smile on her pleasant face, detached herself from the group and came forward. "Hello, Brianna. It's nice to see you again. Remember me? I'm Louise Gardner."

"And this is her house." A taller woman whom Brianna recognized as Diana rose from the couch and came to greet her. "It's the only one large enough to handle so many of us. And we all wanted to see you again."

As Brianna was introduced to the women, many of whom she had seen the day before, she realized she had been wrong in thinking the women looked so much alike. As she became familiar with them, she saw that there were definite differences, nearly as striking as would exist in any group.

Louise, for instance. She had a shy retiring manner, a sweetness about her, that was in stark contrast to Diana's strong assertiveness. Others were beginning to stand out from the crowd, too, as she said a brief word to each.

"Please sit down." Louise patted an empty chair, rather anxiously, Brianna thought, as she sat down on the comfortable flowered chintz. She caught the troubled look the woman gave Diana and wondered if there were undercurrents here she didn't understand.

"What is it that you want to know about us?" The question came from a large woman with straight black hair and overpowering features whom Brianna remembered was incongruously called Lilly.

"Now, Lilly, let's wait until Brianna has her tea," Louise said firmly.

All eyes watched her face as Brianna sipped the familiar fragrant brew. Perhaps this was a good place to start. "This is delightful tea," she said, again raising the cup to her lips. "I've never tasted anything quite like it. How do you make it?"

Alta shrugged. "This particular tea is a mixture of several herbs. Catnip, lemon verbena, elderberry flowers, a touch of foxglove—"

"Foxglove! That's poisonous!" She set the cup down so hastily it clattered in its saucer.

"We certainly don't use enough to be dangerous," Alta said calmly. "Just enough to stimulate the heart a bit. Mixed as it is, it gives a definite feeling of well-being."

Brianna looked at her in astonishment. She had been right about there being a stimulant in the tea, but she hadn't suspected it might be harmful. But all the other women were drinking it, too. Very carefully, she picked up the cup. This might be a test.

Louise gave her a sweet, apologetic smile. "Daynew women have always used herbs, Brianna. There is nothing to hurt you."

The other women sipped unconcernedly, and Brianna did the same. If she were to gain these women's trust, she had to show a little trust, too. And it *was* delightful tea.

There was a small murmur of approval, and Brianna decided it was time to go on with her interview. "That's just one of the things I'd like to know about you. For instance, I suppose the art of herbal medicine has been passed down for generations."

"There has always been a woman skilled in medicines," Alta agreed.

"How is the skill passed along?"

"From mother to daughter, usually. For instance, my mother taught me."

"I'm so glad you came for me today," Brianna said, leaning forward impulsively. "Stories of your past must have been passed along, too, just as these herbal recipes. I'm so anxious to learn all about it."

"We talked it all over, and we decided there is no reason not to cooperate with you," Alta said firmly, her eyes raking the room like an alert hawk. There was a murmur of agreement, although Brianna noted one or two women, including Louise, just looked stolidly at the floor. There might still be some disagreement among them, she decided, but the majority had acquiesced to cooperate.

The women talked, and Brianna scribbled hastily in her notebook. They didn't tell her anything startling, but she knew it was still too early. She didn't yet have their full confidence. She would start with easy, nonthreatening questions, get them used to seeing her around. What she was getting from them now was interesting, but she knew they were deliberately being superficial.

She started to ask another question, but was interrupted by the sound of heavy boots walking up onto the porch. All heads turned to the door as it swung open and a man stood on the threshold, glaring around at the assembled women.

"Chad!" Louise rose quickly and hastened to her husband. "I didn't expect you home so early."

"Too early," he said, a sour expression on his square face, as he continued to survey the women.

Alta Thompson shot him a malicious glance. "Didn't you remember this was our meeting day, Chad?"

He didn't answer, his eyes going from face to face. When he saw Brianna his frown deepened and a flush darkened his weathered skin. For a moment she thought he was going to say something, but he only muttered something under his breath, turned and left the room, slamming the door so hard the frame house shuddered. The room was quiet until the sound of his footsteps died away.

Louise still looked at the door, a worried frown on her face. "Oh, dear, I'm sorry. I thought Chad would be at work."

"It's Saturday," Diana reminded her dryly.

"I know—but he was supposed to move his jammer to another site to be ready for Monday."

"You defer to that man too much," Diana said.

There were murmurs from the women, both of agreement and protest, but Louise herself looked troubled. She shot Diana a defiant look. "He's my husband. Perhaps if you were married you'd understand."

"I understand," Diana said. "That's why I'm not married. Come on, Brianna, let's get on with the questions."

Although there was no further discussion of Chad and his obvious disapproval of the gathering, the mood had changed. The women were restive, their glances going often to the door. Brianna caught the exchange of furtive looks, and snapped her notebook shut. She had better arrange to see them another time; Matt would be waiting for her.

She glanced at her watch and caught her breath. She had no idea it was so late. She should have left Matt a note. It would be quite late by the time she got back to the campground, and she already knew Matt was not the most patient man she'd known.

Matt knew the campsite was empty when he was still several feet away from it, the knowledge coming in an intuitive flash, although he continued on and made a thorough search. He stuck his head into the camper, called her name, then sat down gingerly on the picnic bench, ready to spring up at the sight of her walking toward him down one of the trails. Perhaps she had just stepped away for a few minutes.

Damn it, he had told her he'd only be gone a couple of hours, and he'd hurried to be sure he didn't keep her waiting. In fact, he'd cut some things a little short he'd been so intent on getting back to her.

As he sat there, the only sounds the wind in the trees and the scurrying of unseen little forest animals crackling in the underbrush, his initial uneasiness turned to active worry. Where could she have gone? Ordinarily he wouldn't have been concerned, but he couldn't get it out of his mind that her camp had been vandalized just yesterday. And she had promised to wait right here for him; was she the kind of woman who couldn't be trusted to keep her word?

He hated to think so; honesty was about the most important thing there was. Something must have happened. Perhaps even now she was in danger, hurt, frightened . . . his chest suddenly constricted.

He forced himself to give up that line of thinking. The best thing to do was to drive around and see if he could locate her.

His jaw clenched and his hands tightened into fists. When he did, he would give her a lecture about irresponsible actions. Not that it would do much good. She was impulsive by nature, rushing in without considering the consequences. Or thinking about how people might worry about her!

By the time he was in his pickup and cruising down the road he was very nearly as angry at himself as he was at Brianna. Angry at his own reaction to her absence. He wasn't much good at kidding himself and he knew very well that his anger was only a small part of what he was experiencing. The larger component of his dark mood was fear—fear for her safety, and it angered him that concern for her should affect him so intensely. This reaction wasn't what he wanted or needed.

Where would she go? Hope Mercantile was too far away to travel on foot. If she were walking. Perhaps someone had come by, picked her up, forced her— He shook his head, sending a dark lock of hair falling over his forehead. Absently he pushed it back with a bronzed hand, and his lips thinned in derision at his reactions. He was acting like a mother hen with a lost chick and he didn't like it; he should have insisted she leave Hope immediately.

He forced himself to loosen the grip on the steering wheel, and took a deep breath. He was overreacting, and he didn't know why. She was really just an acquaintance, although admittedly an attractive one. One who felt indescribably exciting in his arms, but a woman who had no permanent place in his life. True, he felt responsible for her while she was in his territory, but the thought that she could really be in danger was ridiculous. He was just irritated because she hadn't been waiting where she said she would be.

He had been prepared to take her directly to his house, and the expectation had sent a warm glow all through him. He thought of her in his spacious house, sitting in front of the open fire in the evening, coming down the stairs in the morning, her face soft from sleep. Mostly he thought of what might happen in between.

He shook his head angrily. He was thinking of more than her safety when he invited her to his home. And he didn't want that type of involvement. He wanted her gone.

He turned the wheel abruptly just in time to miss a collision with the pickup that hurtled toward him around a sharp bend in the road. Chad's old blue pickup. He pulled over to the side of the road and stopped as Chad braked, too.

He rolled down the window and grinned at Chad. "Hi. Speeding a bit, weren't you?"

"I could say the same for you, Boss." Chad's frown vanished and his familiar grin split across his square face.

"Get the jammer set up?"

"Uh—just going up there now."

A shadow darkened Matt's eyes. He was surprised that Chad hadn't done what he had expected him to do, but it didn't really matter. There was plenty of time.

"You haven't seen Brianna around, have you?"

Chad's face changed subtly, his eyes darkening, his smile less pronounced. "Looking for her? Matter of fact, I have. She's at my place, gabbing with the women."

Matt frowned slightly. Brianna hadn't said a word about going there. Had something come up suddenly? Well, at least she was safe. "I thought you all had decided not to talk to her," he said slowly.

"Who can understand women?" Chad shrugged. "I guess they all got bored and decided talking to her would break the monotony."

In spite of Chad's casual tone, Matt thought the man wasn't too pleased about Brianna's presence, but he didn't pursue it. Everyone at work kidded Chad about keeping Louise on a tight rope, and maybe he was afraid Brianna would strengthen her willpower. Nevertheless, Chad's domestic arrangements were none of Matt's concern, although he suspected Louise might be a little more pliable than most of the Daynew women who had a reputation for being headstrong.

"I'll go on over and give her a lift," he said, easing onto the road.

As he drove toward the Daynew village his relief at learning Brianna was safe and accounted for turned to irritation. She could at least have let him know where she was going! By the time he drove up in front of Chad's house, he was thoroughly disgusted with her lack of consideration. His mood wasn't helped any by the sight of her coming out the door; he watched, his throat tight, as her slender body moved gracefully down the path toward him. She looked so lovely and delectable, vibrantly alive. He wanted to take her in his arms and assure himself that she was all right, kiss her senseless, then shake the stuffing out of her for worrying him.

"Matt!" She came hastily toward the car, a rueful smile on her face. "I'm sorry I didn't get back in time—"

"Or leave a note," he said gruffly.

She paused, alerted by his tone. "I would have left a note, but I thought I'd be back before you got there. Anyway, no harm's been done," she said brightly.

No harm done! How like her to dismiss the entire episode so selfishly. She didn't know how he had worried! He leaned across the seat and opened the door. "Get in."

For several miles they drove in stony silence with Brianna glancing occasionally at his profile. Finally she spoke. "I know I was thoughtless. I apologize. After all, you are kind enough to let me stay with you and I shouldn't have inconvenienced you by just leaving without a word—"

"It's not the inconvenience," he said stiffly. "Something could have happened to you."

"Happened to me? Like what?"

"Are you forgetting your campground was vandalized?" he asked dryly. "I thought you were scared. Or do you want to stay with me just because you like my company?"

He caught her outraged look out of the corner of his eye and grinned inwardly. She deserved it for the concern she had just put him through.

"I've been thinking about the campground," she said coolly. "I guess, deep down, I suspected it was trashed by the Daynew trying to scare me away. But I was wrong. They are quite willing to cooperate. It must have been an animal, as you thought."

"Maybe."

"Anyway, there's no reason to bother you now. If it was the Daynew, they've changed their minds. I can stay in the camper and I won't cause you any trouble."

"I'd feel better if you stayed at my place tonight."

"I'll be quite all right."

He turned to look at her, and was glad she had averted her head to look out the window. His own unruly emotions must be written all across his face. She was sitting there so stiffly, the very rigidity of her posture making her look fragile and vulnerable. A woman needed a man's protection. Her hair glowed, her skin appeared nearly translucent in the light of the sun that shone through the truck window, and he saw that she was biting her luscious lower lip with delicate, pearllike teeth. She was too delicate, too feminine; he wasn't going to risk anything happening to her.

"I'm taking you to my house," he said brusquely.

She swung toward him, ready for battle at the commanding tone in his voice. "Matt, I know I asked to stay with you, and believe me, I appreciate your agreeing. But things have changed. There isn't anything to be afraid of."

"Probably not. But I'll enjoy the company. And you must be about ready for a shower."

She sighed, admitting to herself that a night away from the camp would be welcome. "I'll need some things."

"We'll stop by the camper. Just stay the night, and in the morning I'll drive you back to your camp. And you can think about leaving Hope," he said abruptly.

Her head snapped up. "I thought we'd already had that argument."

"I like my point of view better all the time."

"Matt, you can't order me around like you do everyone else," she said stiffly. "Maybe you're El Patron of Hope, but you're not responsible for me. I can look after myself."

"Yes, I could see how well you were doing about two o'clock this morning." Matt knew it was an unfair shot, but he had to bring her to her senses.

"Very well, I admit I was afraid. But now I've talked to Alta Thompson, and I know the Daynew."

"*Know* the Daynew? In a couple of days?" He lifted an incredulous eyebrow. He had played with the Daynew, gone to school with the Daynew, and he sure as hell didn't know them. For instance, why was Chad so upset today?

"Okay," she said suddenly, slumping back against the seat. "So I don't know them all that well—yet. I'm really grateful for a place to stay tonight." The smile she gave him set his pulse racing. "But forget about my leaving, Matt. I've just gotten started."

Both stared straight ahead as he drove up the circular driveway and stopped in front of his house.

Brianna stared out the window at the imposing structure before her. She didn't know what she had expected, but it certainly wasn't this. This house looked like the abode of some medieval baron instead of the home of a backwood logger.

It was huge, rambling over the elevated knoll in two wings composed of peeled logs fastened together in the Finnish style, each log cut to fit exactly over the other, but that wasn't all that made it so impressive. It was its look of age, of solidity, of permanence, as though it had been there forever.

Now she took in the details: dark shake roof, recessed windows that looked as though they belonged in a fort, fieldstone steps that climbed to a massive entry door flanked by narrow lights. Perhaps it was Matt's unassuming manner, his casual dress, but she had never expected him to inhabit a place like this.

"Like it?"

"It's a bit overwhelming."

"And not at all what you expected to find around Hope," he said, jumping down to open the door for her.

"It's not how I pictured you living," she admitted.

"Ah! So you've thought about how I exist." He grinned and took her arm firmly as they walked together up the stone steps.

She moved away. She was ambivalent toward the way Matt had overridden her protests, insisting she come here even after she had told him there was no longer any need for it. Just another instance of his controlling, possessive nature. She had agreed because, after all, it had been her idea in the first place, but she was determined to keep things on a purely formal basis. And his touch threatened that determination.

He merely took her arm again. "I know you can take care of yourself," he said dryly, "but please allow me to be mannerly. My mother always told me to be mannerly; doesn't cost a thing to carry them around."

She smiled, mollified. He was just being charming, and what was wrong with that? She was overreacting. "I never thought your place would be so huge," she said.

"My great-grandfather built the first few rooms," he said easily, steering her through the door. "After him, Stuarts just kept adding on haphazardly. My dad built the last wing. I can't imagine why; I'm an only child and I sure rattled around here."

"So am I—an only child." She thought briefly of the difference in her life and Matt's. She had lived in rented homes, homes that were pleasant, efficient and easy to manage, necessary qualities since her mother worked and her dad might be anyplace around the globe. This old mansion was probably full of hidden corners, fantastic hiding places.

But it would be lonely, too.

Matt took her hand and pulled her along the hall, and she caught only fleeting impressions of high-beamed ceilings, paneled walls, comfortable furnishings.

"I'll give you a tour later. Right now, I'm hungry. Are you?"

She hadn't thought about it, but it had been a long time since breakfast, and that had consisted only of coffee. It was now well into the afternoon. "Starved," she agreed.

They entered the kitchen, a large square room with varnished log walls and brown tiled floor. There was even an open fireplace.

"This is the older part of the house," Matt said, his gaze following hers. "I hope Mrs. Clayton left us some food."

He moved to the refrigerator and returned with a platter of cold chicken and sliced tomatoes, which he put on the sturdy wooden table that dominated the middle of the room. "There should be plates and stuff in that cabinet."

Brianna set the table as Matt foraged for more food, and soon they were seated across from each other. Brianna looked at the enticing meal, but her mind was on something else. "You said Mrs. Clayton left the food," she said slowly. "She doesn't live in, then?"

His eyes sparkled, and Brianna felt herself blushing. "No, she doesn't live in," he answered. "She comes in for a few hours during the day, fixes lunch and dinner, and does the dishes."

So they really were alone. She felt the vital energy that surrounded him like a nimbus crackling across the space between them, shooting sparks of sexual awareness, and couldn't suppress an involuntary shiver. He kept his eyes on her face until she lifted her gaze to his. His eyes were dark, mesmerizing.

"Afraid?" he asked softly.

Chapter 7

She deliberately chose to misunderstand him. "Oh, no, I'm not afraid here," she said lightly. "I *would* have been if Mrs. Clayton hadn't left us some food. I get the definite impression you're not a cook."

"Your impression is right," he said cheerfully, allowing her the subterfuge. "I've heard all about the new fashion in men, but thank God it hasn't reached Hope. Househusbands?" He raised a dark eyebrow as he reached for a jar of horseradish. "Not for me. Besides, if Mrs. Clayton hadn't come through I'd have expected you to whip up a little something with your feminine hands."

She saw the teasing glint in his eyes and replied in the same tone. "I'm afraid you would have been out of luck. I can open a mean can of soup, but that's about all. We'd starve together."

"Is that one of your main requirements for a man? That he be able to cook?" His lips quirked in a knowing smile that made it suddenly hard for Brianna to breathe.

"What makes you think I have requirements?"

"You must have thought about it," he insisted. "The kind of man you'd like to marry. Or whatever." His grin was absolutely wicked.

She was definitely not going to encourage his flirting. She leaned back in her chair and put her fork down carefully beside her empty plate. "I know the type of man I like." And it's not you, her tone clearly said.

But did she really know the type of man she liked? The thought of Roy flashed through her mind for the first time in days. They had so much in common, students together in a field they both enjoyed. She'd thought she loved him enough to marry him. He was sweet, gentle, understanding, treated her as an independent woman—until his interests conflicted with hers. Then he reverted to that masculine selfishness that must be present in all men.

Matt wouldn't have to revert; it was all there in his every word, every action. Pure virility ready to engulf any unwary female, to make her body sing, while she forgot every idea she ever had in her head! He'd probably expect such things as coffee in bed and some docile dummy would consider herself fortunate to bring it!

"What kind of woman do you like?" she asked sweetly. "The kind who walks three steps behind?"

"Not at all," he said, his grin widening. "If there's danger ahead, I'd like someone out front sweeping the way." His smile faded and he turned his compelling gaze on her. "I never put it into words before; maybe I never even sorted it out in my head. But I'll know her when I see her."

A dozen butterflies began skittering around in Brianna's stomach. Something in the deep tone of his voice touched her physically and her throat tightened to the point where she found it hard to swallow. She bit her lip nervously. It was time to change the subject. She glanced at his empty plate.

"If you're through, I'd like that tour of the house you promised."

He rose immediately, and Brianna followed. She would have liked to clear away the dishes, but after their conversation touching on male and female roles, she couldn't bring herself to do it. She'd make it up to Mrs. Clayton, she promised.

The tour was a good idea; the charged atmosphere between them softened to friendly camaraderie. Although she was still keenly aware of Matt every minute, she was too engrossed by the house to let it overwhelm her. The place reflected the differing personalities of its various owners: in the decoration and furnishings, varying from clear classic lines to the baroque; in the record collection, which contained everything from country and western to classical; in the library, where paperback romances stood alongside Gibbon's, *Decline and Fall of the Roman Empire* and Mark Twain's *Letters from the Earth*.

She reached up and took a slender volume from the shelves and examined its title. She had revised her estimate of Matt as a hick after their first meeting, but now she was beginning to suspect he was even more complex than she had suspected; if he had read even half of these books he was an educated man.

He laughed, apparently aware of what she was thinking, and placed the book on the shelf.

"Let's get back to the living room. It's a little chilly now that the sun's going down. I'll get a fire going and we can talk about your time with the Daynew."

Back in the large, well-proportioned living room with its high-beamed ceiling and broad expanse of windows, she sank into a comfortable well-upholstered chair and watched appreciatively as Matt knelt on one knee to strike a match to the kindling. His dark blue denim jeans stretched tautly across his firm buttocks and thighs, and the muscles of his back and shoulders rippled under his shirt as he reached out to hold the flame to the wood. She wished she could get over the feeling that she was holding her breath, waiting for something inevitable to happen.

She wondered if he would come to sit beside her, and sighed with what she supposed was relief as he turned and sat down in a chair across from her, leaned back and crossed his booted legs at the ankles, his eyes holding only a friendly regard as they sought her face.

"So," he said, "what did you find out about the Daynew?"

"Today was just a preliminary discussion but they were friendly; I think they are going to open up to me."

He frowned slightly. "It does look like it. I'm surprised."

"Why?" She was immediately on the defensive. "Don't you think I'm competent to interview them? Or to gain their trust?"

He raised his hand to stop her words and smiled. "I'm sure you are. No, it's just that I've never known them to be so open with a newcomer before. Usually they stay well away from strangers."

"Surely they must have gotten over their anger at that earlier anthropologist by now, realized that everyone isn't like him."

"They're over the anger, I suppose. But they're still wary, always have been. I wish my great-grandfather had been a little more forthcoming in his journal; I always had a feeling there was something between the lines."

"Your journal!" She had forgotten she planned to return it to Matt. "Did I tell you I have it? My dad picked it up at an estate sale. Naturally I'll return it."

"I always wondered what happened to it," he said easily. "I suspected that anthropologist stole it after Mom let him look at it. Maybe we can go over it together."

"I doubt we'll learn very much new; he mentions the Daynew only briefly. Did you know that they are skilled herbalists?"

His mouth quirked in amusement. "I know they make some powerful tea. Keeps you on a high for days. Old Alta makes a real witches' brew; give me coffee every time."

"The skill is passed down from mother to daughter; apparently they were a matrilineal society." She smiled, remembering Chad's annoyance at finding the women assembled at his house. "Maybe they still are—your friend

Chad didn't seem too happy at finding us all together, but he didn't lay the law down, either."

Matt frowned thoughtfully. "I've sensed something brewing with the men, but I can't put my finger on it. Did he say anything?"

"No, just muttered something I couldn't understand...."

Her voice trailed away under Matt's steady regard. For a moment they were silent, awareness growing uneasily between them. She watched his face and caught the exact moment when his expression changed from friendly interest to something much more intense. Spellbound, she watched his blue eyes darken to near indigo, his jaw tighten. She was fascinated by his mouth: a wide, generous mouth with lips that were firm without being thin. Then there was the tiny cleft in his chin. She wondered how it would feel to run a finger lightly down his square jaw, down to touch that intriguing indentation, then gently caress his mouth....

From the flare that leaped into his eyes, she became increasingly aware that her thoughts might have been completely transparent; she clenched her hands at her sides to be sure they wouldn't betray her by acting on her musings and looked wildly around the room, searching for anything to break her concentration on Matt.

It didn't help much. The flames flickered softly on the open hearth, crackling as they bit into the dry wood. Matt allowed the evening shadows to drift into the room, darkening far corners, intensifying the glow from the fire. The fitful blaze illuminated a fur rug in front of the hearth, and Brianna withdrew her gaze hastily. She'd just had the unaccountable vision of Matt's lean length stretched out there, the embers glinting on his dark hair, playing over his bare forearms, deepening the bronze of his skin. Irresistibly her gaze returned to his.

"You look very good sitting here, Brianna," he said softly. "I like the way the gleam is putting red highlights in your hair."

His bronzed hand was absently stroking the velvet-covered arm of his chair; Brianna had the sensation that it was really smoothing her own blond locks, and her pulse raced.

As though unable to sit a moment longer he rose abruptly and stood with his back to the burning nook, hands clenched behind him. His face was shaded but Brianna could feel the torment in his regard and it sent little shivers along her bare arms.

Had she made a mistake in coming here? She had known that the sexual affinity between herself and Matt was like dry tinder, waiting for only a spark, but she had told herself she could keep it under control. She could be aware of the desire but she didn't have to give in to it. Now, looking at Matt standing just a few feet away, she wondered if she had been overly optimistic.

"I've thought of you sitting there, just like that," he said softly, "with the firelight playing across those luscious lips..."

"Matt..." Her voice was so tremulous she hardly recognized it.

"Dreamed of it..."

She started to reply, but her answer choked in her throat as, with a low growl, he moved toward her, covering the few feet between them in one stride. Kneeling in front of her, he clasped her to him with such vehemence that she gasped. He buried his face in her shoulder and she felt his harsh breath on her skin, heard his incoherent murmurs as his lips moved over her smooth skin. She was enveloped by the warm, musky scent of him, felt the powerful pounding of his heart through his flannel shirt.

After an agonizing period of time, time in which she felt every cell in her body turn toward him in sweet, desperate yearning, he drew back slightly so his eyes were level with hers. Slowly, like a man in a dream, he raised one hand and drew it gently along the length of her hair, pulling her head closer, his intense gaze never leaving her face.

"I've never seen eyes like yours," he whispered almost as though talking to himself. "Golden, tiger eyes. Beautiful. Full of enchantment."

She should say something, break this moment, but any movement was completely beyond her. She could only stare back at him, see the pupils darken to black, experience the compelling force of his personality.

Again, he stroked her hair, then tangled his fingers in the long strands, his gaze never leaving hers. His earlier frenzy was under control, but this slow, sure look into the very depths of her being was even more impossible to resist. It was as though he were deliberately calling forth some passionate response that she hadn't known existed in herself.

He bent toward her, his mouth grazing her soft lips in a feather touch, then tasted again, this time more firmly. As though it were the most natural thing in the world, her lips opened to him, and she was aware of nothing but the sweet, incredibly arousing texture of his mouth. Then he deepened the kiss, pressing her close, exploring, demanding, awakening her entire body to tremulous response.

Drawing back a little, he ran his lips over her cheek, while he pulled her even closer in a fierce embrace. Her head fell back, leaving her throat vulnerable to his kisses. Propelled both by the force of his arms and by her own need, she slid from the chair until she was kneeling with him, face-to-face, her body pressed tight all along the long, lean length of his torso.

His arms tightened around her waist, pressing her against him. Was the thundering heartbeat reverberating through her chest hers or his? Then he lowered his hands to the sweet swell of flesh just below her lower back and pulled her even closer. She gasped and shuddered as she felt the urgency of his desire.

Time ceased to exist as they clung together, mouth to mouth, body to body, held motionless by the force of the wild current of sexuality that coursed between them.

Without releasing his grip he rotated her gently and lowered her back onto the fur rug in front of the fire. She gazed up at his face as he bent above her, and desire ignited every nerve of her body. His eyes were in shadow while the light from the flames highlighted his broad cheekbones, accentuated the harsh outline of his features. Time fell away; he was a fierce, primitive lover, a man whom she knew instinctively would demand every atom of her being to respond. The knowledge was both exhilarating and frightening.

"You have no idea what you look like," he said roughly, "with your hair spread out behind you like golden wings. A princess..."

She raised her arm to draw his head to her lips. For endless moments they clung together, lost in the wild sensation. Her body quivered with hungry desire. She was mindless, drugged by his touch. One part of her knew this was going too far; she had never meant for this to happen. The other part, the old, primitive part that assured the survival of the species, strove to bring him even closer.

With what was left of her mind, she tried to wrest control from her blazing emotions. She had known this would happen if she relaxed her guard, and she had resolved not to let things get out of hand. But the entire episode had happened so naturally, so inevitably, that she'd had no time to erect her defenses.

Apparently her body communicated her ambivalence to Matt. He drew back and looked searchingly into her face.

"Do you want this, Brianna?" His voice was husky with need as he moved mere inches away to look deeply into her eyes.

Did she want it! It took every ounce of control to meet his questioning gaze when what she longed to do was pull his head back down to where she could luxuriate in his kiss, feel his hands spread liquid fire all over her body. But that was the problem. She wanted him, wanted his heated body, wanted his intimate caress, but that could never be enough. Years of conditioning came to her rescue. In spite of her body's demands, she knew that Matt was not for her. She needed more than one night's passion. For her, passion had to be paired with love and commitment. But this was perilously late to remember that!

"I—I'm sorry..."

She felt the effort it took him to regain control: saw his mouth contort, the tendons of his neck go rigid, then relax, heard him take long, tortured breaths. Then she felt a surge of relief as he smiled down at her, then leaned over to kiss her quickly on the nose.

"Don't be sorry—ever. It was my fault. Really, I didn't plan on seduction."

"Me, either," she said shakily. "I certainly didn't mean to tease, to let you think..."

"Probably something in the air," he said lightly, moving away until he was lying beside her on the rug, propped on his elbows, looking down into her face. "Something happens to us every time we get within kissing distance. If I didn't know better, I'd say we were attracted to each other."

"But we both know better," she smiled. "Since you spend all your time trying to persuade me to leave the country."

"And you consider me a redneck primitive."

"Well, I'm changing my mind about that. It's certainly not why I—I didn't want to go on."

"You don't have to explain." His voice was gentle.

"I'd feel better if I did. It isn't that you don't—appeal to me, Matt. How could I deny it?" Her mouth twisted in a wry smile. "But we both know it's just a physical attraction—and that's not enough for me."

He gave her a lazy grin. "It's something. Don't underrate it."

"I'll be leaving in a few days. Not as soon as you'd like perhaps, but soon."

"I know," he sighed. "And you don't want to start something you can't finish. Well, I don't, either, for that matter."

He rose and reached for her hand, then pulled her lightly to her feet. "I'm not too sure how long I'll remember that, though, with you looking so enticing."

She ran her hands down over her hips, smoothing the rumpled material of her slacks, and gave him a tremulous smile. "Perhaps I'd better leave..."

"Don't be silly. I won't lose control again. I may think about ravaging you, but that's as far as it will go."

She wished his swift grin that showed flashing white teeth was a little more reassuring.

But he was as good as his word. They spent the next couple of hours in friendly conversation, although she couldn't quite get over the feeling they were carefully skirting an abyss. When Matt finally showed her to her bedroom he gave her a smile, half a salute, and left her, ambivalent and unmolested, at the bedroom door.

She had a long, luxurious shower, toweled herself dry, and walked across the thick carpet to the large double bed. At another time she would have been intrigued by the old-fashioned furnishings: the ornately carved oak dresser with the beveled mirror above it, the oval bedside table whose highly polished surface held a green-shaded reading lamp, a canopied bed with a carved headboard. Now she was too concerned with what had happened between her and Matt to do more than give it a cursory glance.

She pulled the cool sheets up over her heated body and lay still, her eyes staring into darkness. Sleep would be impossible until she had come to some understanding of her own reactions.

She would have liked to believe that Matt, with his forceful, masculine needs, his urgent desire, had swept her off her feet, but she knew that was not true. She had been a willing, even assertive, participant. And she had to be honest with herself. She had been attracted to men before, had even made love before, but she had never felt this wild, aching need, this incredible passion with anyone but Matt. And it didn't make sense; she hardly knew the man. It could be nothing but a chemical reaction accentuated by proximity and her own sense of isolation.

But could something that powerful be entirely physical? Admittedly Matt was an impressive specimen, with his rock-hard body and sizzling masculine energy, but was that enough to explain his compelling attraction? As she came to know him better, she was afraid it might be more than that. He was intelligent, humorous, energetic. In another time, another place, she might have found much to admire, even to love.

But Matt was of his time and place, not hers. His obsessive need to care for, guide and protect was only the other side of the coin of control and possessiveness. His need to shield the Daynew was patronizing, and his concern for her reduced her to the status of a child.

Why was she even concerned about his qualities? One thing she knew—Matt and the community of Hope were linked. This was his home, but this wilderness backwater could never be hers. When she had her Ph.D. she would get a job at some university where she could use her talents fully, apply for grants that would enable her to continue her research, and then think about the other side of her life—love and a family.

She squeezed her eyes tightly shut, trying to block out his face. If she could only forget that just a few doors away he was lying there in bed, maybe staring into the dark as she was. And she had only to go to the door, walk down the hall, and his arms would tighten around her, his warm body would welcome her...

She tossed angrily in bed and muttered between clenched teeth. "Brianna Royce, you are impossible!"

The next morning Matt drove her to her campsite, waited while she slid from the cab and then drove hastily away; she watched the pickup until it was out of sight, then glanced at her watch. Ten o'clock on a Sunday morning; Matt was as eager to get rid of her as she was to go.

When she had come downstairs this morning, Matt was already up. Neither mentioned the night before, though she knew it was on both their minds. They had been ill at ease with each other over the scanty breakfast they had prepared together, taking great care not to meet each other's eyes. She suspected, though, from glimpses of his haggard face, that Matt hadn't slept any more than she had. When she suggested she should get back to her van and work on her notes he had quickly agreed. He had left without mentioning when he would see her again.

Well, that was what she wanted. Anyway, she had plenty to do. Although she wouldn't be able to talk to some of the Daynew women today—she had the definite impression they preferred to see her when their men weren't home—she could always visit with Alta Thompson. She gathered that the old lady lived alone, although Diana apparently dropped in every day. It was Alta she needed to see anyway. She had the definite feeling that the woman held the key to the Daynew.

The ground shook slightly, but she paid little attention. She was becoming as accustomed as everyone else to the occasional ground tremor. None had been as violent as the first one she'd experienced.

She walked on into her campsite and glanced around the small space. Everything seemed just as she had left it—nothing slashed, nothing overturned. She should have stayed here last night and spared herself the emotional upheaval.

Her mind was elsewhere as she wandered over to the picnic table. For some reason she was loath to get started on her interview with Alta. It was hard to admit it, but the memory of Matt's kisses was more compelling than the thought of spending the day with the eccentric old woman.

Although she had been as anxious as Matt to forget last night's episode, she admitted to herself that she had half hoped he would suggest spending Sunday together. Just as friends, of course. The isolation of this place was beginning to wear on her. Her trips with her father to remote places had been of limited duration, and even there she had been surrounded by people—her dad, his helpers, sometimes officials of the country where they stayed. Aside from that, her experience had been in the city where you were never *really* alone. There was always the telephone, the roar of traffic—something to remind you that people were close by.

She was only a few feet from the table when she saw it. She hesitated, her heart pounding, then came a few feet closer. She wasn't sure what it was, but she knew she hadn't left anything on the table. Someone had been here.

Then she recognized the objects, and let out her breath. There was nothing threatening about the vegetables arranged in a circle on her table. Ears of dried corn, summer squash, bunches of ruby-red radishes. Someone had come, found her gone, and left her a gift.

She came a little closer, and her eyes narrowed thoughtfully. Strange that the vegetables were arranged in a circle, with one situated right in the center. She reached out to touch the ear of corn that stood, still in its husk, in the center of the circle.

It was only when she looked at it more closely that she began to feel uneasy. The husk had been fashioned into the shape of a skirt, the cornsilk arranged like a cascade of golden hair, and the features of a face—eyes, mouth, nose, had been crudely painted on. It was a doll of some sort.

A voodoo doll? Of course not. There was nothing malignant in the doll's appearance. Although it was crudely done, it reminded her of some of the pictures she had seen of the statuettes that had been found in the remains of nearly every ancient Paleolithic site—little feminine figurines the archaeologists called "venuses." Apparently likenesses of the female form were universal.

Nevertheless, there was something disquieting about this one. She sank onto the bench, replaced the little figure in the center of the vegetables, and stared at it, thinking of the significance of its presence. Someone had visited her camp and left her a message. A message of acceptance and friendship? Or a warning?

Chapter 8

Matt arrived at the logging site early Monday morning, long before he expected any of his men. It wasn't his usual practice, but then nothing seemed to be going as usual these days, he thought, scowling as he pulled to a stop beside the road. For instance, he usually got a good night's sleep, something that had eluded him for the past week. He didn't usually toss and turn all night, tortured by thoughts of a tall, slender woman with golden hair and tiger eyes.

He jumped lightly from his pickup, his boots kicking up little spurts of dust, and breathed deeply of the crisp mountain air, inhaling the scent of pine and blooming huckleberries. He always enjoyed the fragrance of the woods early in the morning before the logging started and the earlier freshness was interspersed with the scent of diesel and dust and the pitchy resin of fresh cut logs.

Gazing out over the green timbered slopes that faded to a blue haze in the distance, he was filled with the sense of belonging to this place. Its unfettered space gave a man scope, room to be himself. Although he enjoyed an occasional change of pace in Boise, he could never think of living anywhere but right here in Hope. There was a sense of permanence about this sparsely peopled landscape, which, although it might be illusory, was nevertheless powerful.

He heard the distinctive sound of a diesel engine and turned to look at the logging road he had just driven up. Soon a pickup rounded a bend; he recognized it at once as the battered old vehicle that he used to transport some of his men from the place where they congregated mornings outside the Hope Mercantile.

Frowning, and a little uneasy, he saw that the only occupant of the ancient truck was the driver, Jeff Clark, and he walked to meet him. Jeff, one of the few non-Native Americans that he employed, was a short, wiry man around twenty-five, with a mop of blond hair, pale blue eyes, and a face that reddened rather than tanned in the high mountain sun. Now that face was fashioned into an expression of anxiety.

"Morning, Jeff, what's up?" Matt asked, taking in Jeff's worried countenance. "Where's your passengers?"

"Wish I knew, Boss." Sighing, Jeff rested his arm on the pickup door as he squinted at Matt through the open window. "I waited half an hour but nobody showed up. Then I called your house to see what to do, but you weren't home. Figured you might be up here."

Matt's face turned a dark red as he began a slow burn. This was almost unprecedented, but somehow not unexpected. He recalled vividly how the men had been acting the past few days, congregating in little knots that dispersed like running water as he drew near; furtive glances at one another when they thought he wasn't looking; conversations trailing off as he came toward them. Their behavior both hurt and puzzled him. He was aware that he had never been allowed into their innermost circle, but he had thought they trusted him more than their recent actions indicated.

It had all begun with Brianna, he thought, clenching his jaw. His men had been uneasy, restless, ever since she met with them that evening at the schoolhouse. Somehow, in a way he didn't understand, it was her fault.

"Did you check at the store?" he demanded of Jeff. "Did any of them call in?"

"Not a one."

Muttering a low curse, Matt turned away. "You might as well go on home," he called over his shoulder as he headed for his pickup. "I'll see what I can find out, but by the time I round anybody up it will be too late to start working today."

Reaching inside the cab, he picked up his radio-telephone to contact the trucks and stop them before they started the long haul up the mountain. The drivers weren't going to be too pleased at losing a day's work anyway, and it would compound their annoyance if they got all the way here merely to turn around and drive back.

When he had done everything he could, Matt started the long drive back down the twisting road, his face set in a mask of anger. How could the men be so irresponsible as to just not show up? He wasn't the only loser; they were losing a day's pay. And if one of his contracts was terminated because of failure to deliver logs, they would be forfeiting more than that.

Along with the anger and frustration came a dawning sense of apprehension. He had pushed the thought away, but he admitted now that he had sensed something else among the Daynew men the past few days. Something more than distrust.

Fear. It was in their averted eyes, in the way they drifted away at his approach. If they were afraid of something, they might not be as easy to handle as he hoped.

Again he thought of Brianna. She was the catalyst, but maybe he shouldn't blame her too much. If there were actually something to fear, if the Daynew weren't just being infantile, then it was possible she was in danger, too. He didn't think her camp had been vandalized by a marauding animal, in spite of what he had said to her. The destruction had seemed too deliberate. It was probably meant to frighten her. But why?

His body tensed and his hands tightened on the wheel as he remembered the feel of her body through her thin nightdress when she had launched herself into his arms the evening he had gone to her campsite. In spite of her bravado, her prickly independence, she was a woman, and she was frightened.

He remembered, too, the burst of passion that had snapped his control and propelled him across the room to clasp her frantically against his chest. He didn't like that. He didn't like losing control, and he didn't plan on it happening again. He had fully intended not to see any more of her after what had nearly happened between them when she was in his home. He didn't like his reaction to her, and she wasn't his responsibility. But if she were really in danger...

He shoved the accelerator to the floorboard in angry frustration. He was going to have to get to the bottom of this, and he didn't want her wandering around like a loose bullet while he was doing it. She would be safer—everyone would be much safer—if he didn't let her out of his sight again.

It was early; she might still be at her camp. He turned in that direction, deciding on a course of action as he drove.

He didn't falter in his intent, although the sight of her did strange things to his chest. She was sitting at the picnic table, her head bent forward, making some notes on a lined yellow pad. The first thing he noticed was the morning sun glinting on her hair. He hesitated, swallowed, then walked toward her.

Somehow aware of his approach although he wasn't making a sound, she raised her head and watched him walk toward her. He saw her face change, as her first look of warm welcome was swiftly covered by cool appraisal. He wondered if his ambivalence had shown in his face as clearly as her emotions were reflected in hers.

"Matt, this is a surprise. And your timing is perfect. I was just getting ready to leave."

"Great. Then we can leave together."

He hadn't realized how autocratic he had sounded until she frowned slightly and snapped her notebook shut. "Maybe *we* aren't going in the same direction."

"I think *we* are," he said tightly. "You want to study Daynew, don't you? Their charming little ways and unusual actions?"

At her bewildered look, he wished he hadn't been quite so brusque and sarcastic. He needn't take his disappointment out on her.

"Is something the matter?" she asked.

"You could say so." He struck his fist against his thigh, knowing some vague, unknown enemy was the real target. "None of the men showed up for work this morning."

"Is that so unusual? Maybe they just wanted a day off."

"It's unusual, all right. We've functioned for years as a smooth team. They know as well as I do what's riding on our finishing the sale."

"What is?"

He shrugged. "Stuart Logging operates on a tight budget. It wouldn't take too much to put us under."

She frowned. "Maybe it's not as serious as you think. Anyway," she said, tossing her hair back from her face and flashing him a look of challenge, "it's *me* you seem angry with. What has all this got to do with me?"

"I'm not sure. Nothing. Or everything. If you'll come along with me, perhaps we can find out."

She glanced at his face and without another word rose and went into the van. A moment later she returned, carrying a light sweater. "Let's go, then," she said coolly. "Perhaps I can figure out what you're talking about."

As she walked toward him, he felt a tightness in his throat and his initial annoyance turned to confusion. He watched the graceful swing of her hips, the confident tilt to her shoulders, the proud way she carried her head, and he found it difficult to swallow. He wasn't much given to introspection, but he had a flash of insight. Did he want her gone because of her effect on the Daynew or because of her effect on him?

They rode in wary silence until they arrived at the gravel road in front of a neat little house. Then Brianna turned an inquiring face toward Matt's set profile.

"This is Chad and Louise's house."

"So it is." His voice was as grim as his set face as he jumped from the cab. Brianna was out her door before he could come around to her side. He waited, then grabbed her by the arm and they walked hastily up the path.

Although he'd been to Chad's house many times before, he couldn't suppress a feeling that something was different today. Was their approach being observed through the slit in the curtains? Or was anyone even home?

Then he realized what was different. Chad usually saw him coming and had the door open wide before he reached the porch. Now it was like approaching a stranger's place.

Pulling Brianna along, he strode up onto the porch. The door remained firmly closed. Well, it wasn't going to be that easy for Chad. Without any hesitation he raised his fist and pounded on the door.

There might have been movement within the room, but the door remained closed. He pounded again, harder. Nothing. He raised his hand again, then lowered it as the door swung open and Chad peered out.

"Come in, Boss." Chad gave Matt an uneasy smile, nodded at Brianna, his eyes hooded, then stepped back into the room to allow the two to enter.

Matt strode into the middle of the room, and wasted no time coming to the point. "What happened? Did you all forget it was a workday?"

"Well, no," Chad said, glancing at his wife who huddled in a chair in a far corner of the room, her gaze on the floor. "Sorry we couldn't make it."

Matt followed Chad's glance and puzzlement began to dilute his anger. Had Louise been crying? Her eyes looked suspiciously red. He turned back to Chad. "That's not much of an answer. Is there some trouble you'd like to tell me about?"

"Oh, no." Chad refused to meet his eyes, and Matt's sense of concern intensified. Chad had always been the most forthcoming, the most open of all the men. He considered him his friend. Now he hadn't even asked him to sit down. Had they interrupted something? A quarrel, perhaps? But why was the man being so evasive?

"Then what is it? You know we have to keep those logs rolling in or we're all out of work. And why did all of you pick today not to come in?"

"I'm sure sorry about it, Boss. But you see, it's kind of a religious holiday..." The man looked extremely uncomfortable.

"Religious holiday? I don't know about any holiday at this time of year," Matt said.

"It's an old one," Chad said lamely. "We don't always observe it, but when we do it takes a lot of preparation."

"Well, why does it keep you from working?" Matt demanded impatiently. "Can't you prepare for it in your spare time?"

Again the eyes slid away from his, but Chad said nothing.

Feeling as though he were fighting the wind, that there was nothing solid he could hang on to, Matt sighed in defeat. He wouldn't get anyone to work today.

"I want to see you at work in the morning," Matt said curtly. "All of you!" Without awaiting a reply, he strode angrily out the door. Brianna, who hadn't said a word, followed closely behind him.

When they were once more standing outside by the pickup, Brianna looked up into Matt's perplexed face. "What do you make of all that?"

"I don't know," he answered slowly, "I wish I felt more optimistic."

"What holiday could he be talking about?"

"None that I know of. It's just an excuse."

"What are you going to do now?"

"I don't know that, either." He took a deep breath. "Talk to some of the others, I guess. Not that it will do any good.

These men stick together. When something is agreed on, they all follow along."

"Maybe there really is a holiday of some kind."

He grinned down at her, his irritation with the Daynew momentarily displaced by the look of her face turned up to his. Lovely. "It's news to me," he finally said. "If it is a holiday, it's the first time they've celebrated it since I've known them. But you're the one who knows anthropology. You tell me."

She shrugged. "It could be anything, I guess. Almost all primitive people celebrated the beginning of summer. The summer solstice. Midsummer's Eve. It was a big event in the various pagan religions, especially among agricultural people. But I don't know that the Daynew celebrate it. Besides, the summer solstice is still a couple of weeks away."

He frowned thoughtfully. "If that's what it is, I can't afford for the men to be off work for two weeks. I'll have to think of something to get them back on the job."

"I was going to see Alta Thompson today before you came along and spirited me away. She promised to tell me some of their old myths. Would you like me to try to find out what holiday is taking place?"

Smiling down into her upturned face, he reached for her hand and squeezed. He liked the feel of it—long fingers, smooth skin. "Sure. It might help. In the meantime, I'll talk to the other men. I'll drive you over to her place."

Brianna shook her head. "I don't think she lives that far away. She gave me directions the other day. It's quite a distance by road, but it's just a short walk down that path."

She gestured to a barely visible trail and Matt nodded, then jumped up into his truck. "I'll be back for you later in the day," he called through the open window. He watched her in the rearview mirror until he rounded a bend, a little worried about leaving her. But she couldn't get into much trouble with old Alta, and he'd be back in a few hours. He was surprised and a little displeased at the rush of emotion he felt; she looked so vulnerable standing there alone that he'd wanted to turn around and insist she stay with him all day.

Left alone, Brianna hesitated a moment, then walked toward the path that led from the gravel road. She had no trouble locating it; it was a well-trodden trail, and Brianna suspected that many of the Daynew found their way to the old woman's place daily. After all, she was the tribal healer, the herbalist, and many people, thoroughly civilized in most ways, probably still subscribed to the age-old practices.

She had just spotted the house, still several hundred feet away and nearly hidden by the dense foliage that surrounded it, when she heard a flurry of footsteps behind her and turned quickly.

"Louise!"

"I'm glad I caught up with you." Louise gasped for breath, then her words came in a rush. "I wanted to talk to you before you got to Alta's."

"I was just at your house," Brianna said, giving her a puzzled look. "Why didn't you talk to me then?"

The glance Louise gave her was nearly contemptuous. "In front of Chad? And Matt? No, I wanted to speak to you alone."

"Something is going on, isn't it? Can't you tell me what's happening, Louise?" Brianna looked into the woman's flushed face, and met her worried eyes. "I sensed when I was at your house the other day talking to all of you women that there was a disagreement about something. Was it about my interviewing you concerning your history? Why don't you want to talk about it?"

"Why did you have to come here?"

Brianna hesitated, surprised at the heat of the woman's outburst. She tried to frame a calm, reasonable reply. "Louise, I only want to talk to you; surely there's no harm in that."

"There is danger," the woman said slowly. "It may already be too late."

"Danger? To me? I can hardly believe that."

"Not only to you, you fool! Danger to us!" Louise hissed.

As Brianna gasped and stepped back a few paces, startled by the woman's vehemence, Louise narrowed her eyes and studied Brianna's face. For a long moment she stood absolutely still, her eyes probing fiercely. Then a look of resignation came over her features, her shoulders slumped, and she whirled around and hurried back down the trail. Brianna barely heard her last muttered comment. "But I can see there's no use talking to you."

More puzzled than ever, Brianna continued down the path to Alta's house. As she came nearer, her pulse quickened; it was markedly different from the others. This was more like a Native American's house should be! Instead of boards, it was constructed of peeled logs set upright in a circle. The roof was of old, weathered shake shingles. The two windows she could see were very small, and the entrance was a high, narrow door also made of weathered, peeled logs.

Its appearance of antiquity was further enhanced by the willows and sod that had been piled around the outside of the structure, probably for insulation, Brianna decided. Whatever the purpose, it made the dwelling resemble a large beehive.

As she came closer, she saw that the house had something in common with all the others. The entry was flanked by posts, but although these two were more massive than those on the homes of the other members of the tribe, Brianna saw that they were similarly decorated with deeply etched, ornately carved knotwork. Her excitement intensified; the overall impression was one of age, of the mellowness of time passing unrecorded.

She stepped onto the porch and, as though she were expected, the door swung open revealing Alta Thompson—but a more impressive Alta Thompson than she had seen so far. The elderly woman wore a full-length robe encircled at the waist by a braided sash and caught with an intricately fashioned gold clasp. Her long gray hair was held close to her head with a wide band, then fell loose in profusion over her shoulders. Perhaps it was her commanding manner that made her seem so much taller than Brianna remembered, but whatever the reason the woman's presence was slightly intimidating. Brianna raised her chin to meet her eyes squarely. The woman's intense gaze clung to hers, and Brianna moistened her lips to speak, fighting off a chill of fear. Had she again misjudged the woman?

As though aware of the impression she had made, and regretting it, Alta relaxed visibly, smiled and held out her bony hand. "Brianna. I hoped you'd visit me. Please come in."

Unaccountably reluctant, Brianna nevertheless stepped inside the doorway. Then, glancing around the small room, she forgot her initial hesitation, engulfed in a blaze of excitement. This room was more what she would have expected of the Daynew! Her trip was becoming worthwhile.

Even though it was broad daylight outside, the room itself was shrouded in gloom, partially because of the narrow windows that let in only a small amount of light, and partially because of the bundles of dried herbs that hung from the low ceiling beams like inanimate animals. The aroma contributed to Brianna's sense of claustrophobia—a heavy dark scent that permeated the entire house; scent of basil, rosemary, nettle, willow, catnip, monkshood, rue—and many others she couldn't begin to identify.

As her eyes adjusted, she saw the room contained the common necessities of living: table, chairs, a bed pushed against a wall and covered with a throw of bearskin. On the stove a kettle whistled merrily, and Brianna forced herself to relax. The room was unusual, but it was what she had hoped for when she undertook her study of the Daynew. It was nothing to be frightened of.

As Alta bustled about, finding her a chair, pouring tea, Brianna relaxed further. This was the perfect atmosphere in which to ask the kind of questions she wanted to ask.

After a few minutes of inconsequential talk, Alta pulled her chair closer to Brianna, her eyes darkening with excitement. "Now, dear, exactly what do you want to know about us?"

Brianna whipped out her notebook. "Do you know any of the old myths? For instance, where did the Daynew come from?" Her experience had been that almost every tribe had a creation myth; the way the Daynew explained their presence might tell her a lot.

Alta settled back. "The story of the Daynew goes back years and years, before time began. A lone man came to the People. He led us through many dangers. He led us here."

Brianna's interest mounted. A lone man. Where had she heard that before. Then she remembered; the Mandan had said they were led to safety by a lone man. They had built him a shrine.

"Was the lone man a god?"

Alta gave her a shrewd look. "A god? No, he was just a man, according to the old ones."

"Did you have a god, goddesses? What do the old stories say about that?"

"There was a goddess, of course," Alta said, darting a quick look at Brianna as though to gauge her reaction. "Or so we were told by the old ones."

Brianna smiled with satisfaction and made several notes in her pad. Things were developing just as she might have expected. She knew that before the male warrior gods supplanted her, the cult of the goddess stretched to many different areas of the world. Perhaps she went back as far as paleolithic times. Where she ruled, women controlled the mysteries and the knowledge of life.

How exciting if this tribe retained some dim memory of this long displaced deity. It might help prove her theory that people evolved in one place and dispersed around the globe, taking their myths with them.

"Can you tell me a little about the goddess?"

Again Alta Thompson smiled her peculiar, secret smile, but her words were commonplace enough.

"I know only what has been handed down. There are many, many stories about her. One I always especially liked. It seems the People saw the goddess in the moon. When the moon was full the goddess reigned, searching always for her mate, the sun. She could not find him, of course, since he comes in the day."

Alta paused, then continued, her voice taking on a singsong quality that sent little shivers down Brianna's back as she realized she was listening to something that had been repeated thousands of times.

"Her silver light touches everything in the forest as she searches. Then, once every month, he comes to her, his shadow darkening her light, until finally he engulfs her completely. But her death is only temporary; like spring, like seed cast into the dark ground, she recovers, emerges, bursts forth at last in a triumphant blaze of light."

Brianna scribbled hastily, trying to keep up with the woman's voice. "That's wonderful! Just what I wanted. Are there other stories about her?"

The voice droned on, and Brianna wrote as fast as she could, one part of her mind recording the myths and the other congratulating herself on how lucky she was. She had indeed come in time. Alta seemed to be the last in a long line of storytellers and when she was gone there would probably be no one else to keep alive their old traditions. She had found the Daynew just in time. What a coup it would be when her findings were published!

Hours later there was a knock at the door and she glanced at her watch, amazed at how fast the time had gone. It was well into the afternoon.

Alta opened the door and Brianna saw Matt standing in the entryway. He spoke briefly to Alta, then smiled at Brianna.

"Hi. Ready to go? I'll drive you back to your camp."

Brianna gathered her things, thanked Alta profusely, made arrangements to see her again and joined Matt on the porch. The door closed softly behind them as they walked back down the path. Without thinking, she took his arm.

"I had no idea it was so late," she confessed. "She's wonderful, Matt! The stories she tells are priceless."

He bent his dark head to look at her face, and covered her hand with his large palm. The touch felt right, natural somehow, and she didn't pull away. "Well," he said, "I'm glad one of us had a little luck. I talked to some of the other men, but I couldn't get a commitment out of any of them. I just hope they'll be back to work tomorrow."

"Oh, Matt, I'm sorry! I forgot all about asking Alta about the holiday. I just got so involved..."

He smiled at her guilty expression. "That's okay. I doubt it's a holiday anyway—that's their excuse. I didn't get the impression that anything gala is going on," he said grimly.

"What, then?"

"I don't know. I swear, they seem afraid of something, but I'm damned if I know what."

She thought of Louise's outburst, her implication that the Daynew were somehow in danger, and frowned thoughtfully. She had been so excited listening to Alta's tales of Daynew history that she had forgotten all about it. Now she recounted it to Matt, adding her own assessment that it didn't make sense.

"No, it doesn't," he agreed. "Do you have old Caleb's journal at your van? Maybe if we go over it together we might come across something that would explain the way the Daynew are acting."

Half an hour later she lifted the journal from the metal box and placed it on the picnic table. Matt sat down beside her and together they read the old man's account of his life among the Daynew of several generations ago. Brianna made a valiant effort to keep her mind on it, although it would have been easier if she hadn't been so aware of Matt's hard thigh pressing against hers.

An hour later they gave up; they discovered nothing new. Caleb Stuart described the Daynew briefly—their fair coloring, their handsome appearances. They lived much as the other Native Americans he had seen, in round huts covered with hide, roofs thatched with pine boughs. They did seem advanced in metal work. Mostly he spoke of them with disgust; the men, he said, didn't know how to treat women, being woefully henpecked. And the women, though attractive, were much too aggressive to be feminine.

Only one sentence caused them to ponder, but they could make nothing of it. *Course, if I had to put up with what those men put up with, I'd be mightily polite, too.*

"What do you suppose he meant?" Brianna said, sighing and closing the journal.

"No idea," Matt replied sourly. "I'd say Caleb was a typical man of the time—women had their place, and the Daynew women didn't stay there. Probably thought they had flouted a rule of nature."

He turned to look at her, his own face shadowed by the failing light. "There's nothing more we can do. How about coming on back out to the house with me? I'll feel better if I can keep an eye on you."

The thought was appealing, but she was very much afraid of what it would lead to. There was more to Matt, much more, than she had supposed, and it made it even more necessary than ever to stay out of situations that could lead to involvement. She didn't want to depend on anyone, and certainly not Matt who was much too prone to take everything onto his own broad shoulders. Independence was dearly won, and easily lost, she knew. What was it Zorba had said to his young friend when he was advising him about women? *Put a hand on her breast, and she'll forget any idea she ever had.* It wouldn't be true of her!

"I'll stay here," she said. "I don't want to trouble you anymore."

He frowned. "I think it's too late for that, Brianna. I'm already troubled. We're involved in something whether we like it or not. I'm not going to have you getting hurt. Come along, now."

This was the tone that always made her grit her teeth and rebel. "Matt, I'm all right here. I want to get up early tomorrow and see Alta again."

He rose, hoisted one booted foot onto the bench and gazed thoughtfully into the distance. "That's another thing. Why has she suddenly changed? She never gave anyone the time of day before. Why now? And why you?"

"Because I'm a professional, and maybe she likes me!"

He studied her face carefully, then grinned. "Maybe so. That's easy to do."

For an instant she was speechless, touched by the sudden tenderness in his voice.

"Sure you won't come?"

"Sure."

She expected more of an argument, but he merely stuck his thumbs into his jeans, looked down at her as though assessing her thoughts, smiled his sweet wicked smile that set her pulse pounding, and walked away. She couldn't believe it; he was whistling.

She'd won, but it didn't give her the satisfaction she expected. In fact, the sound of his pickup driving away made her downright lonely.

It was well after dark when Matt drove back to the campground and parked a hundred feet away at a spot where he could see anyone who entered or left Brianna's campsite.

He shouldn't have let her get away with it, but he had looked at her set face when he asked her to come home with him, and suspected that further insistence would only harden her resolve. But he certainly wasn't going to leave her alone until he had a better idea of what was going on.

He unrolled his sleeping bag and spread it out under a pine tree, took off his boots and crawled into the nylon sack, sighing with exasperation. Damn that stubborn woman. He wouldn't get much sleep tonight—but then, he thought, suddenly philosophical, he hadn't been getting much sleep lately anyway.

Chapter 9

Brianna spent a restless night, jumping at every faint sound that penetrated the thin walls of the camper. When the first streaks of dawn lighted the sky she gave up on sleep, pulled on jeans and a shirt and went out to look around.

She raised her face to the light breeze, closing her eyes and breathing deeply, then stepped quickly along the path that circled the campground. Everything looked different in the soft half-light of dawn, shadowy and mysterious; in the night or day one knew what to expect, but in this nebulous in-between time where two worlds converged, anything could happen.

Smiling at her fanciful thought, she glanced to the side of the trail and saw a dark shape. At first she thought it was just a shadow. Inspecting it more closely, she saw a recumbent form in a red nylon sleeping bag huddled darkly under the pine tree. Her heart seemed to stop, then thudded wildly. Holding her breath, she inched forward, ready to run at the slightest movement. There might be danger. Why would anyone be sleeping out of a designated campsite and so close to her van?

Then she recognized Matt and her apprehension flared into anger and relief. So this was why he had left so willingly the night before! He'd only pretended to let her win the argument. He'd had every intention of guarding her whether she liked it or not! He had treated her like a child, helpless, unsure of her own mind.

She came closer, intending to give him the benefit of her ideas about arrogant, bullheaded macho behavior, and then stopped as she peered into his sleeping face. The sight of him went straight to her heart like a sharp thrust of pain. This was the first time she had seen him with the barricades down. He looked so young, so vulnerable, that a catch came into her throat and swift tears stung her eyes at the unexpected rush of tenderness.

He lay sprawled on his back, his face turned to the sky. Thick black hair fell across his high forehead, and she remembered the way he habitually brushed it back with a careless gesture. Long dark eyelashes brushed his sharply sculpted cheekbone, in dramatic contrast with smooth bronzed skin. His deep, even breathing moved his chest in a strong, rhythmic motion. Slightly open, his mouth appeared unguarded, defenseless, and she had a fantastic, hastily suppressed impulse to lean down and brush his lips with her own. A powerful need to guard him, protect him—and claim him—swept through her with almost overwhelming force.

Suddenly he opened his eyes, seemingly completely alert, and the moment was broken.

She tried hard to recapture her initial annoyance, but it was no use. "You must be a morning person," she said, knowing that her voice sounded huskier than usual. "You come awake all at once."

"And from the accusing way you say that," he replied, struggling to a sitting position, "you're probably a night person, although in that case I don't know why you're up at this time of the morning." He glanced at the sky, just beginning to show a faint rosy tinge. "It can't be much later than five o'clock."

"I didn't sleep much," she admitted. "To me, it's still night." She watched as he slid from the sleeping bag and knelt to roll it up competently and quickly. "I'm not even going to ask what you're doing here when you have a perfectly comfortable bed to sleep in."

He gave her an amused and sheepish glance. "I would have agreed with you along about two o'clock this morning. The least you could do is have something interesting going on; it got pretty dull just watching your camper."

"I could have told you that. But you were determined to be gallant."

"Well," he said cheerily, tossing his bag into the back of the pickup, "since I was gallant enough to lose sleep over you, you could at least offer me a suitable reward." He turned toward her, his eyes roving appreciatively over her face, her throat, down her slender body, and she was joltingly aware of him as an exceedingly attractive and virile male.

At the insinuating look in his eyes, she felt her cheeks burn, but before she could retort he took her hand in his warm, strong grip and moved toward her campsite. "Now don't jump to conclusions," he said, chuckling softly. "I was thinking of coffee."

"I might even rustle up some scrambled eggs."

He moved immediately to start the fire. By the time Brianna had set the dishes on the table and stirred up the eggs the aroma of coffee permeated the campsite.

She was somewhat ill at ease, the force of the moment when she had looked down at his sleeping face still lingering, and she was glad he dropped the innuendos and just chatted in a friendly, disarming way. When he wasn't playing macho-man, he was really a lot of fun.

"So," he said, lifting his mug to his lips, then cradling it in his hands, "are the Daynew going to disappoint you? Or will you get enough material to make your fame and fortune?"

"Don't think that's a joke. If the rest of Alta's stories are as good as the ones she told me so far, this study could be a real winner for me."

"And that's very important to you—winning?"

"Much better than losing." She gave him a speculative glance. "Don't tell me you don't believe that. You have to be competitive, or you wouldn't be a successful businessman."

"Not necessarily." He looked darkly into his cup. "Or at least, not primarily. I've learned something from the Daynew. Cooperation can sometimes beat competitiveness. Everybody working together."

"In a rural area, maybe. But you'd soon get eaten up with that kind of attitude anyplace else."

"Maybe that's why I like it here so well. I guess you'd find rural life a little—stifling?"

She paused, going over his words. On the surface, it seemed just a casual comment, and yet...

"I don't think I could ever find the scope I need here," she said slowly. "It's so far from the mainstream... I want to be on the cutting edge of my profession."

"A very ambitious, competitive woman." He raised a dark eyebrow.

"Is that bad?"

"No." A tiny muscle jerked in his jaw. "Not as long as she's someone else's woman. I might even admire her. But I'd like to come home to a soft, loving lady. I certainly can't see competing with my own wife."

There was so much going on under the surface of his words that she felt confused, and said the first thing she thought of. "Afraid you'd lose?"

"Afraid we both would," he said softly. Suddenly he smiled, the serious part of the conversation apparently over. "Although there's one thing to be said for an independent, ambitious woman."

"Really? What's that?" She glanced at him suspiciously.

"She can be a heck of a lot of fun to be around. Not at all boring."

His blue eyes held hers and he was smiling that devastating smile that turned her into jelly. If things were different, she thought for perhaps the tenth time—if he didn't live in such a remote area, if they agreed on fundamentals, if their values were the same, if his innate need to protect didn't translate into smothering and control— With a wry inward smile, she broke off the thought. If pigs had wings.

The silence stretched between them, pregnant with unspoken words, and she sighed involuntarily. Better get back to a safe subject like the Daynew.

"I wish I knew what to make of Alta Thompson," she said slowly. "In some ways she's like everybody's old grandmother. A little crotchety, perhaps, but nothing more threatening than a garrulous old woman. Sometimes, though, when she skewers me with those eyes I have the strangest feeling that she's looking right into me. Seeing things about me I don't know myself..."

He laughed. "I know what you mean. She's a legend among the men. I think they'd do anything rather than cross her."

"The women seem to be comfortable with her."

"Oh, yes," he said dryly.

"Except Louise. You know, I keep thinking there's something going on with Louise. She doesn't seem to fit in...."

"Maybe it has something to do with her and Chad's relationship. They're a unit, more so than the others, I suspect."

"They couldn't be jealous of a woman's husband!"

"Why not? Women like to stick together, I'm told."

"That's silly. A man and woman—why that's the primary thing!"

"Now you sound more like the beautiful feminine creature you look like," he said softly.

She stumbled on in confusion. "Well, I never said a woman can't work and be a woman, too. I know I certainly want a man I can love, be friends with..." At the look in his eyes, her voice trailed away. She had never meant for the conversation to turn personal again. "But you don't really approve of women who work," she said lightly.

"All women work. Whether they work at home or at a career, you can bet they work."

"Then it's not the working that bothers you. You'd tolerate a job if that's all it was. But a career—a career that takes up their enthusiasm and energy—that's different."

"I certainly want some of that energy left over for me," he said dryly.

She stared at him across the space that separated them, abashed at how heated the discussion had become. They were just discussing hypothetical situations, weren't they?

He rose, took a final swig of coffee and smiled down at her. "Look, what we both need is a break from the Daynew. How about driving into Boise tonight for dinner?"

"You drive eighty miles for dinner?"

"Sure." His blue eyes glinted with mischief. "Unless you'd rather take a chance on the hamburgers at Hope Mercantile."

"Boise will be fine," she agreed hastily.

An hour later, Brianna parked her van alongside the trail that led to Alta's lodge. She was earlier than she had expected to be, but she hadn't been able to wait for the appointed time. After Matt left she had straightened up the campsite, paced a little, reread her notes, but she couldn't concentrate. There seemed no reason to wait; the stories Alta had told her yesterday had whetted her appetite for more.

She jumped from the camper and walked eagerly along the trail. Alta wouldn't mind that she was early, and she wanted to put in as much time as possible with the woman this morning since she had to be ready to leave for Boise with Matt in the afternoon.

She was still some distance from the house when she became aware of a faint, rhythmic sound floating toward her. Pausing uncertainly, she tilted her head, straining to locate the source. It was a chant of some kind, rising and falling in monotonous cadence. She didn't recognize any words, but the sound itself struck her as slightly menacing, touching some chord of uneasiness deep in her subconscious. Frowning, she walked a few feet farther along the trail, then paused again.

Yes, it was definitely a chant. A low, droning chant that made the hair rise on the back of her neck. It was still difficult to pinpoint the source, but it seemed to be coming from the direction of Alta Thompson's house.

She began to move silently toward the house, uncomfortably aware that she might be considered to be spying. It had taken her so long to win Alta's confidence she hated to risk losing it. She shouldn't have come early. She had an uneasy feeling that whatever was going on in the lodge ahead of her was not for the ears of strangers.

Suddenly the low, insistent sound broke off and she heard several voices raised in sharp argument. Instinctively she slipped off the trail into the cover of the thick brush just as the door of the lodge flew open and Louise Gardner rushed out onto the porch. Brianna was close enough to see her face, hear her voice, and she could tell the woman was upset.

"I won't have anything to do with it!"

The erect form of Alta Thompson appeared right behind the younger woman. She grabbed Louise by the arm, and although her voice was low it came clearly to where Brianna crouched, carrying the authority of unquestioned command.

"That will do, Louise. You know what must be done."

"But what if Chad—" The woman's voice broke and she raised beseeching eyes to the old woman.

"Chad will do as everyone else does," Alta said firmly. "Now, come back on in," she coaxed, her voice suddenly soft and persuasive. "There is much to do."

Louise paused, looking wildly around, then seemed to wilt in the woman's grip. Brianna thought the young woman resembled a recalcitrant child as she was firmly escorted back inside the house.

On trembling legs, Brianna hurried back down the trail. The interrupted chant resumed, following her nearly to her van. It resonated deep inside her body, sinister and insistent, like a dream half remembered. For an instant she was back in her childhood nightmares, surrounded by dark shapes, half-hidden faces.

Later, at the appointed time, she had to force herself to walk back down the trail. But everything was as commonplace as it had been on her first visit. Alta was alone, with no indication that there had been anyone else there a couple of hours ago. She welcomed Brianna warmly, and was as loquacious as ever with her charming tales as they sipped the ubiquitous tea.

Finally Alta settled back in her chair and stretched. "My goodness, that should be enough for one day. I'd like to know a little about you, my dear."

Brianna snapped her notebook shut. "I'm afraid I'm pretty dull. Just a student, really."

The gray eyes flickered strangely as they fastened on Brianna's face. "Oh, not dull. Not dull at all. I wonder what called you here to us?"

"I told you—I—"

"Oh, I know what you said, but there are always many reasons for one fateful action, don't you think? Some perhaps not even known."

Brianna twisted uneasily in her chair. "Really, it's all quite straightforward. . . ."

"Of course. Quite straightforward." For an instant her expression took on the vulpine look of a forest animal; then it was gone before Brianna could quite believe she had seen it. "And you came alone. No young man to miss you?"

Something in the tone made Brianna lift her head quickly, but Alta's expression was only gently inquiring. "No, not really."

"Matt, now, he's a handsome boy. I hear you've been seeing a lot of him."

She bit back a sharp retort. Alta was snooping, but then, wasn't she entitled to a little leeway? Brianna was certainly posing enough questions herself.

"He's been helping me some," she said calmly.

"Yes. Well, you do make an attractive couple."

Brianna rose quickly; there was something about the questioning that bothered her, something more than the idle curiosity of an old woman. There was a smugness, almost a complacency, about the comment.

She said goodbye, realizing when she was halfway home that neither she nor Alta had mentioned anything about what might have gone on in the little lodge earlier that morning.

Brianna leaned back in Matt's high-powered sports car and gazed at him appreciatively through half-closed eyes as he drove expertly along the twisting road toward Boise. He wore a pale blue dress shirt with a string tie, a western-cut jacket, dark twill pants, and highly polished western boots. It might have looked like a costume in other places; here, it exactly suited the rugged country and the man.

She felt a little breathless as she surveyed the strong clean lines of his profile. Strange that she had known him such a short time, but that by closing her eyes she could trace the outline of his heavy eyebrows, his deep-set eyes, strong nose, determined chin with the tiny cleft that cried out to be touched.

She was glad she'd had the foresight to bring along a semidressy outfit from Santa Barbara. She knew from the appreciative look in Matt's eyes that the emerald-green silk sheath she wore, with the high neck and long sleeves, was extremely becoming and more seductive in its simple understatement than something more revealing would have been.

"Did your men come back to work?" she asked, breaking a companionable silence.

He frowned. "No. Oh, a few straggled in, and we got several loads out."

He turned to her, his smile erasing the concern on his handsome face. "But I'm tired of thinking about it. Just for tonight, let's forget about them. Let's keep tonight just for us."

He reached for her hand, and she returned his warm smile. His suggestion was fine with her. She was tired of thinking of them, too, tired of puzzling about their strange behavior. Tired of wondering about the undercurrents of Alta's remarks. With Matt beside her, listening to the steady hum of the engine, seeing the evergreen forest flash by, she could almost believe she had imagined the ominous tone of the chanting she had heard. She had been silly to read anything sinister into it.

They made a quick tour through Boise: the university, the tree-lined streets, the bustling downtown area, then pulled into a parking lot in front of a structure built along the banks of the Boise River. She surveyed the long, low building with a certain surprise. There was an elegance in its clean lines and softly lighted entry that was pleasing. This restaurant could have graced any metropolitan city, and she said as much to Matt.

"Yep," he agreed, coming around to open her door. "But here you can park."

When they were seated at a table with a view of the river, she surveyed the expanse of white tables glowing in the soft lighting, the well-dressed diners, the waiters moving smoothly in their dark dinner jackets, and turned to Matt. He certainly looked right at home; a different person from the rough logger in his diesel pickup. She was seeing another facet of this endlessly intriguing man.

He met her look and grinned, and suddenly he was the same Matt.

"My dad said the first time they put a tie on me and brought me to town I stood on the corner all day. I thought I was tied up."

"Oh, Matt, was I that obvious? I just didn't expect all this. I'm not really a snob."

"I know you're not," he said gently. "Would you like a drink?"

They decided to skip the cocktail and settled on a bottle of wine with dinner. As though deliberately repressing his blazing sexuality, Matt talked easily and pleasantly, and Brianna relaxed. They were having their after-dinner coffee, strong and black with a shot of brandy, when Brianna looked up to see a man standing by their table.

"Hello, Matt." The big, hearty voice went with the man; his well-tailored suit covered a sturdy body, and his face was broad and pleasant with full lips, prominent nose and shrewd blue eyes. "Didn't mean to interrupt, but I wanted to tell you I think I've got just the property."

"Great." Matt gestured to Brianna. "Brianna, this is Gregory Parks, Boise's best realtor—and a good friend. Greg, Brianna Royce."

The man's eyes assessed her swiftly and thoroughly, he glanced at Matt, then smiled broadly. "About time, Matt, about time. I thought you'd never fall, but when you do, you do it properly."

Brianna hoped her flushed cheeks weren't obvious in the soft lighting. Was the affinity between herself and Matt so obvious that anyone could see it?

"About that property," Matt reminded his friend dryly.

Still smiling, the man turned back to Matt. "The site is perfect for a mill, and the price is right. Want me to move on it?"

"Probably. Phone me with the details tomorrow," Matt said.

After Gregory Parks had moved away Brianna turned to Matt.

"You didn't mention you were building a mill."

"It's just in the planning stage," Matt said. "I've been thinking of expanding for a while, putting in a mill to turn out kits for log houses. Give me something to do in the winter."

"You're full of surprises. I guess I envisioned you sitting by the fire in the winter, sipping brandy while the blizzard howled outside the windows."

"You do make it sound attractive. But a little lonely." His eyes held hers until she dropped her gaze to her plate.

It had been a successful evening, she thought later, as Matt pulled into her campsite. Although the physical attraction was certainly there, coloring and deepening their conversation, lending excitement to the most mundane comments, it didn't overwhelm them. Their talk ranged over a variety of subjects; there were only two exceptions. They didn't discuss her work and they didn't talk about the Daynew. That was fine with her. In the elegance of the fine restaurant, with Matt beside her looking so absolutely appealing, the Daynew seemed far away, not only in distance, but in time. A people of another century. And was her work so relevant that it had to be the focus of every discussion?

She knew Matt better now, but she knew also that his basic view of life remained unchanged. A man loves a woman, provides her with a home, children, takes care of everything that comes up. Tonight it was a seductive thought, to sink into Matt's arms and dissolve in a sea of desire. He made her feel dizzily feminine and most women would think she was crazy to resist.

"What was he like?" Matt said softly, breaking into her thoughts.

"Who?" She played for time.

"The man you thought of marrying."

When had she discussed Roy with him? Then she remembered that in a very general way she had talked about the young man. Matt was able to pick up on her innermost thoughts in a most disconcerting manner.

"He was intelligent," she said. "Ambitious."

"Not like me." He grinned.

"Your intelligence was never in question," she said dryly. "At least not from the time you first opened your mouth.

And I'm changing my mind about your ambition. You sounded very enthusiastic about your idea for the mill."

"Why didn't you marry him?"

She thought of answering the question vaguely, but Matt's directness seemed to require an honest response. "His career always came first," she said. "I was expected to accommodate." Her lips curved in a sad smile. "He made the discoveries; I did the typing."

Matt studied her face in silence; she was glad he didn't reply. Although she hadn't been aware of it at the time, now she could have given another reason for not marrying Roy. *He didn't make my body sing, my heart leap.* Could she possibly, against all reason, be falling in love with Matt?

"Sure you won't stay at my house tonight?"

She shook her head, smiling. They had discussed this for the better part of the last half hour. Matt was reluctant to leave her at the campsite, but she determined that she would prove she was able to stay by herself. What use was it to proclaim your independence if you ran for shelter at the first sign of trouble? Her growing awareness of her deepening feelings for Matt made it even more imperative to stay out of temptation's way. She'd proven she could withstand physical attraction, but his dry humor, his sparkling intelligence, his old-fashioned consideration for her feelings, were every bit as seductive as his blazing sensuality.

"I don't want you hiding out watching over me, either," she said sternly. "Get some sleep."

Matt finally agreed, and after a thorough check of the campsite and making sure she was safely locked inside her van, he started for home.

He was still uneasy, though, as he headed for his house several miles away, and not at all sure he could keep his promise to leave her unguarded. He hadn't discussed all his concerns with Brianna; after all, it was a man's duty to protect a woman from worry as well as physical danger.

Still, he had to respect her wishes. He couldn't help but admire her courage and intelligence, and respect her desire for autonomy.

He wondered, too, if he had been seeing her work too narrowly. She was surely dedicated, and he had to admire that. Might there even be something to her ideas that myths impacted on the present?

He shook his head impatiently. It was the present that interested him, and in the present he was losing money as most of the crew stayed away. Those who returned today had acted downright weird, tense, uneasy. Something was brewing. He'd even overheard what might have been an enigmatic threat against Brianna. A troublemaker, one of the men had said.

He drove up to his front door and vaulted out, leaving the car parked in the driveway. It was nearly one o'clock. He would put it away in the morning.

He ran lightly up the steps and reached for the door handle, then paused as he saw the note tacked just at eye level. A cold sense of foreboding ran down his back, as he reached for it and held it under the entry light. It was a piece of lined scratch paper with some scribbled words, but the words leaped out at him like hammers, every one a hard blow to his chest:

Get her out of here if you want to keep her alive.

He didn't stop to try to puzzle out the handwriting, or to see if whoever tacked it to his door had left some sign by which he could be traced. He was aware of his blood thundering in his ears, of his heart thudding against the wall of his chest. Later he would track down the cowardly man who left threats and then slunk away in the night. Later he would find him, and by God, he would punish him. Right now he was driven only by the desperate need to get to Brianna.

He should never have allowed her to stay alone. Even now, she might be in trouble. Jumping into his car, he gunned the powerful engine, roared out of the driveway and sped along the dark road to her campsite.

Chapter 10

Brianna sat on the mossy bank by the edge of the stream that ran a few yards from her campsite, legs pulled up and arms encircling her knees, head bowed so that her hair fell over her clenched hands, and gave herself up to the rhythm of the water. It had been wishful thinking to believe she could sleep after Matt left her. She was much too keyed up, her senses too achingly tuned to desire, to even make the pretense.

She had tried to relax inside the camper, but the small enclosed space fueled a growing sense of claustrophobia. She needed to move, to pace, to think. So she had thrown a light blanket over her shorty nightgown and stepped out of the stifling quarters into the warm summer night.

This time there was no sense of fear at the isolation. The dark trees that encircled her seemed benign, like guardian sentinels; the moon, although not yet full, gilded the forest with silver and gave her a clear view of both her campsite and the little enclosure where she huddled on the grass with the blanket lightly around her shoulders. Crickets called lazily from the bushes and water rushed over the stone bed of the creek with an insistent cadence.

She wondered briefly why she wasn't afraid, then realized there was a different mood about the forest tonight: a sense of poignant waiting, as of something holding its breath. She didn't understand it, but she accepted it.

She lifted her head at the drone of an engine, heard the abrupt silence, and then the sound of footsteps running down the trail. In a near trance brought on by the wine, the mood of the forest, her memories of Matt's touch, she came slowly to her feet, letting the blanket slide to the ground. Somehow, it was no surprise to see Matt rushing through the clearing toward her van. Was this what she had unconsciously been waiting for?

"Matt," she called softly.

He stopped in midstride, wheeled around and peered into the soft darkness, then moved abruptly toward her. The moon gave sufficient light to show the anxiety in his face as he covered the distance between them in a few giant strides.

"Brianna! Are you all right?"

He didn't wait for a reply, just seized her arms and pulled her to him. He held her so fiercely that she gasped for breath; she couldn't have answered if she'd wanted to. Both hard arms tightened around her convulsively and he pulled her even closer against his heaving chest.

"My God, if anything had happened to you—" He broke off and raised one hand to tangle in her hair as he pressed her head against his shoulder. For several endless seconds they stood pressed together, tremulous body to tremulous body, not moving, not speaking, the only sound the harsh rasp of his breath warm in her ear.

Finally he took a deep, gulping breath, loosened his grip a bit and raised his head so that he could see her face. He searched it intently, as though to look into her innermost being, then spoke in a husky whisper. "Are you all right?"

"Why wouldn't I be?" she replied, her voice as husky as his.

"Thank God. But you shouldn't be alone outside in the dark like this. What are you doing? I left you in the camper. . . ."

"I'm not alone now, am I?" she said softly. "Besides, I'm not a doll. You can't expect me to stay right where you put me." The gentleness in her voice took any possible sting out of the words.

"If I thought you would stay where I put you," he said, smiling now that his initial concern had been alleviated, "I'd be a little more confident about your safety than I am now."

"Has something else happened?"

"Nothing to worry about now."

She didn't press it. She wasn't at all sure she cared, with this fire running through her veins. Whether he had come because he feared for her safety, or whether she had somehow called him with her thoughts, she wasn't sure. Right now all that mattered was the feel of Matt's warm hands on her back through the thin material of her shorty nightgown, the muscles of his chest absorbing the thrust of her breasts against him. He was holding her so tightly that the wisp of silk over her thighs presented no obstacle to the stiff material of his twill pants rubbing against her flesh. Desire coursed through her, tingling all through her body, glowing in the pit of her stomach, aching sweetly in the juncture of her thighs. She felt incredibly weak, incredibly strong, all at the same time.

"Nothing to worry about," he repeated, his voice sounding hoarse in his throat as he lowered her slowly to the grassy bank. For a moment she wondered what he was talking about, then realized he was still commenting on some possible danger to her. "But you're going to catch pneumonia out here dressed like this," he continued.

"I had the blanket . . ."

He followed her gaze and went quickly to spread the blanket over the damp moss. The moist minty scent floated up to her, as he put his arms under her legs and swung her around until she was lying on her back on its cozy softness.

Just in time, too, she admitted. Her legs were so weak she couldn't possibly have stood much longer.

He knelt beside her, stripped his jacket from his back and placed it gently over her chest. Then he stretched out beside her, pulling her against his hard, muscular body, enveloping her in his warmth. Her shivering changed; she wasn't cold anymore, but nevertheless she trembled, her body arching toward his as she felt his urgency.

For one flickering instant her conscious mind regained control. She shouldn't be doing this. She knew where it was leading and this time nothing would stop it. But her flash of hesitation was just one discordant note in a symphony of desire that surged and swelled with irresistible force. She knew now what she had been waiting for as she sat alone by the stream, knew why the forest had not been frightening. She had known somehow that Matt was on his way to her.

He put one hand behind her head to draw her to him in a long, impassioned kiss. She welcomed him with a burst of fire, seeking, giving, demanding as much as he. As he ran his other hand up under the jacket that covered her, teasing, then capturing her breast as his mouth continued to ravage hers, she impatiently thrust the jacket aside. She wanted nothing between them.

She broke away long enough to raise herself above him, and she swiftly unbuttoned his shirt, baring his broad chest with the sprinkling of dark hair to her seeking hands and mouth. She heard him catch his breath, and it spurred her on.

When his shirt was off he moved away long enough to pull off his boots and trousers while she divested herself as quickly of her nightgown. Then, with a long, quavering breath, she stretched out beside him and he reached hungrily for her, his mouth and hands and every part of his body wildly demanding.

He teased her, stroked her, worshiped her, until she couldn't stand it a moment longer. She met him with a frenzy as uncontrolled as his own. Every cell of her body burned with aching need.

As she clung mindlessly to him, inviting his entry, she had a sudden strange sensation that for one blink of time she was somewhere above them, watching and approving the inevitable mating. This had happened before; it would happen again. It was ordained. Then she was back with Matt, every nerve tingling and sparking from the force of the life current that held them together.

Time ceased to exist as they strove together on the blanket beside the stream, only one entity under the unwavering eye of the moon. She no longer knew where her flesh ended and his began; every atom intermingled as their breath came in unison, their hearts pounded in perfect rhythm, sexual heat fused their separate cells into one body. The rhythmic thrust and counterthrust was as ancient as the species, as compelling as the tides. When she gave a long, drawn-out cry of ecstasy he matched it with his own.

Then there was silence. Completely sated, unable to move, she gloried in the feel of his moist weight on her body. With one finger he idly stroked her cheek as his mouth moved gently at the base of her throat, sending little afterspasms along her spine. She didn't try to understand his murmured, incoherent endearments. For now it was enough merely to experience this overwhelming joy. A joy so fierce, so consuming, that quick tears sprung to her eyes.

The tip of his finger touched the moisture and he raised his head, concern evident in his indigo eyes. "Brianna, what is it, sweetheart? Are you all right?'

She tried to laugh, but the sound came out half-choked and nearly inaudible. "I think you asked that question just before we got started on this. I've never been better. I just feel—overwhelmed."

"Am I too heavy? Shall I move?"

In reply, she turned slightly so that they lay face-to-face, touching along the full-length of their damp bodies. Her breasts pressed against the moist springy hair of his chest, she felt the hard muscles of his abdomen, recognized the quiescence of his manhood, which was threatening to become not so quiescent again. His breath was hot on her cheek as he reached over her recumbent form for his discarded jacket and draped it over her back.

His lips brushed softly against hers. "I didn't mean for this to happen," he said huskily. "I was just so concerned about you, then so glad you were safe...but I'm glad it did happen," he said firmly. "You are incredibly beautiful, desirable..."

She didn't reply, and he looked searchingly into her eyes. "Sorry?"

"No...not sorry," she breathed. She would never be sorry that this incredible thing had occurred between them, even though it would never be repeated. As some semblance of sanity returned, she recognized the episode for what it was: a moment of shining beauty encapsuled in time. Although they had been strongly attracted since the moment they met, they might never have succumbed if the circumstances had not been just right: she, alone, vulnerable, aching with desire, spurred on by the unearthly mystery of the night; and Matt, frightened for her safety, had claimed and protected his woman in the old, ancestral way. What had happened had been allowed by ancient primitive emotions deep in their subconscious, emotions that had for a few moments usurped control from the newer, rational brain.

But only for a moment. She shivered.

"You're cold." Matt came to his feet all at once like a cat, drawing her up beside him and draping the blanket around her naked form, then folding her against his hard body. "Come on. We'd better get some clothes on. You're shaking."

Safely ensconced in his arms, she peered around the little enclosure, aware for the first time of how open it might be to unseen eyes. But she needn't have worried. Only the forest, dappled by the moonlight, looked back, she sensed, not the malignancy she had imagined at previous times, but bland unconcern.

Matt gave her a little push toward her van, along with a pat on the bottom. "Hurry in and get something on; we'll come back for your van tomorrow."

"But—"

"You're coming with me. And we don't have time for arguments. It's late."

She started to protest further, then realized she was resisting Matt's orders from mere habit. Cutting off her nose to spite her face? She wanted to be with Matt for the rest of the night, to wake up with him tomorrow. If this were all they were to have, she wanted all of it.

Early the next morning Matt drove toward the logging site, his mind still occupied with Brianna. And other parts of him as well, he admitted wryly, aware of a faint stirring in his groin. She had looked so peaceful, so—so at home—in his large, rumpled bed that he hated to leave her this morning. He wanted to be there when she awoke, to kiss the sleep from her face, to feel her lips quicken, to— With a quick jerk he shifted down for the steep grade he routinely anticipated, and heard the grinding of the gears with sheepish frustration. He should keep his mind on what he was doing, but this morning he wasn't sure he had a mind.

He didn't want to feel the way he did. What transpired between them should never have happened, and might not have if he hadn't felt such vast relief at seeing her unharmed that the only thing he could think of was to take her in his arms. He couldn't regret it, but it had certainly complicated things.

He had left the keys to the sports car by her bedside table where she would be sure to see them when she woke up, but nevertheless he knew he wouldn't be away long. She was a siren, calling him back, a fever in his blood. He was going to do one thing, though, he vowed, setting his jaw in fierce determination. He was going to find out who had left the note warning him that Brianna was in danger. And why.

When he pulled up at the site he saw immediately that although he was early his crew was there before him. Puzzled, he watched the big log loader swing around and deposit a log on the waiting truck, saw Joe West run along the log deck and lop off limbs with his chain saw. The operation was going smoothly and efficiently.

His smile was grim. So his crew was back. Fine. But they had a few things to explain.

He strode into the middle of the road and gestured sharply, then waited as the men gathered in a circle around him. For a moment he studied their faces silently, trying to read their mood, but it was useless. Sheepish smiles, blank faces, innocent eyes.

He put his hands on his hips and glared at each one in turn. "All right," he said harshly, "who is going to tell me what's going on? Why are you all back today?"

Joe West wrinkled his forehead. "But I thought you wanted us back."

"Well, of course I did! But that's not the point—"

"We've already got three loads out, Matt." This was Chad speaking up, and Matt turned to him in relief. If anyone would tell him anything, it would be Chad.

"That's fine. But I still want to know why you all quit at once. And whether you have any idea of doing it again." His eyes raked them all impartially.

Chad came close and spoke softly. "Let them go, Boss, and we'll talk."

Matt nodded and sent the others back to work, then walked with Chad to the pickup where they could talk privately. "Okay," he said, looking at his friend's broad face, now twisted in an expression of anxiety, "Talk."

"As I told you before, we had to get ready for the holiday, but everything's been settled. At least for now. We talked it over; we're back to work."

"That doesn't tell me very much. What did you have to settle?" Matt demanded.

"Oh, things... You wouldn't understand." From the manner in which his gaze drifted down, Chad looked as though he'd found something very interesting in the tips of his boots.

"Try me," Matt ground out.

Still Chad looked everywhere but at Matt, his face expressionless. "We did what we could. It's over."

"The holiday's over?"

"Our part's over."

Matt thought of demanding more of an explanation, then realized it was useless. The man was talking in circles. But he wouldn't let him be so evasive about the threatening note. He'd find out if he had to fire the man. Or beat him to a pulp, which was the way he felt right now.

"Okay, we'll drop it. For now," he said shortly. "Suppose you tell me about the warning I found tacked on my door last night. The threat about Brianna Royce."

His tone was so implacable that Chad looked up quickly, saw his stony face, and spoke hastily. "It wasn't me."

"But you know very well who it was."

Chad didn't answer, and the rage he'd been controlling since he began talking to the man boiled up in Matt, threatening to destroy his calm manner.

"Answer me!"

Chad stared back for a long moment, then sighed, his heavy shoulders slumping. "It wasn't me. That's all I can say about it. But if I were you, Boss, I'd pay attention to it." He turned abruptly and strode back toward his loader, leaving Matt staring helplessly after him, clenching and unclenching his hands.

With a muttered curse, Matt shrugged, knowing he might as well give up for the moment. What did he really know about the Daynew, when you got right down to it? Friendly people up to a point, good workers. But in his great-grandfather's time, these men were savages. Was the veneer of civilization thinner than he supposed, and his attempt to bring them into the modern world all for nothing?

He felt unaccountably dejected. He had wanted to help them, had believed it was in their best interest to leave their past behind.

To hell with them. Was Brianna right? Was his concern misplaced? Did they know as well as he did what was good for them?

He stared at Chad's retreating back, but he didn't really see him. He was again on the bank of the stream with Brianna, experiencing a bewildering depth of passion he had never known before. A passion that he reluctantly suspected went beyond the physical, although he nearly blushed at the ridiculous thought. He almost felt as though he knew her on some deeper level, as though her spirit somehow called to his.

And that showed how far her crazy ideas had taken him from the realm of common sense! He shook his head as though to clear out the conflicting ideas. It was true that her independence and intuitive nature were alluring. Could she be right that he was too rigid in his thinking?

He hit the fender of his pickup with his clenched fist, then winced angrily at the pain. She was making him as crazy as she was! If he didn't love her, he'd let her stay right here in Hope and take her own chances....

The thought had come out of nowhere and he stood stock-still, staring at nothing. Was it true? Was he beginning to love her? If so, he had better stop it right now!

Because, in spite of last night's passionate interlude, nothing had really changed. She would complete her work, go back to her world, and he would be alone.

He stepped up into his pickup and drove back down the road, vaguely depressed. He had never thought of himself as alone before. And it was going to be inevitable. His knowledge of how deeply he felt about her made it even more imperative that she be kept safe, and he wasn't at all sure he could protect her in Hope. He sensed that Chad was still afraid of something, and the threat against Brianna had been real. It was absolutely necessary that she leave. The thought deepened his depression, and he swung the wheel savagely. Until she did, he couldn't afford for their emotional involvement to deepen; somehow, he had to stay aloof.

Feeling drugged by the night's glorious lovemaking, Brianna moved slowly around the empty house, showering, breakfasting, idly wondering when Matt would return. The interlude with Matt had sapped her energy, left her body tingling and vibrantly aware, her thought processes unaccountably dull.

She smiled as she saw the keys on the table, appreciative of Matt's thoughtfulness. She wasn't stranded, although she wasn't sure she would go anywhere just yet. She should get back to work, of course....

The knocker thudded against the heavy front door and she wandered slowly toward it. A friend of Matt's, probably, and maybe she shouldn't answer. Maybe he wouldn't want anyone to know she had spent the night here.

Imperiously the sound came again, and she shrugged. For all she knew the entire town of Hope was already aware that she had come home with Matt. News seemed to fly in some way that escaped her city-tuned sensibilities.

To her surprise, it wasn't a friend of Matt's. Diana Thompson, Alta Thompson's daughter, awaited her on the entry steps. As tall as Brianna, clad in jeans and a long overblouse, hair pulled back from an impassive face, the woman met her eyes silently.

"Come in," Brianna said, stepping back to motion the young woman inside. "This is a surprise."

Diana stayed where she was, her manner indicating plainly that she had no time for superfluous chitchat. "Mother wishes to see you."

Okay, she could be just as direct. "How did you know where to find me?"

The young woman shrugged. "You weren't at your van. Where else would you be?"

Although the words were said in a matter-of-fact tone, Brianna couldn't help feeling that there was a subtle satisfaction in them. She thought of refusing; she didn't particularly trust Diana. The young woman said very little, but her gray eyes were shrewdly observant. Still, if Alta wanted to see her right now, she had better go. The old woman had been so cooperative that she had best placate her; she was the key to the success of her project.

"Wait till I change."

As Diana waited on the side steps of the entry, Brianna hurriedly changed from Matt's oversize robe to the slim pants and long cotton shirt that she had collected from the van last night. Remembering the last time she had left without leaving word for Matt, she scribbled him a hasty note and joined Diana on the porch.

She supposed Diana had driven, and was surprised when the woman walked quickly around Matt's house and plunged into the woods. She detected no trace of a trail, but Diana moved quickly and with complete assurance. Even though she couldn't see through the surrounding trees, Brianna was very good with directions, and she knew they weren't going toward Alta's house.

They had walked perhaps ten minutes when Brianna began to be concerned. Diana seemed to be taking much too much pleasure in keeping her running behind her, only occasionally casting a look back over her shoulder.

"Where are you taking me?" Brianna gasped, struggling to keep up with the other woman. "This isn't the way to your mother's place."

Diana turned and gave her a long, contemplative look, a look that sent a faint shiver down Brianna's spine. Then, without answering, she plunged on into the forest. Brianna suddenly wondered if Diana were guiding her against her will. Was this tall, taciturn woman one of those who wished to have nothing to do with Brianna and was only complying reluctantly with her mother's wishes?

She concentrated on keeping up as another twenty minutes went by. She was absolutely certain now that Diana was leading her in circles, and her uneasiness increased. Surely the woman wouldn't harm her, but there was no doubt that she was making certain that Brianna was completely lost. If her guide vanished now, it would take her ages to find her way out. If she ever did, she thought glumly.

She considered demanding an explanation, but rejected it. Diana's back looked too uncompromising, and if the

Excitement boiled up in Brianna until she could hardly speak. Could it be true! But how could it not be true? The marks on the stone looked exactly like ogham, the ancient lettering of the Celts!

It wasn't out of the realm of possibility; she remembered the controversy about the Mandan Indians, and how for centuries some people believed they were a lost band of Celts. Had those ancient wanderers come even farther, and ended up here on the shores of a lake in Idaho?

Her earlier apprehension was completely forgotten. If she could prove this, it would stand the world of anthropology on its collective head!

But her colleagues would be hard to convince, she knew. She could anticipate the questions. Why had she been the only one to discover this? Soberly she suddenly realized it was a good question, and turned to Alta.

"Why are you showing me this, Alta?"

"You wanted information about the old days of the Daynew." The woman's glance was dark and secretive.

"And I appreciate it. Do the Daynew still come to this shrine?"

"No, it has been a long time since my people believed," Alta said simply. "Now all prefer the new religions." Her face darkened and again Brianna felt the chill of fear. She hurried on.

"There have been other anthropologists, other people," she stumbled along.

"But none who could understand," Alta said simply. She held Brianna's eyes in a deep, compelling look of intimacy, a look of a secret shared that seemed to probe her soul. Shaken right down to her shoes, Brianna wished she knew what that secret was.

Chapter 11

Matt, it was incredible! There is no way it could be there—and yet it was!" Brianna's voice sparkled with excitement as she looked across at Matt.

He couldn't match her enthusiasm. Standing in front of the fireplace, hands clasped behind his back, Matt looked at Brianna's vivid, upturned face and frowned slightly. *She* was incredible. She absolutely glowed with enthusiasm: her odd golden eyes encircled by black-rimmed irises danced with delight as she tossed her head to send her hair flowing back over her shoulders in a cascade of gold. She had been siting in the soft, upholstered armchair, bare feet and long legs tucked underneath her, but she couldn't sit still. He watched her jump up and pace a few steps, then collapse back into the chair.

"A druid's circle? I'd say that's pretty incredible, all right," he replied, one dark eyebrow rising slightly in obvious skepticism.

"So you don't believe me! But it's true!" She elevated her chin and gave him a level glance. "I assure you I can recognize a druid's circle when I see one."

"Not just a haphazard circle of stones left by a retreating glacier?"

She bounced up again as though on springs, her enthusiasm forcing her to some kind of action, and continued speaking as though she had not heard his comment. "I should have seen it right away. It was all there! The spiral decorations, the geometric designs on all the houses. The linear lines of Ogham. Even the gray eyes, light hair. Everything points to the Celts!"

"So why didn't you notice it?" he asked dryly.

"Because it was so unexpected. I just never made the connection until I actually saw those stones, with the dolmen in the center. Matt," she said earnestly, taking his arm and looking up into his morose face, "this could be the discovery of the century!"

"Or a joke by Alta." Matt hated to douse her enthusiasm, but he thought she was stretching a long way to her conclusion. "Look, I don't know much abut this. And I agree that hardly anyone believes that Columbus was the first person to arrive in America after the Native Americans made it over the Bering Strait thirty thousand years ago. But you certainly don't think the Celts beat Columbus here by a couple of thousand years!"

"Why not?" she demanded. "New evidence is being found all the time. The Phoenicians, Celts, Basques, all may have gotten to the new world by 1000 B.C., maybe earlier. Traces of Celtic settlements have been found all through New England!"

He sighed and moved to the couch, slouched down, crossed his long legs at the ankles and regarded her moodily. He'd always known she was credulous, her mind so open her brains might just fall out, but this was carrying things a little too far. "Isn't there some controversy about that theory?" he asked softly.

She shot him a suspicious glance. "How do you know so much about it?"

He grinned at her challenge. He suspected she considered his interests were confined to his business, and it amused him to bait her. "There was a series about it on Uncle Bob's Children's Hour."

She flushed slightly, shrugged and spread her hands in apology. "Sorry. I didn't mean to sound pompous. But if you know that you also know the story of the Mandan Indians."

"A lost Welsh tribe," he agreed. "Never proven."

"Or disproven," she insisted. "Oh, it's pretty sure they didn't arrive with Prince Madoc as late as a lot of people thought. But there's absolutely nothing to prove they didn't reach America much earlier, spread out from New England—"

"And a group of them got as far as Idaho," he finished. "Pretty farfetched."

"Then how do you explain the druid's circle. The ogham?"

He really couldn't explain it, but he wasn't ready to jump to the conclusions Brianna had apparently reached. The Daynew a band of lost Celts! Ridiculous.

"You said yourself all primitive people have certain common elements in their religion and history. And didn't you also say the spiral is a common decoration?"

"Nothing this specific," she insisted, pacing in front of him, head down, lower lip caught between her teeth.

"You may just wear out my rug," he said dryly.

She continued as though he hadn't spoken. "Matt, we really know next to nothing about the groups who peopled the Americas. There's a tremendously wide variety among the natives. Why is it so outlandish to think a group of Celts made it as far west as Idaho, and more advanced than their neighbors, isolated themselves, kept their culture, their religion?"

When he didn't immediately reply she paused and gave him a beseeching look. "Cut off from their roots, their myths their only history, they might very possibly have kept the old ways intact for years, though hidden."

He regarded her thoughtfully, his skepticism beginning to waver. Her enthusiasm was contagious; if he weren't careful, he might end up thinking she wasn't entirely crazy. He'd come home this afternoon to find her waiting in his living room, bubbling over with news of her discovery, and they'd talked of nothing else for hours.

"Tell me again just where this circle is located," he said. "It seems strange to me that I've lived here all my life and never heard of it."

She shrugged, refusing to meet his eyes. "I'm afraid I don't really know," she admitted. "Diana took great pains to get me totally confused."

He remembered Chad's warning, and his mouth tightened. So she had been stumbling around lost for hours, and someone, he was convinced, meant her harm. Fear for her safety made his tone harsher than he would have wished. "You mean you went off in the wilderness, just like that?"

Immediately she elevated her chin. "Matt, I'm here to learn about myths. Learn about the Daynew. How can I possibly do that if I stay here in your house all the time?"

For a full moment they glared at each other, then Matt sighed and turned away. He hadn't told her about the latest threat; perhaps he couldn't expect her to be as concerned as he was.

"Are you hungry?" he asked abruptly.

She looked slightly surprised. "I guess I am. I'd forgotten all about it."

"Well, let's whip into the Hope Mercantile and get a hamburger. I'm getting a little tired of druid circles and weird writing, and displaced Celts; I'd like to get back to reality."

She hesitated, then grinned impishly. "Well, I'd say the hamburgers there will certainly jolt you back to reality, all right."

For the remainder of the evening they kept up an uneasy truce. Occasionally Matt caught a questioning, almost pleading look in her eyes as he resolutely kept the conversation impersonal.

It wasn't just his skepticism about the druid's circle that bothered her, he suspected. Undoubtedly she was confused, maybe even hurt, at the abrupt change in his attitude since last night's lovemaking. Once or twice she had tried to touch on the subject, but his remote reply had silenced her and she had too much pride to pursue it.

She couldn't know how much it cost him to hold her away, he thought, but he didn't dare relax his guard for an instant. If he did, he just might say, *I love you* and then they would have to deal with it in some manner. If he didn't hold her, didn't kiss her, didn't feel her heart beating against his chest, maybe his fancy that he actually loved her would prove just that—a fancy—and go away.

After they had devoured juicy hamburgers and crisp french fries, played a game of pool, and Matt had toured her around the area until he couldn't think of another place to show her, he drove her to his home. He was quite proud of himself. He hadn't touched her once, and she, although he caught an occasional baffled look in her eyes, didn't mention the night before, either. Perhaps she had decided to treat it as he had: an aberration in both their lives, dangerous, not to be repeated.

Only for a minute did his resolve waver. She stood at the foot of the winding staircase that led to her room, and put out her hand. "Matt..."

There was something so vulnerable in her voice. His throat felt dry and pain laced through him. Swallowing, he enveloped her hand in his, acutely conscious of the delicacy of the bone structure, the softness of her skin.

"Yes?" His voice sounded gruff to his own ears. If she mentioned the lovemaking now, if she asked him to come up with her, what would he do? Did it really matter if they had one more enchanted night? How much worse could he feel than he already felt? He held her outstretched hand, feeling the touch down to his toes.

But she had something else on her mind, he finally realized. She was frowning thoughtfully. "Matt, there was one more thing about Alta's chanting and the druid's circle..."

He waited as she brought the words out painfully. "I felt—I felt as though everything there was familiar, somehow."

He didn't like the cold feeling that coursed through him, but he forced a smile. "Well, it probably was familiar. You've seen plenty of pictures of Celtic ruins and you studied ogham writing in school."

"Yes, I suppose so." He heard her sigh as she turned, and head bent, walked slowly up the stairs. She didn't look back, and he watched her slender back until she turned into the hall toward her room. Then he let out his breath in a harsh sigh.

He hoped she would sleep well. God knows he didn't expect to.

The familiar argument began again first thing in the morning as they sat together at the breakfast table. How could she look so delectable so early in the morning, he wondered, running his hand over his freshly shaven face. He'd stood under a shower for fifteen minutes, and he still felt the effects of the past few sleepless nights. But she seemed unaffected, he thought morosely, as he watched her gulp down her orange juice and take a burned piece of bread from the toaster and smear it with Mrs. Clayton's strawberry jam.

"Have to hurry," she announced happily. "I'm meeting Alta in a few minutes. She's taking me to the druid's circle again."

Matt looked up sharply, then set his coffee mug down firmly on the table. "I don't think that's a good idea, Brianna."

She sighed with exaggerated patience. "Matt, be reasonable. How can I finish my dissertation if I don't get any material?"

"How are you going to find the circle? You don't even know where it's located."

"Alta will guide me."

"And get you thoroughly lost again, I suppose."

"Well, I can certainly understand why they don't want just anybody knowing where it's located. It has to be a secret. It's a religious shrine, for heaven's sake. A place where they used to practice all kinds of ceremonies."

"And you won't be able to find your way back alone, either, I suppose," he growled, wishing he knew how to persuade her to drop the entire thing.

"I don't need to! Alta will bring me back."

"Okay," Matt said decisively, rising to carry his plate to the sink. "Then I'll go with you."

"Matt, what's the matter with you! You know Alta won't talk when you're around. Besides, don't you have work of your own to do?"

He gave her a long, hard look, saw the angry resolve in her face, and shrugged. Perhaps he did seem a little unreasonable since she didn't know about the warning that had been pinned to his door, but Chad's enigmatic words still rang in his ears.

I'd take that threat seriously if I were you. Well, damn it, he did take it seriously. He would see that she got out of Hope the minute she could be persuaded to leave, and in the meantime he'd be very sure nothing happened to her, whether she liked it or not.

For now, there was nothing he could do. He couldn't imprison her, although it might not be a bad idea, he thought, his lips tightening.

He waited until she had gone, then went at once into his office and pulled a sheaf of maps down from the shelves. Brianna had said that the stone circle was located in virgin timber, untouched by loggers. Well, that made it easy; there were very few places on this mountain that Stuart Logging had not been over.

But there was one. He had been told that in his great-grandfather's time a bargain had been struck with the Daynew. The loggers agreed to stay out of a tiny strip of land; in return the Daynew would make no complaint about logging anyplace else on what they considered their domain. The agreement might have no legal basis. The Daynew owned no land now, the forest service or the large lumber companies having taken over most of their ancestral land, but each successive Stuart had honored the agreement.

He located it quickly, and frowned. Strange that he had never even walked through it, but perhaps that was because the strip was quite well protected by the Daynew village on one side, a large canyon on the other. There was plenty of open space without it, anyway; it had never been necessary to invade that tiny strip of primeval wilderness.

He didn't follow Brianna immediately. Judging from the look in her eyes when she left, she probably didn't trust him at all and might even expect him to follow. He didn't want a confrontation, but he had to assure himself she was safe. He would go by another route and remain just behind her.

Half an hour later he parked his pickup alongside the road and dived quickly into the trees, not at all bothered by the absence of a trail. He had long ago learned to tell directions by the angle of the sun or the manner in which the moss grew on the tree trunks.

He was somewhat surprised, though, as he penetrated deeper in the gloom; the place was unique. Even in wilderness areas trees usually didn't grow as thickly as this; they were often pruned by fire, drought, disease, even if they did escape man. But he soon saw that this area was different. It gave him a strange feeling, almost as though he had taken a giant step back in time.

He reached out to run his hand over the rough bark of a pine. The trees were unimaginably huge, their girth making it seem they had grown undisturbed for thousands of years. The undergrowth, brush and fern and trailing vines, reached above his head, making it difficult to find his direction. He smiled thinly. So much for his previous assumption that he knew all about the Daynew. Although he had often camped with them, fished with them, hiked with them, they had never once led him to this secluded grove.

Their secretiveness hurt, but he brushed it aside. Perhaps it was understandable. They had years of distrust to overcome. He was slowly bringing them around; it just took time, that was all.

He stopped and took a deep breath, his eyes probing the forest gloom. Which way from here?

He heard the crackle of brush and for a second he tensed, considering the possibility of a wild animal. Then, recognizing the woman who stepped out in front of him, he relaxed and smiled. "Diana. What are you doing here?"

"I guess I could ask you the same, Matt," she said easily, not moving from her stance by the trunk of a huge Douglas fir. Its ancient limbs threw shadows on her face, making the contours suddenly unfamiliar.

He surveyed her more closely, alerted by the coolness in her voice. On the surface, she was the same, familiar woman he had always known. The one he had gone to school with, danced with, once even had a slight crush on. But now she looked different.

It wasn't her clothes; she wore faded denim jeans over her long legs, sneakers, a brightly colored, sleeveless cotton blouse. Her long dark hair was pulled back from her strongly featured face and tied with a red kerchief, and huge, dramatic earrings fell against her neck.

The earrings held his attention. He had never noticed it before, but now he realized all the Daynew women wore geometrically patterned earrings that, since he had talked to Brianna, he recognized as a variation of the Celtic Cross. Could Brianna possibly be right?

It was Diana's eyes that were different, he finally decided. They were cool and remote. They met his gaze unwaveringly, dark and solemn, holding not a trace of the friendliness he usually found in the Daynew.

"Just out for a walk," he said easily, wondering why he had to explain anything.

"Shouldn't you be at work?"

This was becoming rather strange; she didn't move from her position; it was almost as though she were barring his way.

"Oh, the boss can take one day off," he said, moving forward to step around her.

Before he reached her, he heard the sound of footsteps to his right, and another woman materialized out of the shadows. He knew her, of course, but her expression was as solemn as Diana's. Before he could question her, another woman stepped smoothly out of the gloom on his other side.

Not at all concerned, but definitely puzzled, Matt greeted the women, then started to move forward again. He didn't quite know how she did it, but Diana was in front of him, definitely blocking his path.

"Hey," he said easily. "What gives? If I didn't know better, I'd think you lovely ladies didn't want me hiking around here. Secrets?"

Diana smiled. "You know us women, Matt. We just like to get away from the men for a while."

"Sure. I understand." He looked at her face, stern in spite of the smile, and then glanced at the other two women. Suddenly he knew that if he tried to go forward he might be met by all the females of the tribe.

He debated what he should do now. A no-win situation, whatever it was. His men often talked about the penchant of the Daynew women for "hen parties," gatherings to which no men were invited. It was understandable since the tribe had once been matrilineal. He knew himself that Daynew women still took a strong part in tribal affairs. Even though they had all adjusted fairly well to western culture and the men were now the undisputed breadwinners, the women probably still clung to some of their old ways.

Making up his mind, he said goodbye, turned and walked back the way he had come, uneasily aware of their somber eyes on his back. He didn't like it, but after all, it was Daynew land, and he was trespassing. Brianna was probably in there someplace with old Alta, allowed in because she was female. It irritated the hell out of him, but he didn't see what he could do about it unless he wanted to make a real scene. And his relations with the Daynew were touchy enough right now, with the men acting so weird; he didn't want the women complaining about him and stirring things up further.

Anyway, Brianna was safe enough, he thought sourly, with that ring of women guarding her. If he hesitated to break through that barricade, how much more unlikely were any of the Daynew men to do so. And that must be where the threat was coming from; Chad had as much as admitted it.

Suddenly the ground rolled sharply under his feet and he caught a tree to steady himself. Were the tremors getting more frequent lately? Probably not. They usually came in cycles, but he hadn't heard of a really strong one since his great-grandfather's time. He wished that were all he had to worry about.

Brianna sat on the stone dolmen, writing furiously in her notebook. Everything was so peaceful; it was as though the outside world didn't exist. On one level she was aware of the light breeze playing in her hair, the sound of a jay, the crisp scent of pine, but most of her attention was concentrated on Alta. Now and then she glanced up at the old woman, not quite believing how lucky she was.

Once started, the woman proved to be a fountain of information, and the stories she was telling now sent chills of excitement all along Brianna's spine—fantastic stories about the very beginning of Daynew mythology.

"What else do you know of the land you came from?" Brianna prompted.

"A green and beautiful land," Alta chanted.

"There was a great war," Brianna reminded her. "The barbarians forced you out. Who were the barbarians?"

Alta seemed nearly in a hypnotic trance, repeating words that had echoed through time. "They called themselves the Sons of Mil."

Brianna's heart raced, but though she tried to get more details, that was all Alta had remembered of the ancient conquerors. She switched to another subject.

"You told me the old ones worshiped a goddess," Brianna said, prompting the old woman. "Can you tell me about her?"

Alta looked up suddenly, her eyes catching Brianna's in an intense gaze. She smiled almost furtively.

"What would you like to know?"

"Everything!" Brianna said, her voice ringing bell-like in the little clearing. "For instance, how long have the Daynew worshiped her?"

Alta shook her head impatiently. "I told you. The old ones said the goddess has been with us since the beginning."

"What do you call her?"

"Danu. She is the Goddess Danu," Alta said shortly.

Brianna looked at her, somewhat puzzled by her tone. Had she offended her in some way? Alta seemed to be expecting her to understand something, but she had no idea what it was.

"This Goddess Danu, tell me more about her."

Alta shrugged. "The story goes that she guided us through many lands. She came with us here, lived here, until the coming of the white man. Then she left us."

The woman spoke so bleakly that Brianna looked up quickly. This was a myth, wasn't it, a story of long-ago times? "Why did she do that?"

"Who knows? I know only what was told to me. Our people were quite primitive in those days. They had strange beliefs." The feverish eyes swung to Brianna, and something furtive moved in their depths. "It was even said that one day she'll return."

"Is this her shrine?" Brianna gestured around the enclosed circle.

"I am told it was. It was also where the old ones came to read the heavens, learn what the future held for the tribe."

Brianna scribbled furiously, hardly noticing the time as the day wore on. Alta's stock of anecdotes seemed endless, and for the most part she seemed just as eager to impart them as Brianna was to receive them.

It was only occasionally that Brianna felt a flash of misgiving, a feeling that Alta was communicating something to her wordlessly, imparting some secret knowledge that she was on the verge of understanding. But she dismissed her vague uneasiness. This was the first time in years the old woman had found anyone interested enough to listen to her ancient tales. Of course she was excited.

As she wrote down the words of the loquacious old woman, an idea began to form in Brianna's mind, an idea so preposterous that she didn't even want to admit it to herself. She would wait until she could bounce it off Matt. With his steady common sense, he would surely point out the holes in her hypothesis.

As she walked in the door of Matt's house she paused, taking in the tantalizing aroma of something baking. Only then did she realize how hungry she was. She had spent the entire day with Alta, much too interested to be hungry. Now she hesitated, wondering about Matt's mood. He hadn't been too happy with her when she left this morning, his overprotectiveness almost daunting in its intensity. Did the man think he had to take care of the entire world? She hoped he was over it. She slung her notepad on the coffee table and followed the aroma into the kitchen.

"Hi." Matt shut the oven door and turned toward her. He pushed back the lock of dark hair that had fallen across his forehead, a gesture that made her pulse pound a little faster, and gave her a wide smile. "Mrs. Clayton left a chicken roasting. All we have to do is keep an eye on it."

He looked so doubtful at the prospect that Brianna nearly laughed. "I guess we can handle that."

"Let's have a sherry while we're waiting." He took down two fragile, long-stemmed glasses and poured in some amber liquid from a crystal decanter. "Did you have a productive day?"

"Very interesting." At least they weren't going to take up the argument where they left off. She accepted the sherry and walked to the table and leaned against it, her sherry forgotten in her hand. "Matt, I think I've found out something extremely interesting."

"More interesting than displaced Celts?" He grinned, lifted his glass in a quick salute, then took a drink.

"You'll think I'm crazy—"

"Probably," he interrupted, "but don't let that stop you."

Ignoring his comment, she continued breathlessly. "I think I've found more than just Celts. I think I've found . . . the Tuatha De Danann!"

He nearly choked and set his glass down hastily on the table. "What did Alta put in your tea? The Tuatha De Danann! The fairy people of old Ireland!"

She shot him a quick glance. "What do you know about the Tuatha De Danann?"

"Brianna, you are talking to a man whose father was Scottish and whose mother was from the 'auld sod itself!' Not hear of the fairy people? She told me bedtime stories about them."

"Did she tell you they were real?" she demanded. "Oh, not fairies," she said hastily, seeing his face. "It's only recently that people have been learning about the mysterious Tuatha De Danann. People of Danu."

He merely raised an eyebrow and she continued as though trying to convince herself. "A matrilineal people called the Dananns lived in Greece in about 1250 B.C. It was the old story—they were driven out but some of them apparently reached Ireland. They took their goddess with them. Around 500 B.C. or earlier, they were defeated by other invaders, the much more primitive Milesians."

"And they took to the hills," Matt said slowly, "hiding out. And the invaders found them so advanced they considered them magic? Fairies? Is that what you're saying?"

"Some of them did," she agreed, meeting his eyes squarely, but wincing inwardly. Now was when he would laugh at her. "Others came to America, fought their way across the continent—and live today as the Daynew!"

"Wow! Is your dissertation supposed to be fiction, Brianna?"

"Look at the evidence," she said severely. "The Day-new. In the old days, followers of the Goddess Danu. Tuatha De Danann—People of Danu. Forced out of 'a green and verdant land' by the Milesians. The Daynew have a myth about being conquered by the Sons of Mil. The druid's circle..."

"The Celts had the druid's circle—not the Tuatha De Danann!"

"The Tuatha De Danann had their druids also. Besides, I think they may have been branches of the same people," she said stoutly. "In fact, the later Celts probably borrowed the whole thing from the Tuatha De Danann—the White Goddess was worshiped in Ireland until Christian times. The White Goddess—Danu."

"Aren't you doing a lot of supposing?"

"Not as much as you might think. The more we dig into the past of these mythical people, the more we find out about them. My theory will take some proving, but it's not impossible."

He sighed. "Well, you'll sure make a stir when you publish this idea!"

"That's just it—I have to be sure. It all holds together, but I have to find out more."

He looked up quickly. "Then you won't be leaving—soon?'

She could have sworn there was disappointment in his voice, and she felt a quick rush of depression. What was the matter? Matt had been a different person since the night they had made love—remote and reserved most of the time, bursting with anger at others. She realized she had been perilously close to falling in love with him, and had suspected a depth of feeling in him that, if it existed, he was certainly keeping carefully hidden.

But what did she want him to say? Anything permanent was out of the question for them. Perhaps Matt's way of ignoring the problem was the sensible thing to do.

But it wasn't her way. She placed her empty glass on the table and deliberately caught his gaze. "Matt—we've got to talk."

Chapter 12

Talk?'' Matt reached for the decanter and poured another drink, all his attention seemingly on the amber liquid that flowed into his crystal glass. ''I thought that's what we were doing.''

Brianna bit her lip to forestall a sharp retort. He couldn't be that dense; as usual, he was pushing her away.

''Yes, talk,'' she said firmly, her eyes on his carefully bland face. ''Matt, some things you just can't ignore....''

He sipped carefully from his drink. ''I'm sure you can't....'' Then, as though weary of the sparring, he jerked impatiently to his feet. ''I could say I'm sorry, I suppose. I didn't mean to take advantage of you.''

''Don't apologize!'' How could he trivialize what had happened between them! Treat it as a casual episode that an apology would gloss over! And to say that he had taken advantage of her, as though she had no will of her own, was insulting.

''There is nothing to be sorry for,'' she said stiffly. ''Neither of us meant it to happen. I—I just thought I should make it clear that it won't happen again.''

At his swift look, she felt her face redden. He must think her presumptuous. Matt had given no indication at all that he wanted it to happen again. In fact, his actions suggested not only that it would not happen again but that it had never happened in the first place! "I mean," she floundered, "I don't want you to think—"

He came to her in one stride, caught her shoulders in his hands and yanked her to her feet so that she had no alternative but to look directly into his eyes. His fierce gaze riveted her to him as surely as his unrelenting hands. He was scowling, his lips a thin line, only inches away, and his words seemed to come through clenched teeth.

"Brianna, I don't think anything. Let's drop it. We were both carried away—the situation, the moonlight. But don't worry—I don't want an involvement any more than you do."

His words cut cruelly. So she had been right all along. That passionate interlude meant nothing to him. She meant nothing to him.

"I just wanted to be sure," she said weakly. "I didn't want you to get the wrong idea. I mean, I don't take such things lightly, but on the other hand, you shouldn't attach too much significance to it—"

He let her go so quickly that she swayed and reached for the table to keep her balance. "Which is it?" he said briskly. "You don't take lovemaking lightly? Or you don't attach much significance to it? Or are those two positions as contradictory as I think they are?"

How had he put her at such a disadvantage? Her words certainly mirrored her own uncertainty. She surveyed him thoughtfully. His expression indicated she had hurt him in some way, though she couldn't see how. Nevertheless, certain things had to be said. She didn't know why, but it was important that he believe she would never have made love to him if she hadn't felt something—something very nearly like love, even though it couldn't lead anywhere.

"I just think things should be clear between us." She raised her head and gave him a defiant stare.

He turned and sat down, lean muscular legs straddling a chair, his elbow on the table as he lowered his head to run his hand restlessly through his hair. "Brianna, what do you want of me?"

"Nothing! But things have been so strained between us for the past few days I thought we should talk about it."

"Will talking make a difference in your plans?"

When she didn't answer, he sighed and raised his head to give her a twisted smile. "Some things can't be changed, Brianna. I like my life as it is. You have every intention of leaving just as soon as you get your material. Can't we just say it was a lovely interlude, and leave it at that?"

Her throat constricted so that it was hard to force out the words. "That's it? A lovely interlude?"

His gaze wandered over her face as though he were famished for the sight of her. She felt it like a physical touch, and her heart beat a little faster, her knees seemed made of water. When he spoke, it was like an intimate caress. "A very lovely interlude," he said huskily. "One to remember all my life. After you've gone."

"Oh, Matt—"

The shrilling of the telephone cut off whatever she had been about to say. He held her gaze for seconds longer, as though unwilling to break the contact, then got slowly to his feet and walked into the living room. Wandering in behind him, she watched him pick up the phone and heard him bark harshly into the instrument.

"Matt here."

There was a pause; she saw his body stiffen as he listened silently for a few seconds, then slam down the phone with a muttered curse. He turned toward her, revealing a face set in hard anger.

"I'll be back in a few minutes." He was already striding toward the door.

"Where are you going?" She hurried after him, clutching at his arm.

"Just a little trouble with the crew; nothing for you to worry about."

"I'll come with you."

"It's not necessary—" He broke off as he saw she was paying absolutely no attention to his words. "Hurry up, then. We have to go to the Hope Mercantile."

They drove in silence, Brianna trying to steady herself against the jolts as the pickup bounced along the road toward Hope. Matt was driving much faster than usual, and he seemed to hit every pothole. She suspected he was taking out his anger and frustration by speeding through the twilight. How much of that anger and frustration pertained to her, and how much to whatever problem awaited them at the Hope Mercantile, she didn't know. She glanced at his profile and decided not to ask any questions.

With tires skidding on loose gravel, he pulled up in front of the store and jumped from his cab, not waiting for Brianna to scramble down on her side. Nevertheless, she was so close behind him when he swung open the door to the little restaurant-bar and then stopped abruptly that she nearly collided with him.

She stared unbelievingly, then took an involuntary step backward. It was a scene of complete chaos: chairs overturned, tables upended, bottles of beer, full and empty, scattered around the floor like bowling pins after a strike. Half a dozen men were scattered around nearly as haphazardly as the bottles: two of Matt's crew sat quietly on the floor, legs outstretched looking foolishly and quizzically at one another; another man was stretched out prone beside them; several others were methodically turning over whatever chairs had remained upright during what must have been an epochal fight.

The noise level turned the entire scene to a surrealistic dream; it might have been a country and western song accompanying the madness, but the volume was turned so high that all Brianna could discern was a wall of sound.

Matt surveyed the room quickly, then strode to the bar where one man was sitting alone, an expression of bewilderment on his face. When he saw Matt he slid from the stool and came quickly forward.

"What's going on here, Jeff?" Matt demanded.

Jeff seemed to shrink under Matt's angry gaze. "Just what you see. The crew came in for a beer after work like they always do—but they didn't go on home."

"I can see that, all right," Matt said dryly, watching another man slide slowly down a wall and then collapse on the floor. "But what started it? They've never done this before."

Margie came slowly from around the bar where she had taken refuge, put her hands on her ample hips, and surveyed the inebriated men with a sour look. "Of course they've never done this before. If they had, they'd all be in jail. Get 'em out of here, Matt, before I change my mind and call the sheriff anyway."

Matt gave her a quick, conciliatory smile. "Thanks for calling me, Margie. I'll take care of it. And the damage, too, of course." From the disgusted look he gave the men, Brianna suspected the cost of the damage would be deducted from the paychecks.

Matt swung around to Jeff. "Have you got a pickup here? None of these guys will be driving tonight."

While Jeff went to bring the pickup closer to the door, Matt moved among the men, ordering, cajoling, doing whatever worked with the men still on their feet. It was easier than it might have been. Matt's arrival seemed to have sobered them somewhat, and they moved, stumbling and shamefaced, to the door.

One by one he and Jeff herded those who were still mobile outside and dumped them into the bed of the pickup. Then they turned their attention to those who had passed out, carrying them out and depositing them with their friends until finally the bar was cleared.

Matt ran his hand through his hair and turned his attention to Jeff. "Think you can get them home, Jeff?"

"Yeah," Jeff said with a wide grin. "I can get them home. I can't do much about what their wives are going to do to them when I get them there, though. Going to call off work tomorrow?"

"Why? Just because these men got bombed? No way," Matt said, his eyes glittering dangerously. "If they're not at work tomorrow I'll come out and pull every one of them out of bed."

When Jeff had left, Brianna, who had been sitting quietly on a stool observing the exodus, touched Matt briefly on the shoulder.

"Does this happen often?"

Before Matt could reply Margie spoke up. "Like I said, this has never happened before—and I sure can't understand it. Here, have something to calm your nerves."

She poured two cups of coffee and set them before Matt and Brianna, then poured one for herself. "Thanks for coming right over, Matt. I didn't like to disturb you, but these guys were set on tearing the place apart."

"I'm glad you called. But sorry they trashed things." His expression was grim as he glanced at the wild disorder. "Any idea what started it?"

Margie took a sip of coffee as she gazed thoughtfully into space. "Not really. They came in after work like they usually do. Most nights they have one beer, maybe two, then head for home. Tonight they just didn't go home." Her brow wrinkled as she tried to reconstruct the scene in her mind.

"Was it a fight? Somebody insult somebody?"

"No, not like that at all. They were quiet, moody. Not much joking like there usually is. In fact," she said, her eyes narrowing, "they hardly talked to each other at all."

Brianna shared Matt's and Margie's obvious puzzlement. From what she'd seen of them, the Daynew always seemed to be laughing, joking, teasing one another. When the silence lengthened, Margie gave Matt an oblique look.

"Matt, this is going to sound crazy..."

"Go ahead," he said dryly. "I'm getting used to that."

"It was almost like the guys were afraid of something...something they didn't want to talk about. But they threw those chairs around like they had a demon by the throat."

The words sent an eerie chill down Brianna's spine, and from the expression on Matt's face, she suspected he was affected, too. But he merely finished his coffee, stood, and took Brianna's arm. "Thanks again, Margie. I'll send somebody in to help with the mess."

His hand still on her arm, they walked together into the darkening night. Still without speaking, he helped her into the cab, and they started home.

There were too many unanswered questions to permit Brianna to remain silent no matter how unwelcome her comments would be.

"Matt, all those men work for you, don't they?"

"Yes." His profile was faintly outlined by the starlight, enabling her to see the rigid set of his jaw. "At least everybody on the crew wasn't there—maybe I should be grateful for that."

"But why? Margie said they usually don't get drunk."

"I wish I knew why! I wish I knew a lot of things! All I do know is these guys have been acting weird ever since you came."

"Me! You're blaming that on me!"

He took a deep breath. "Oh, I'm not saying it's your fault. But you're a catalyst of some kind, Brianna. I can't help feeling they're afraid of something, just like Margie said..."

"Surely not of me!"

He glanced over at her and his agate eyes softened. "Well, we can't figure it out now. Do you think the chicken will still be any good?"

She had forgotten all about the chicken simmering away in the oven, and she glanced quickly at her watch. They'd been gone a little over an hour. "It should still be okay. I hope."

They pulled up in the circular driveway in front of the massive entryway to Matt's house, and Brianna reached for the door handle. Matt reached over and covered her hand with his. "Wait a minute, Brianna."

A little shiver of excitement flickered through her, and she glanced back at his face. But he wasn't looking at her. His gaze was directed at the entryway.

"Somebody's waiting for us," he said softly.

Following his gaze, she made out the outline of a man standing under the light. Her first instinctive shock at the unexpected appearance faded as she looked more closely, her muscles relaxed and she leaned back against the seat. Although his features were in shadow she recognized the broad shoulders and sturdy physique of Chad Gardner.

"What's Chad doing here?" she whispered to Matt.

"I don't know," he said grimly. "I was glad he wasn't at that fiasco tonight, but maybe I was a little premature." Loosening his grip on her hand, he slid across the seat and stepped down from the cab.

"Something wrong?" he asked, taking the steps two at a time.

Brianna, just behind him, was able to see the look of relief on Chad's features as he turned to Matt. "Not sure. I mean, yes, there's something wrong..."

Matt gave him a sharp glance, opened the door behind him, and gestured the man into the hall. "Well, what is it?"

Still Chad hesitated, and Brianna saw the ambivalence in his face. Then he took a deep breath, squared his shoulders and looked directly at Matt. "Don't like to bother you with this kind of thing, Boss. Seems like something I should handle myself." He shifted his weight from one foot to the other. "But—the point is, I can't—I don't know what to do."

"Perhaps we could decide that if you told me what's the matter," Matt said dryly.

"Louise is gone."

Now that he had actually said the words, Chad's reserve broke like a damn in a high flood. "I don't know where she is. She's *always* at home when I come in from work. You know I hardly ever stop at Hope Merc—she knows I'm coming home. But she's not there—she's not anyplace."

"The other women?" Matt said. "Maybe she was just visiting, and didn't notice the time."

"No," Chad said stubbornly. "She wouldn't do that. Especially—not now."

"Why not now?" Brianna said, picking up something unusual in Chad's tone.

He glanced at her, then back at Matt. "You've got to help me find her, Matt."

"An accident, maybe? Have you called around?"

"As much as I can." Again he threw a strange dark glance at Brianna, then turned back to Matt. "I—I'm scared."

Brianna knew how much it had cost the man to say that, and she glanced at Matt's somber face. He, too, was taking this very seriously. But surely the woman couldn't be in any danger. Not in this bucolic place, surrounded by friends and family. But perhaps she had gone for a walk, slipped, hit her head...

"Let's get a few people together and start searching," Matt said, heading toward the phone. "Some of the Daynew men aren't going to be of much use, but the women can help—"

Chad grabbed his arm. "No."

"No?" Matt's voice betrayed his surprise. "But surely they would be the ones most likely to know where she was last seen—"

"Just us," Chad said firmly. "We'll look for her ourselves."

Matt started to protest, but a look at his friend's determined expression stopped him. "All right. But we need a place to start. Have you any idea at all where she might be?"

Chad shook his head, and Brianna realized he was nearly out of his head with worry. "We just look," he said doggedly. "That's all."

Matt shot Brianna a glance over the man's head. She understood. It was up to them to find Louise and they apparently weren't going to get any clues from Chad.

Plunging into the forest in the dark seemed to offer the least reasonable alternative, and since Chad was so sure that she wouldn't be with any of the other women, the only avenue open to them was to cruise the mountain roads around the village, hoping they would stumble upon the woman through pure luck. It didn't seem to offer much hope, but at least it pacified Chad until they could organize a search party. If they didn't locate Louise tonight, Brianna decided, they had no choice but to alert the authorities.

For hours they cruised the twisting mountain roads, the headlights of the pickup only a brave, thin shaft of white in the darkness. Shadows shifted and strange shapes loomed beside them, menacingly until they came nearer, only to find they were roadside boulders or overhanging branches. There was little talk, and the monotonous hum of the engine sounded louder than ever in the dark silence.

Several times they went back to Chad's house and he made a quick walk-through, then returned, shoulders slumped, eyes desperate, and they resumed their futile search.

Brianna's eyes were beginning to feel the strain of peering into the darkness. She sat wedged between the two men, acutely aware of the tense atmosphere. She knew the same thought was in all their minds. This was hopeless. Even if Louise were in some ditch along the road, would they ever spot her? It didn't seem likely, but still they searched.

For the third time they pulled away from Chad's house and Matt steered the pickup onto a logging road that branched out from the main thoroughfare. "Chad," he said, breaking a lengthy silence, "don't you have anything else to go on? Think. Was there anything unusual about today? Did Louise plan on doing something special?"

Chad stared out the window into darkness. "No, nothing unusual. The women were going to get together this morning. I guess they did. I asked Diana and she said Louise was there, but she left early. That's the last anyone's seen of her."

Matt frowned. "The women were meeting? I saw Diana early this morning in the woods behind the village."

Brianna whirled toward him. "You were there! Why?"

"I—er—I thought you might want some company," he said lamely.

"You were following me." Her voice didn't contain the outrage it would have under other circumstances. She resented being spied on, but Louise's disappearance seemed to drain his action of importance.

"You saw Diana in the woods?" Chad turned sharply to Matt.

"Yes—her and a couple of the other women."

"Then the meeting wasn't at Alta's house," Chad said slowly.

The road made a sharp twist and Matt turned the wheel sharply. The headlights shone ahead of them, illuminating approximately one hundred feet of gravel road. They all saw it at the same time. Brianna gasped and Matt braked sharply; she felt Chad stiffen, then give a sharp exclamation.

A form stumbled along the road ahead of them, weaving slightly; as the lights caught her the figure threw up her hand, blinded by the glare, but Brianna had time to see her face, and her heart raced. They had actually found her—a needle in a haystack! Louise!

Chad was out of the pickup before it came to a full stop and by the time Matt and Brianna came up to them he was holding his wife tightly in his arms. With one hand he pressed her head into his shoulder, while with the other he pulled her tightly against him. Finally he held her away and gazed fearfully into her face.

"Louise, what happened? Are you all right?"

She smiled up at him and Brianna had a quick sense of being an unnecessary bystander at a tender scene. "Why, of course... what are you doing here, Chad? Where am I?"

Chad's gaze fastened on her face, consternation written on his features, and Brianna felt a little shiver of alarm. The woman seemed to be in a daze.

Matt put his hand on Chad's arm. "Let's get her home."

They climbed back into the pickup, Louise perched on Chad's lap, and drove the short distance back to the Gardner house. Louise babbled on incoherently, but they were able to make very little sense out of her account. She had just fallen asleep, she said, and when she woke up it was dark. She was just on her way home.

That was the reason they had finally located her, Brianna supposed. If they had just waited at her house she would have eventually arrived.

She found a nightdress, and they soon had Louise in bed, sleeping soundly. Chad hovered around the bedroom, unwilling to be separated from his wife by even a few feet, and Brianna, dead on her feet, yawned widely.

Matt touched her briefly on the shoulder. "We've done all we can do here. Wait in the pickup; I'll be right out."

She started out the door, then hesitated as Matt's voice drifted out to her. "Okay, Chad, let's have it. You must know more about this than you're saying. What happened to Louise? It looks to me like she's been drugged."

"Maybe," Chad said briefly.

"Why?" Matt demanded.

There was a long silence; Brianna stood on the step, knowing she was eavesdropping, yet unwilling to walk on. She was fond of Louise. This concerned her, too.

When Chad's reply came his voice was hard and unyielding; he didn't sound like the same man who had ridden with them as they searched for his wife.

"I've tried to tell you—get her out of here!"

Brianna's heart thudded against her chest; they were talking about her!

Matt's reply was just as cold. "You have given me a lot of vague warnings, Chad. My men tied on a spectacular drunk tonight, something they haven't done since I've known them. God knows who will be at work tomorrow. And now Louise comes stumbling along, obviously drugged. I insist you tell me what's going on."

Brianna heard footsteps coming into the living room, but she didn't move. This was the first she had heard of any vague warnings, and she was as interested in getting to the bottom of things as Matt was.

"Boss, I wish I could tell you more," Chad said, a defensive ring to his voice. "But I don't know much myself. I just know you'd better get her out of here."

"Brianna thinks she has a right to be here," Matt said. "And I think I agree with her."

"You act like you're falling for her," Chad grumbled.

"That has nothing to do with it!"

"Well, whether she has a right to be here or not, she'd better go," Chad said. "Don't say I didn't warn you."

She didn't want Matt to realize she'd been listening, especially in view of Chad's charge that he was emotionally involved with her. She hurried down the steps and was in the pickup when Matt got in the other side. He slammed the door so hard the pickup shook, and she decided not to question him until later. But she wasn't going to let this drop.

Entering his house, they were assaulted at once by the acrid smell of something burning.

"The chicken!" both cried at once.

Brianna dashed to the kitchen and pulled open the oven door. Smoke boiled out at her, stinging her eyes so that she could barely see into the oven; but she saw enough. Matt peered over her shoulder as she stared incredulously at the blackened carcass—what was left of the chicken.

They turned toward each other, laughing helplessly. With one accord they moved together and clung as gusts of hilarity rocked them, the spasm leaving them both near collapse.

"The chicken!" Matt gasped.

"The chicken!" Brianna cried. Mrs. Clayton couldn't even trust them to attend to a simple chicken!

Weak with emotion, Brianna sank onto a chair, gales of laughter still overcoming her at intervals. "I'm not sure why that was so funny—" she finally managed.

"Me, either," Matt said, collapsing beside her, still holding her hand. "Relief, probably—this hasn't been a real funny day up to now. And we still have to eat," he said, his laughter subsiding as he cast a dubious look at the blackened fowl.

"Then let's get to it." Brianna rose and stuffed the chicken in the garbage can while Matt opened all the windows. After they had cleared the room of the worst of the odor, Brianna pulled a can of tuna from the cupboard, and Matt, grinning, chopped up an onion and celery. The resulting tuna sandwiches might not have pleased a gourmet cook, but Brianna was happy with the result. Judging by the way he wolfed them down, she decided Matt must agree.

Later, they went into the living room where Matt struck a match to the fire that Mrs. Clayton had laid. He didn't switch on the lights, relying on the blaze to partially illuminate the large room. Light flickered off the high beams and painted the fur rug in front of the fireplace a shimmering copper. The flames, the meal, relief from the tension of the day, soon had its effect. Both lazed in comfortable chairs, feet toward the fire, tired, but loath to go to bed.

"You have the makings of a great cook," Matt said. "I don't know when I've seen a can opened with more expertise."

"You didn't do too bad, yourself," Brianna replied, smiling dreamily into the flames. "You'll win if awards are ever handed out for eating whatever is put in front of you."

There was a companionable silence; Brianna didn't know what Matt was thinking, but she was just luxuriating in the peaceful setting. Really, it was wonderful here, better than she would have imagined. She had a sense of seclusion, but not isolation. She was grateful that he had allowed her to stay at his house. The thought of being alone in the campground wasn't at all appealing.

She hated to break the rapport between them, but she had to find out what Chad meant when he demanded Matt send her away. She had been surprised at the vehemence in his voice. There had been instances in the beginning perhaps meant to drive her away: the vandalizing of her camp, the strange offering left on her table, but since Alta had championed her she had thought the threat, whatever it was, was over.

"Matt, why is Chad so insistent that I leave Hope?"

He stiffened, then turned his dark head toward her. "You heard?"

"Yes. And I wish you would tell me what it's all about."

He ran his hand through his hair, and sighed. "I wish I knew; the men think you're stirring up something, but I don't know what."

"Do you want me to leave?" She hadn't meant to say that, certainly not in that entreating tone. As she whispered the words she knew she was asking about more than the Daynew; she was asking Matt what he felt about her. She dropped her eyes in confusion.

Matt saw the color burn across her cheeks as the reflection of flames skittered across her face. Did he want her to leave? No! Absolutely not! He wanted her close to him, pressed against his heart forever. He wanted her just where she was, at home in his house, which was also her house. He wanted to see her at breakfast, sleepy-eyed and tousled; he wanted her in his bed. God, how he wanted her in his bed! Observing her now through narrowed eyes to hide his own reaction—her flushed cheeks, her lower lip caught between her teeth in embarrassment at her revealing question, he was nearly certain that he loved her.

And completely certain that nothing could come of it. She wasn't made for this country. Her future lay far away, with the excitement and achievement of her chosen life of science. He had only to see the way her eyes sparkled when she talked of her work to know she wasn't the type of woman to sit docilely by the fire, or to have dinner waiting when he came home. And, in spite of the way she made him feel, he didn't want any other kind. He was almost sure of that.

"Do I want you to leave?" he repeated. "I think it's probably a good idea. I don't know what's brewing around here, but I suppose it could be dangerous."

Dangerous for me, he could have added, but didn't. From the long look she gave him, he wondered if she had heard him anyway. Pain twisted his heart as he saw her shoulders slump in defeat. He would have flattened anyone else who put that dejected look in her eyes. It would be so easy to move across the inches that separated them, kiss her until those golden eyes blazed with passion. So easy and so irrevocable. He clenched his hands so they wouldn't betray him.

"I suppose I might as well leave soon," she said, not meeting his eyes. "I don't want to cause any trouble, and you've done enough for me as it is."

"Have you all the material you need?" It wasn't what he wanted to say, but it seemed appropriate.

"I could spend years listening to Alta, but I have enough now to write the paper I intended to write...."

"And the Tuatha de Danann?"

"I'm not sure I'll mention them. It's such a far-out theory...."

How much longer were they going to talk about everything except what was on both their minds, he wondered. The fragile look of her as she sat in the chair, head down, one bare arm flung over the side in a gesture that was almost supplicating, tore at his heart. She needed warmth, she needed protection, she needed comfort....

She needed him. Almost as much as he needed her. She would leave tomorrow or the next day, and nothing could change that. Not even one more night of ecstasy in her arms.

As though his thoughts had reached out to physically touch her, she turned her head to meet his intense gaze. He saw her eyes flicker, darken, then burn with molten flame. And he was lost.

In the grip of a force as relentless as that which moved the tides, they rose and came toward each other. Slowly, inexorably, as though walking through deep water, they drew together. He put his arms around her shoulders, drawing her close, drawing her into him as the sweet currents of desire ravaged all his senses. Running his hands down her back, he cupped his hands over the swell of her thighs, pressed her desperately against his hardened body, thrilling to the spasms that shook her slender frame.

Arms tightly entwined, lips drinking rapture from heated lips, they sank together onto the fur rug in front of the fire, and passion swept them into the old, primeval world that belongs only to a man and a woman together.

Chapter 13

Brianna walked down the trail to Alta's cabin, barely aware of the light morning breeze carrying the astringent scent of pine or of the raucous chatter of blue jays quarreling in the undergrowth. Her mind, like her senses, was concentrated solely on Matt.

Last night's lovemaking had seemed so inevitable that she didn't waste time feeling guilty, but it didn't change anything. All that was left to do was to say goodbye to Alta, tie up a few strings in her notes and then leave Hope. For good.

The finality of the decision colored the mood of the morning; it might have been snowing as far as she was concerned. But leaving was the only decision possible. Even if Matt wanted her permanently, she could never accept his obsessive need for control. It would soon poison the relationship; that quality was so integral in Matt's personality that he could never allow her to be her own person.

Still mulling this over, she looked up when Alta opened the door and gave her an ingratiating smile.

"Come in, come in," the woman said. "I was hoping you would be early. I have such a lot to tell you today." She stood aside and gestured Brianna into the room.

Brianna hesitated, then walked on in. It was silly, but the room, with its wood beams with bundles of herbs hanging like giant bats, always triggered in her a vague sense of uneasiness. She much preferred talking to Alta in the open meadow of the druid's circle, but it didn't really matter; she didn't plan to stay long today. Just a fervent thank-you, and goodbye.

Brianna sank into the proffered chair, and Alta bustled around, heating water for tea, reaching for ingredients from various dried herbs. The aroma was powerful, pungent and dark, and for a second Brianna felt almost dizzy. But the tea Alta soon placed in her hand revived her quickly.

She thought of Louise as she sipped the tea, increasingly puzzled. Matt suspected Louise had been drugged. Perhaps Alta knew something about it. She smiled at the older woman over the rim of her cup, wondering how to broach the subject.

"I'm still a little sleepy today," she finally said. "We spent several hours last night searching for Louise. I suppose you heard about it."

Alta said nothing, but her back stiffened slightly.

"Chad said she had been to a women's meeting," Brianna continued.

"What did *she* say?"

"Well, frankly, she didn't say much of anything. She seemed slightly incoherent, almost as though she'd been drugged."

Alta shrugged a bony shoulder. "That Louise. Always out of step. Yes, she was at the meeting, and perhaps she drank a little too much of something."

The words were faintly contemptuous and Brianna glanced at her in surprise. It was the first time she had heard a Daynew woman criticize another. Why was Louise out of step? She debated asking, and then changed her mind. The dynamics of the Daynew were nothing to her now. She was going to say goodbye and then leave for Boise.

Alta made a dismissive gesture, reducing the problem of Louise to insignificance, and turned burning eyes to Brianna. "I have something to tell you." She paused and Brianna could almost feel her excitement. "We made a decision yesterday at the meeting that I'm sure will interest you."

"I've something to tell you, too," Brianna said. "I came over to say goodbye. I want to thank you so much for all your help. I know I have enough to write a marvelous paper, and I'd better get back and start on it."

Alta whirled toward her so swiftly that she shrank back in the chair, startled and obscurely afraid. For an instant she didn't even know the other woman; her face was flushed, her lips tight, and her eyes flashed with strong emotion. Anger? Incredulity? Determination?

"You can't go yet!"

The force behind Alta's words were as surprising as her menacing visage. Brianna's initial shock was followed by outrage. It was endemic to this country; now even Alta was telling her what she could and could not do!

"Why not?" she asked coldly.

Alta, perhaps realizing she had gone too far, smiled ingratiatingly, her rigid posture softened, and she reached for Brianna's hand. "Forgive an old woman. I was just so disappointed. There is so much more I would like the world to know about the Daynew."

Mollified, Brianna smiled back tentatively. "I've time now. What more should I know?"

"I've told you about the goddess. How she dies and is resurrected. I've barely mentioned the ceremonies that assure her return."

Brianna looked rather doubtfully at the woman's face. Alta's words were so fervent that she wondered just how long it had actually been since the Goddess Danu played an important part in the tribal life. Alta was speaking in the present tense. Was she just an old woman confusing past and present? Or was it remotely possible that even now some of the older Daynew held to the worship of the White Goddess? The thought sent a pleasurable thrill down her back. If so, she had stumbled on an anthropologist's treasure trove.

"Anyway," Alta said briskly, "you can't go just yet. We would all be so disappointed. I told you we made a decision. We are going to hold a festival for the goddess just like we did in the olden days. We haven't performed the ritual for years, but after talking to you these past few days, we thought it was a shame to let our old ways be completely forgotten."

"But I really should..." Brianna hesitated, caught between a strange foreboding and a desire to see an actual festival celebrating the goddess. A festival that hadn't been performed in modern times! It was a opportunity too good to pass up.

But why the uneasy feeling? She remembered when she and Matt had confronted the men of his crew the first time they had stayed off work. One man had given the excuse that they were preparing for a religious festival. Could this be it? If so, why had the man acted so weird?

Alta apparently read the ambiguity on her face, and rushed on in a effort to convince her. "We want you to be our honored guest. You will be seeing something that we haven't performed for years."

That was exactly what Brianna was thinking, and from Alta's triumphant smile, she suspected it showed on her face. What difference did a few more days make? She had come all this way to study the Daynew and now they were offering to let her witness a performance that any anthropologist would give his right arm to see. So what if she didn't understand their motives for staging it just now? Perhaps, as Alta intimated, her questions over the past few days had made them remember their roots, and they liked her enough to involve her.

Besides, staying for the festival had an added advantage. Her heart beat a little faster and she dropped her eyes on the off chance that Alta could read her mind. She would have a few more days with Matt.

Whether Alta really was a mind reader, or whether the idea occurred naturally to the sly old woman, Brianna had no idea, but she suspected her next words were not as casual as they seemed.

"I understand you're staying at Matt Stuart's house. Much more comfortable than the campsite."

"Much," Brianna agreed.

"And Matt," Alta continued. "He's a wonderful young man. I've known him all his life and they don't come any better."

"He...he seems nice," Brianna agreed, wondering where the conversation was leading.

"Nice!" Alta laughed, her shrewd gaze on Brianna's flushed face. "He's a fine, strong, potent young man! Responsible, bright, a man any woman could be proud of!"

Brianna watched Alta's face closely, as the woman enumerated Matt's qualities. She agreed—oh, she definitely agreed—but it seemed strange to hear Alta praise his sterling virtues! Was it possible the woman had been drinking? Her manner was always intense, but now she seemed feverish, almost as though she were burning with some secret knowledge.

"A king among men," Brianna said dryly.

"Indeed." Alta gave her a long, narrow look, and then changed the subject. "So will you stay? All of us will be so disappointed if you leave now."

Wondering at her own misgivings, Brianna agreed. Why did the invitation bother her? She should be absolutely thrilled at the prospect. And she was. But there was something about Alta that she couldn't quite put her finger on. Did she imagine a sly, triumphant gleam in the woman's eyes? Perhaps she was imagining it, but she thought the woman seemed stronger, more assertive, than she had been the first time she saw her. Was it possible that she was walking into danger?

She rejected the thought immediately. She could accept that someone had apparently tried to scare her away, and she knew the Daynew men believed she was stirring things up. That probably explained everything. Perhaps the men thought the old ways were silly, and didn't want them revived even in theater. The earlier anthropologist had made laughingstocks of them, reporting that they were primitive and backward. They probably didn't want anything like that to happen again.

But as for actual danger, that was ridiculous. This was the twentieth century, Hope was less than one hundred miles from a large urban center. They even had television, for heaven's sake! How sinister could they be! She had better keep a tighter rein on her imagination.

Later, leaving Alta's house and the atmosphere that was unaccountably oppressive, she decided to stop by and see if Louise was feeling better. Alta had certainly not been very sympathetic, she thought; she had almost hinted that the woman was a troublemaker.

Stepping quickly along the trail, her spirits regained their usual buoyancy. She was going to see a ceremony that most people thought extinct—and even better, she was going to have a few more days with Matt. What was he doing now, she wondered, unconsciously touching her finger to her lips in remembrance of his kiss.

Matt was having his own problems and at the moment his main concern was keeping them in the correct priority. He should be thinking only of getting the logs out, but memories of Brianna kept intruding.

From the cab of his pickup he surveyed the remnant of his crew that had made it to work after last night's debacle. Enough to keep the logs rolling to the mill, but not enough to soothe his temper. If the crew kept up this erratic performance, he just might lose a contract, and the entire community would suffer.

He thought back over everything that had happened since Brianna had arrived in Hope, trying to puzzle out the significance. The attacks on her, while not life threatening, were vicious, and not at all like the Daynew he thought he knew. Still, they must be responsible, and the knowledge blackened his already dark mood. He had worked so hard to help them assimilate into the mainstream, and this was a definite setback. Or was Brianna right and his sense of responsibility demeaning; after all, they weren't children.

Anyway it would soon be over. Brianna, whom he was sure was the catalyst in some way he didn't understand, would be gone, and things would get back to normal.

He clenched his jaw, trying to fight back the depression that thought provoked. Things would never get back to normal; not for him. He loved her. He couldn't deny it any longer. But in this case, love wasn't enough. She was like some beautiful, ephemeral butterfly who had lighted in Hope long enough to give him a glimpse of what life could be, and then went on her way, leaving him nothing but dreams and memories.

Butterfly wasn't quite right. She was more solid than that. So warm, so vital, so responsive. And even more than her physical attraction, which he had never underrated, was the inner core of the woman herself. He would never have suspected that Brianna was the kind of woman he really wanted—courageous, intelligent, independent—a woman with a dream of her own.

His lips tightened until they were almost white. She was also a woman whose safety, he was becoming more convinced every hour, depended on his getting her out of here.

Abstracted as he was, he managed to drive to the various work sites, giving orders, making decisions, as he did every day. The crew seemed subdued, and he didn't try to lighten the atmosphere by so much as an occasional joke. If they felt guilty, it was because they damn well were!

Late in the morning, after assuring himself that everything was running as smoothly as possible, he drove down the road toward the Daynew village. Chad had assured him that Louise was feeling much better, but the man hadn't met his eyes when he said so. It wouldn't hurt to talk to Louise.

He would just drop by and see if there was anything he could do.

The thought made him smile sheepishly. Brianna would consider his concern another indication of his need to take care of everybody, whether they wanted him to or not. She didn't understand he had this responsibility...

He was still several hundred yards away from the Gardner cottage when he saw Brianna walking down the trail toward the house. His heart beat faster and he clutched the steering wheel more tightly. Even from this distance, he had no trouble recognizing her. The set of her shoulders, her slender back, the way her hips moved in a soft, swaying cadence somehow at odds with her determined stride, all were achingly familiar. His mouth felt dry as he watched her climb the path to Louise's front door, even while he cursed himself for a fool.

In that instant he knew that although she would soon be gone from his life, he would never get over her.

He jumped from the cab and reached her before she entered the house.

"Hi. Looks like we had the same idea." He seized her arm to steady her.

"Yes, it looks like it." She turned to him with a welcoming smile. In spite of the smile, he wondered briefly if something were wrong; he thought she seemed a trifle upset, although he couldn't have said what made him think so.

Before they could say anything else the door opened and Louise smiled a shy welcome. His hand still protectively on her arm, Matt urged Brianna forward, his eyes on Louise. She didn't look any the worse for her night's ordeal, except for the circles under her eyes and an unusual pallor.

"Come in," she said. "Sit down." She spoke quickly but still graciously. "I guess I was a lot of trouble to you two last night. I'm really sorry. Have you time for tea?"

Both refused the tea, but they sat in the indicated chairs as Louise moved to the couch and plopped down. "I'm sorry Chad disturbed you," the woman continued. "I was quite all right. It was really nothing."

"You seemed—" Matt hesitated. What could he say? You seemed drunk? Drugged? Neither implication would be appreciated.

She smiled gently at his discomfiture. "The truth is, we women got to talking, and perhaps I had a little too much wine."

Matt didn't know why he suspected she was lying; her eyes were guileless enough and her smile as gentle as always. But he had never seen anyone act as Louise had acted last night from "just a little wine."

Forestalling any further questions, Louise turned to Brianna with a bright smile. "How is your research coming along, Brianna? Will you be leaving us soon?"

Brianna glanced at Matt, then back at Louise, and he was aware of some hesitation in her voice as she replied. "My work is coming along fine. But I've decided to stay on a few days. Alta has invited me to attend your midsummer's eve festival. I'm sure you know all about it," she said hurriedly.

There was no mistaking the lock of shock on Louise's face, Matt thought. It very nearly matched his own consternation. He had heard of conflicting emotions, but he never expected to feel them so intensely. His heartbeat increased until it pounded in his ears and a rush of pure elation coursed through him. Brianna was staying! The thought ran like music all along his veins. He wanted to run, to jump, to shout it to the world. Brianna wasn't leaving!

Another part of him seemed to be looking down an abyss. A dangerous chasm. He wanted to sweep her up, shove her into her van, and get her out of here quickly. The latter thought intensified as he saw the obvious agitation on Louise's features before she produced a bland smile.

"Well, that's very nice, Brianna. But if you'll excuse me now, I have to start dinner. Chad usually comes home for lunch when he can." She rose from the couch in obvious dismissal.

Somewhat nonplussed, Matt and Brianna said goodbye hurriedly and walked silently to his pickup. Only when they were several hundred yards down the road did Brianna turn to Matt with a doubtful frown.

"I'd say she was in a hurry to get us out of there."

Matt nodded, puzzled himself by Louise's manner. Usually she—and all the Daynew—were polite and cordial to him no matter what their underlying feelings. He spoke slowly. "To me, she seemed perturbed about the festival. I guess I am, too." He glanced at Brianna's averted face. "I thought this morning you had definitely made up your mind to leave Hope."

"Well, I had. But when Alta told me about the celebration, I knew I just couldn't miss it."

Matt caught the defensiveness in her tone and frowned thoughtfully. "This celebration—it's the first I've heard of it."

"Alta said they hadn't performed it for a long time."

"Why now?"

"I suppose because my questions got them thinking about the old days. Maybe they feel a need to go back to their roots."

"Maybe." He swung the wheel to avoid a boulder that had fallen onto the road, his frown deepening. "I'm not at all sure I like it."

"It could be fun! Do you realize it's completely unique? A celebration for the Goddess Danu—there's been nothing like it for years."

"Just what does this celebration consist of?"

"I don't know—Alta didn't say. We can only guess what it used to be like, and I suppose it's changed in the years the Daynew have been isolated. It has something to do with planting and harvesting, full moons, propitiation of the goddess to make the earth fruitful, but no one's really sure. It was a mystery—a woman's mystery."

He grinned. "Men not invited?" Getting no response, he pressed on. "I suppose it involved some kind of offerings?"

"I'm sure it did. It will be interesting to see what the Daynew come up with."

"I wish you wouldn't go, Brianna," he said, his jaw suddenly rigid and his voice hard. "I wish you'd leave right now."

He heard a tiny gasp and knew he had hurt her, but he couldn't retract the words or the wish. He didn't know why he felt such foreboding about the coming festival, but he would be much easier in his mind if Brianna was far away. Easier in his mind, he reminded himself. Not easier in his heart.

Out of the corner of his eye he saw her bite her lip, and her words sounded stiff and angry. "This festival is extremely important to me professionally. And I can take care of myself, Matt. I've been doing it for a long time. You don't need to add me to your list of dependents."

He was silent as they drove for several minutes through the tunnel of conifers. Could she really take care of herself? He didn't think she knew at all what she might be getting into. He was certain *he* didn't! He decided to change the subject. "Brianna, did you notice the bruise on Louise's arm?"

"Yes, I did," she said slowly. "It almost looked as though someone had clamped down hard on her arm. Chad?"

"Never. Daynew men don't manhandle their women."

"Maybe she fell last night and hit a rock, or something."

He kept his eyes on the road, not wanting to see the same concern in Brianna's expression that he knew must be in his own. That was probably what it was...a fall against a rock. What else could it be? He just imagined he had seen the lingering imprint of fingers gouging into her bare skin.

Although the next few days passed slowly for Brianna, she was aware that they were a blur of hectic activity for the Daynew women as they prepared for the festival. She knew she was no longer welcome at the village while they carried on their secret preparations. She ran into some of the women occasionally at the Hope Mercantile, and several times she offered to help, only to be met with smiling refusal. Their manner was purposeful, mysterious, as their eyes glanced off hers much in the way stones skipped across the surface of a deep lake.

Her relationship with Matt was just as ambiguous. Although she still lived in his house, she saw very little of him. He was either at meetings in Boise, or constantly with his crew. From his few terse comments, she gathered his men were as erratic as ever, coming and going as they pleased, evasive, moody, disruptive of any schedule. She noticed a growing tension around Matt's eyes and an increasing abruptness in his manner.

She was beginning to feel very much a fifth wheel. Although Alta assured her the festival was in her honor in gratitude for her reminding the Daynew of their origins, she certainly didn't seem very necessary to the proceedings.

Feeling left out as she did, she was doubly surprised one morning when she heard the thud of the brass knocker a few minutes after Matt had left for work, and opened the door to find Alta standing on the stone steps. She smiled with pleasure at the sight of her friend; the woman was garbed in her familiar brown robe with the green sash, her long gray hair was banded by the usual scarf, and she exuded her usual air of calm authority.

"Good morning!" Brianna bubbled. "Won't you come on in? How's the festival coming along?"

Alta ignored her questions until she was settled comfortably on a couch in the living room.

"Preparations are well underway, dear. I've been concerned, though. We've been neglecting you, we've become so immersed in the details. It's been years since the ritual has been performed, and there are so many things we have to keep track of. We certainly want to get it right," she said firmly.

"I can well imagine."

"I'm encouraged, though." Alta leaned forward confidentially, her voice low and stirring. "The portents are all favorable; everything should go well."

"The portents?"

"According to the old stories, there are portents. The increase in the earth tremors, for one thing. It is said—by the olden ones, of course—that the earth tremors signal her readiness to return."

A strange little shiver went down Brianna's spine. It was as though she had stepped back in time. Alta's statement about portents had been made in such a matter-of-fact tone of voice that Brianna wondered if she weren't taking this playacting a little more seriously than she had expected.

"But I came for something else." Alta rose from the couch and, with a dramatic gesture, handed Brianna a brown paper package tied with yellowed twine. "We have all talked it over. It doesn't seem fair for you to be just an observer. We would like you to take part."

"Take part!" The paper crackled like dry parchment in Brianna's grasp. "But I don't know how... I don't know what..."

"Your part would be very simple," Alta said, "and really much more fun for you than just watching everybody else. I've brought you a costume. I'm sure you'll love it. It's hundreds of years old."

"But—"

"Don't worry about not knowing what to do. We'll show you as we go along."

Brianna started to renew her protests, but gave up, somewhat amused by the autocratic old lady's way of ignoring all objections. She wasn't quite sure how it happened, but when Alta walked out the door, Brianna still had the package containing the costume in her hands.

The woman turned on the step, her robe swirling around her legs, and delivered her parting instructions. "The moon will be full tomorrow night, Brianna. The perfect time. We'll come for you."

Still speechless, Brianna watched the ramrod-straight back, the proud head as Alta strode across the circular driveway and disappeared into the woods. She was more ambivalent than ever. She should have refused. Being an observer at a pagan ceremony was one thing; being a participant was another.

But what a marvelous opportunity! Who else in her field would be able to boast that they had actually taken part in a ceremony to honor the White Goddess! Her sense of foreboding was ridiculous, and she would just ignore it.

She wasn't completely innocent of the nature of the festival, of course. Her research had given her an inkling as to the rites performed in those far-off days when the old religion was dominant in the world, but she also knew those initial practices had softened and changed thousands of years ago. It had been eons since the worship of the goddess had consisted of anything more than throwing sheaves of corn and barley into midnight bonfires, or dancing around the maypole...

Of course, the ceremony would be unusual; possibly even primitive. But it certainly wouldn't be dangerous. Things such as she was imagining may have happened thousands of years ago, but they certainly could never happen in this modern world.

Chapter 14

Brianna perched on the couch in front of the fireplace, her own nervousness increasing as she watched Matt prowl the room like an angry panther. Since he had learned she planned to participate in the ceremony, he had hardly left her side.

She caught her lower lip in her teeth, her attention on his lean, hard body as he paced back and forth. With hard corded muscles rippling under his red flannel shirt, powerful thighs pushing against the confines of his faded jeans, he absolutely radiated masculine energy and virility.

Yet that she might have withstood. It was the depth of concern in his eyes, the sensitive curve of his mouth, that kept her firmly entwined in his web.

"You shouldn't worry so much, Matt," she said softly.

He shot her a quick glance, and the expression in his eyes softened. As his gaze roved over her face she felt as though he had actually reached out and touched her with a tender hand.

"You mean a lot to me," he said quietly. "I don't want you hurt."

Her pulse sped up until it pounded in her ears. That was the closest Matt had come to betraying his feelings about her, to revealing his own vulnerability. It wasn't *I love you*, but it must have meant she'd become more important to him than a sexual conquest.

With a deep sigh, Matt tore his gaze from hers and moved to the window that overlooked the driveway. He pushed the drapery aside with an impatient hand.

"It's been dark for over an hour. Maybe they won't come."

"I think they'll be here," Brianna replied weakly. Now that the hour was approaching, she was almost equally divided about the coming ceremony. She still considered it the opportunity of a lifetime, but Matt's obvious concern and her own inexplicable anxiety were wearing on her.

Pushing aside the lock of hair that had fallen over his forehead, Matt strode back to the center of the room, where the costume Brianna was to wear was spread out upon a table. He frowned, reaching down to pick up a fold of the gossamer-light material, then let it fall back in place.

"You certainly don't intend to wear this."

His tone was so accusing that she rose and crossed the room to stand beside him.

"Certainly. Isn't it fantastic, Matt?" She fingered the material, thinking it felt as light as dandelion fluff. "I've never seen anything so old and so exotic."

He might have retorted, but just at that instant a knock sounded at the door. Like an old-time prophet, or Thor about to release a thunderbolt, Matt stood stiffly in the center of the room while Brianna rushed to admit their visitors.

She threw open the door, then stepped back, surprised and delighted at the sight of the five women standing there. They had really gotten into the spirit of the thing. It was a scene out of a fairy tale.

There was Alta, of course, resplendent in a voluminous forest-green robe that had the sheen of velvet. The chain around her waist appeared to be of pure gold, and her headband was embroidered in a multitude of colors in geometric designs. It was her face, though, that made the strongest impression on Brianna; the word that occurred to her was "exalted." The woman's eyes burned with intensity and her mouth was set in a firm line of authority.

The other women were similarly dressed. Brianna had difficulty recognizing them in their green robes with their long hair flowing freely, but she finally placed them. They were all Daynew women that she had gossiped with at one time or another, and had seen frequently in her visits to the village.

Alta swept by her, followed closely by the four women. Her eyes went at once to the costume spread out on the table and a faint knowing smile softened her stern expression as she glanced from the costume to Brianna.

"You haven't put it on yet. Good. We'll help you."

Matt stepped forward, and although he was completely courteous, Brianna had the strong impression he was actually confronting Alta. A current of hostility seemed to flow between them.

"Just where are you holding this ceremony, Alta?" he demanded. "The men don't seem to know anything about it."

Alta gestured to one of the women who scurried off into the kitchen, then turned majestically to Matt. "Of course they don't know anything about it. Brianna must have told you. This is a ceremony for women."

"I don't like it," he said abruptly.

"Probably not," Alta chuckled. She turned to another of the women and gave a brief order. "Lois, help Brianna with her costume."

Feeling helpless at the way things had been taken out of her hands, Brianna allowed herself to be escorted out of the room and helped into the costume. When she returned to the living room Alta was pouring tea one of the women had prepared, and chatting with Matt, who had a sour expression on his face. Both raised their eyes at Brianna's entrance.

She felt a pure, feminine thrill at the awe and disbelief that leaped into Matt's dark eyes. She had taken a careful look in the mirror and knew what he was seeing: her long hair was bound by a headband of antique gold worked in a intricate filigree pattern; the same pattern was repeated in the gold chain that encircled her waist and confined the flowing white, diaphanous material of the robe that fell in soft folds from her shoulders, skimming her full breasts and floating around her legs like mist. Bracelets of finely detailed golden serpents twined around both bare upper arms, their mouths open in an almost audible hiss; and sandals were laced to her feet with golden cords. She knew she must look completely bizarre, out of time, out of place, the stuff of dreams.

The strange, frightening thing was that she didn't feel that way at all. The costume seemed uncannily familiar to her.

Alta rushed forward, a cup of tea in her hand, and offered it to Brianna. "Wonderful! You look just as you should. Here, all this commotion must make you a little nervous. Drink this."

Absently Brianna sipped the tea, her eyes still on Matt's face. His awestruck look was fading, but the look of pure adoration was still there. So was his concern, she soon found.

"I'm going with you," he announced, his gaze caressing her face, then swinging with an obvious challenge to Alta. "Don't try to dissuade me," he said coldly. "I don't care whether I upset things or not. She's not getting out of this house without me, and you might as well accept it."

Alta did not make the objection Brianna expected. Instead she smiled benignly. "Of course, Matt, if you're worried," she said softly. "Though I don't know why you should be. This is just a reenactment of an old celebration—nothing to worry about."

"Maybe," he said tightly. "But something is going on, Alta, and I don't give a damn that this thing, whatever it is, is for women only. I'm going."

He stared implacably at Alta, legs apart, hands in fists at his side. Brianna noted the stubborn set of his jaw and relief trickled through her, in spite of her resolve to handle this herself. She had never dreamed this thing would be so—so realistic. The ominous darkness outside, the women in their robes, her own oddly familiar costume, all combined to cast an eerie cloud over the entire group.

"Well, of course, Matt," Alta said good-humoredly. "You can play Brianna's knight in shining armor if you want to. We'll even let you be a part of the proceedings, if you wish." She nodded to one of the women—Lois, Brianna thought, although they all looked similar in their robes and loose hair.

At the signal, the woman pulled a wreath from somewhere in her voluminous garment and, with a ceremonial flourish, placed it on Matt's head.

Matt, a little shame-faced, sniffed the aroma. "Cedar," he commented. "Okay, when does this show get started?"

Brianna's vague uneasiness was escalating to definite apprehension. Cedar, she remembered, was sacred to the druids, and there was a smug complacency about the women that made her wonder if they had expected Matt's insistence on coming along. Even subtly encouraged it. But at least, she admitted to herself, his company made her feel better. Not so alone. These women seemed so different as they whispered among themselves; aloof, remote, almost as though they were in another world. It increased her nervousness.

But Matt was the same, she thought as she caught his gaze. Strong, dependable, a man would would protect his woman. Why had she ever thought those qualities bad? The knowledge of how much she loved him flooded through her with such force that she felt weak. When they got back from this ceremony she would tell him, see if they could work something out in their relationship...

Her thoughts were interrupted by Alta's low voice. "It's time now—the moon is just coming up. We can leave if everyone has finished their tea. Matt?"

He shrugged and pointed to an empty cup. Brianna thought she detected a little shiver of excitement run through the group as Alta led the procession toward the door.

Once outside, Alta set the column moving in the way deemed appropriate. Head high, back straight, as though marching to an unheard rhythm, she led the way into the darkness of the tress while Brianna, flanked on each side by two Daynew women, followed. Matt, also with his feminine escort, came last. Brianna heard him swear softly as he stumbled over a tree root, and smiled, somehow reassured. This hocus-pocus wasn't getting to him as it was to her.

She admitted to herself that she was becoming definitely afraid as they trudged deeper and deeper into the woods. She even had to restrain herself from turning and bolting, but one look at the women beside her changed her mind. They looked so solemn she suspected they no longer realized they were playacting. And she no longer thought of them as mere escorts; they were more like guards, she thought, her heart sinking.

It wasn't only the soft velvet darkness that caused the hair to stand up on the back of her neck, either. As soon as they had entered the forest the women began a soft, almost inaudible chanting. It grated on her nerves, resonated through her body, and seemed hauntingly familiar. Familiar and sinister.

Glancing off into the darkness, she became aware of strange shapes, amorphous shadows, all keeping the sonorous pace. Called up from some deep recess of time or racial memory, they moved as though they were a dream in her mind. She knew them, knew where they were going...

The thought brought her up sharp. Something was wrong with her mind. It was as though her resistance had been sapped and although she was frightened, she had no alternative but to move along with the procession. She had no more volition than a twig floating downstream, she thought, panic assailing her. What caused that breakage of her will?

The tea Alta had insisted she drink flashed through her mind. She had thought at the time it tasted somewhat different. Now, perspiration broke out on her face and her pulse fluttered. She'd been drugged.

She couldn't face the ramifications of that knowledge. It was too frightening. These women were still her friends, although she had to admit they were caught up completely in their roles.

Her throat constricted as she remembered Matt's empty cup sitting on the coffee table. Had he been drugged also?

They broke out of the darkness of the forest into the druid's circle, and she halted abruptly, her fear momentarily overcome by the sheer, unearthly beauty of the spectacle. The moon had cleared the horizon; it hung in the deep velvet sky, a round, full, golden orb. Its rays illuminated the pillars of stone that enclosed the magic circle of the druids. The brilliant light sparkled on the quartz floor, picked out the flecks of mica in the granite pillars, until the entire scene shimmered and danced in a rhapsody of silver.

She caught her breath as Alta, moving as relentlessly as a force of nature, went to one of the stone pillars and bent down. She extracted something from a cave at the base of the stone and returned to Brianna, bearing the objects as though they represented something of inestimable value. Placing them in Brianna's shaking hands, she fell to her knees in front of her.

Astounded, Brianna looked first at the objects in her hands, then down at the kneeling woman. The light from the moon provided enough illumination so that she could make out a copper tablet in one hand; it was inscribed with the lines that she now knew were ogham, the writing of the ancient Celts. But it was the other object that held her horrified attention.

It was a statue; a statue of gold. It felt heavy and ominous in her hand, even before she made out the various features of the little figure. A statue of the White Goddess—she knew that, even before she saw all the details. The woman was tall and slender with long flowing hair, regular features, and a regal manner. Incredibly she was riding a wild boar, her hair flying out behind her. A shudder went through Brianna like a high wind through a cornfield. The goddess looked wild and powerful and utterly ruthless.

Still, it wasn't the fact that she held the statue of the Goddess Danu in her trembling hand that sent pure panic scuttling through Brianna's veins; it was the fact that the statue bore more than a superficial resemblance to herself that caused her to shake with sheer terror.

On second look she realized it wasn't an exact likeness. Even in the shifting moonlight, she could see that. But it was the same physical type, the same broad cheekbones, long neck, tall, slender body.

Clues she had refused to face washed over her with blinding intensity. The offering of the circle of vegetables with the corn doll in the middle that had been left on her picnic table; the way the Daynew women had been so open with her, inviting her into their group, although they detested strangers; Alta's insinuations that she and Brianna shared a secret; all of it became horrifyingly clear. The Daynew thought she was the White Goddess!

But that couldn't be true. They didn't really believe, did they? They were just pretending, reenacting an old legend. In a moment they would all start laughing, and take her and Matt home.

She looked down at the woman at her feet. Alta's face was upturned toward her, her eyes burning with a fierce, fanatical light, and Brianna's spurt of optimism fluttered and died like a candle in a high wind. She didn't know this woman.

"I knew it," Alta crooned, her voice sending spasms of fear right down to Brianna's toes. "I knew it when I saw you in the meeting. The eyes. The golden eyes rimmed with black. Just like the old ones said. *She will return, and you will know her by her eyes.*"

Out of the corner of her eye, Brianna saw Matt try to shove forward. Immediately he was surrounded by women; a dozen hands grabbed his arms, pinioned his legs as he struggled fruitlessly. The rest of the Daynew women had apparently been the shadows Brianna had seen floating alongside as they were led through the forest.

She watched as Matt fought to free himself, knowing it was useless. Handicapped by an inborn taboo of hitting women, he shoved and pushed, kicked out and flat handed several as they swarmed him. Tears stung her eyes. Could she ever forgive herself for involving him in this horror?

Apparently realizing the futility of doing anything now, Matt stood quietly a couple of feet behind her. She wanted to run to help him, but she felt unaccountably lethargic; it was only with great effort that she was able even to stand. The drug, she supposed. It left her mind clear enough to feel absolute terror of what was happening, but prohibited much physical movement.

Perhaps she could still reason with Alta. It was worth a try. "You can't believe that I'm the goddess..."

Alta rose until her eyes were level with Brianna's, and in spite of her resolve, Brianna felt herself shrinking back. The old woman exuded some strange force that was almost as palpable as a physical touch. Her eyes bored into Brianna's as though she was probing the very depths of her being.

"The portents were all there," she said sternly.

"What portents?"

"First, the eyes. Then you stepped out on the porch, and the earth shook. Just as the stories say. I recognized you immediately."

Brianna recalled the first earth tremor she had felt in Hope; it had sent her flying into Matt's arms. Alta had been lurking in the bushes, she remembered.

"If you recognized me—thought I was the goddess—why did you try to scare me away?" She was edging closer to Matt as she spoke, hoping they wouldn't notice.

Alta laughed softly. "Oh, we didn't. No indeed. That was the men. They were a little recalcitrant at first, but they are over it now."

A terrible suspicion was beginning to form in Brianna's clouded mind. "Why—why were the men recalcitrant?" she whispered. She was close to Matt now. She felt his hand close around hers. It was nearly all that kept her standing.

"The men like things as they are," Alta replied. "They don't want a return to the old ways. The days when women were powerful, mysterious..." She chuckled, and the sound sent a chill down Brianna's back. "I suppose they remember what happened to men long ago."

Matt dropped her hand and made a desperate attempt to lunge forward, and again he was forcibly restrained. He stopped resisting, but his voice rang out loud and angry.

"So you're responsible for the way my crew has been behaving! No wonder they tried to drive Brianna away—the trashed campground, the note on my door. It was all to get her out of Hope."

"And stop the ceremony," Alta agreed coolly. "But they are resigned now. Don't think they will make any move to stop this. They take no part in the festival. They know the ancient mysteries belong to the women."

"You crazy old woman!"

Matt thrust himself between Brianna and Alta, then grabbed her hand and tried to break a hole through the ranks of women, but they surrounded him like dark vultures, cutting him off from Brianna, effectively precluding any movement.

Fear crept around her heart in little icy tendrils, causing her breathing to become labored, difficult, its power accentuated by the immobility caused by the drug Alta had used. Her brain reeled helplessly. How could she have been so stupid? She was a trained anthropologist; she knew something of the rites that had been practiced in the ancient worship of the White Goddess. The Moon Goddess. She just never could have believed, not even in her wildest dreams, that those practices still existed, or that she would become a part of them.

If she were a goddess, perhaps she could make use of it. It was a last desperate attempt to disengage herself from this incredible mess. She drew herself up to her full height and stared commandingly at Alta. "I command you. Let us go. Immediately."

Alta returned her gaze, and Brianna shuddered. She should have known Alta would have no fear of her. In Alta's mind, the goddess was bound by laws as invincible as those that bound herself. Alta was the priestess now, the keeper of the faith, the arranger of the sacred mysteries, and not even the goddess was more powerful.

"Oh, you can't go now," Alta replied calmly. Only by the wild feverish look in her eyes could Brianna have discerned she was in the sway of something ancient and evil. "The festival cannot continue without you."

Desperately Brianna's gaze swept the assembled women, but she knew she would find no hope there. They were nothing but ominous shadows, no longer individual people. Suddenly she knew what they reminded her of—the shapeless, shifting people of her recurring dreams. Now they all moved toward her, arms outstretched, faces contorted in an ecstasy of emotion that sent shivers of revulsion all through her body.

"It's all right." Matt's voice came clearly to her, even in her drugged state. "Don't worry, darling. We'll be all right."

She wished he had a little more to go on. Even as he spoke the women seized his arms and thrust them behind him, tying them quickly, in spite of his gargantuan struggles. They must have taken something to increase their strength, she realized as they pounded Matt to the ground; something from Alta's limitless supply of herbs.

In a second they descended on her, and she winced at the pain of the cord cutting into her wrists as they bound her securely. She heard Matt swear and wondered if they would gag him, but realized immediately there was no necessity for that. She and Matt could scream as long and loud as they wished and no one would ever hear them.

Chapter 15

Brianna twisted and tugged, but the cord only cut more cruelly into her wrists. Tied beside her, legs outstretched on the ground, his back up against the stone pillar as hers was, Matt also struggled futilely, swearing softly and fervently under his breath. She leaned toward him, her lips only a few inches from his ear.

"It's no use, Matt. Even if we could get our hands loose, they've got us roped to the pillar."

"We'll get loose," he said grimly. "Somehow. And when we do—" He didn't finish the thought, but Brianna knew by the tone of his voice and the set of his jaw that he ached to have his hands around Alta's neck.

As though called by the thought, Alta broke away from the group that milled in a circle several feet away and picked up the cedar wreath that had fallen from Matt's head in the struggle. Solemnly, even reverently, she placed it on Matt's head and then returned to the other women.

The action did more than anything else to convince Brianna of the hopelessness of their situation. There had been nothing malicious, nothing vindictive, in Alta's manner. She was merely taking care of a detail necessary for the ceremony. As nothing else had, it convinced Brianna that the woman was unreachable.

The detail of the cedar wreath also brought a thought to the surface that she had been desperately trying to suppress. Now she knew with utter certainty why the women had allowed Matt to attend this ceremony where no men were allowed. If he hadn't insisted, they would have found some other way to get him here. The horror of it soaked right down to her toes.

She should have known. She had read about it in school, but she assumed that if it were still practiced it would only be symbolic. The ritual was ages old, performed by dozens of cultures in many parts of the world before the goddess was supplanted by the male gods. The ritual required the death and rebirth of the king!

So many things were clear now. She remembered Alta's sly enumeration of Matt's many virtues. A fit mate for a goddess; only the best could be sacrificed. It also explained the behavior of the Daynew men. No wonder they were frightened; they remembered what happened to men when the goddess ruled.

She could withstand the horror better if she were only able to touch Matt, make some physical contact. She desperately needed the strength his touch would bring, needed the courage that flowed from him. Maybe she needed the absolution of the contact; it was her fault he was in this situation.

She gazed at his face, seeking to memorize every beloved detail. The moonlight gilded his dark hair with streaks of silver, played across his rugged cheekbones, fingered his firm lips. As she wished so much to do.

Several feet away the women were dispersing, gathering bits of dried branches and twigs and Matt whispered to Brianna. "What's going on now?"

"They're building a bonfire," she whispered back.

"They're also drinking a lot." Matt inclined his head toward the center of the circle where several of the women poured cups of liquid from a large container. "Tea?"

"I expect so."

The thought reminded her; she still felt the effects of Alta's secret compound, but Matt was surprisingly alert for someone who had been drugged. "Didn't the tea Alta gave us affect you?"

He snorted with disgust. "I don't like tea, remember? And I'd never drink the stuff old Alta brews. No, I poured it out when she wasn't looking."

Brianna felt a little better. At least Matt was in control of his senses. They had a chance if they could just break loose from the bonds.

Because she certainly wasn't in control of her senses, she finally realized that something strange was going on in her mind. It must be the concoction that was causing the weird hallucinations. As the bonfire burst into flames and the women began a slow, shuffling march around it, she had the incredible sensation that this had all happened before. The dark, whirling forms, the firelight casting grotesque shadows on the narrow faces, the robes swirling like the wings of giant birds. The scene was chillingly like her childhood dreams.

Fleetingly she wondered if there was a reason other than the tea that made everything seem so familiar. Reincarnation? Racial memory? Or just her drugged state? Whatever it was, the sensation of déjà vu was powerful, and she wasn't sure whether she had read all about the ritual or whether in some supernatural way, she remembered it.

Whatever the basis for her knowledge, she knew with cold, clear certainty that the ancient ritual included the dismemberment of the king, symbolizing winter and the death of the world. And after that, the sacrifice of the goddess so that she could return to earth to be reborn as spring.

A rhythmic pounding began, so soft that at first she thought it was her pulse pounding in her ears. Then the sound became louder, thudding, thudding, thudding, until she thought she couldn't stand it a moment longer. The hypnotic cadence continued, and she saw one woman was beating a drum. The insistent cadence was endless and one by one the women increased the speed and intensity of their dance around the fire.

As she watched, fascinated, Brianna nearly forgot her own danger. She was seeing something from the farthest reaches of human history as the women swayed and jumped wildly in the archaic, long-forgotten steps. Or had they ever been forgotten? Had women performed them all along, the mystery hidden from the male world?

"They look like a bunch of witches," Matt murmured.

"I guess they've been called that," Brianna agreed.

She must be in some kind of dream; nothing like this could be happening. Primitive chants coming from the lips of women who only yesterday had been watching soap operas! She had seen those long slender fingers, which were now beating the repetitive pulsation on an ancient skin drum, just yesterday pouring tea from a porcelain pot!

Matt turned to her and even in the shifting moonlight she could see the depth of tenderness in his eyes. "Don't worry, Brianna," he said softly, "we'll get out of this. But I've got to tell you now. I love you."

She stared back, her heart too full for speech. The danger they faced was unimportant compared to those three words. She could face whatever happened, bear whatever must be borne, secure in the knowledge that he loved her.

"Oh, Matt," she breathed.

He held her fiercely with his gaze, pouring his soul out to her in a look of incredible tenderness. For that moment they were alone, surrounded by a nimbus of love, secure in an impenetrable citadel for two.

"I would have told you anyway," he said. "I've wanted to tell you, ached to tell you, but I guess I was afraid."

"Afraid?"

"That you didn't—couldn't—love me."

Didn't love him! How long had it been since she had accepted the knowledge that she loved him with a deep passion that sometimes seemed more than her body could hold? She had known she loved him, even as she had believed that love had no future, but now she wasn't sure either of them had a future anyway. She could tell him. That would at least make their last hours together easier.

As she leaned toward him to whisper the words she became aware of a change in the frenzied dancers. Startled, her reply froze in her mouth. The women were enlarging the circle, coming closer and closer to the two captives. Darting and dipping, they lunged around the two, in front, in back, while they kept up a wild, eerie wail that matched the rhythm of the drum. It crept right into the marrow of her bones.

Although the women seemed to be in a trance, ignoring the captives except for the wild dance, she recognized some now that they were closer.

"Matt!" she whispered hoarsely. "That's Louise!"

"So it is." She heard him suck his breath in sharply. "Somehow, I never expected to see her here."

She watched the woman closely, aware of something out of place. Although Louise twirled and lunged like the rest of the women, there was something subtly different about her actions. Something more controlled, more purposeful.

The wail increased to howls that seemed to bounce off the surrounding mountains, as the women spun around them at a maddening pace. Occasionally a woman, perhaps worn out by the frenetic pace, stopped by the container to down another cup of the liquid, then returned to the gyre.

The tempest seemed to lose all semblance of order as the women wove in and out between the pillars of stone. Glimpses of their faces showed eyes wild with a strange ecstasy, mouths open and foaming. Brianna knew there was no reaching them now. They were in the grip of something older and more primitive than anything she could conceive.

She shuddered. That feverish trance was probably necessary if they were to work themselves up to the pitch where they could tear apart another human being.

"How long are they going to keep this up?" Matt asked, his gaze leaving Brianna for an instant to take in the women.

Brianna glanced at the sky. The moon was approaching the zenith, and that was probably when the main event would take place. "Not much longer, I think." She forced the words through dry lips. "If you have any ideas, it's time you came up with them."

"Just be ready," he said.

She couldn't imagine why the words comforted her. It was hard to see what Matt could accomplish, but at least the trust she had in him kept her from passing out from fright.

Suddenly she was aware of one of the women coming closer and closer as she danced, her gyrations performing smaller and smaller circles around them. Louise.

She caught a glimpse of the woman's face, and her heart nearly stopped. The eyes were calm and steady; rational, she thought. Whatever was affecting the other women didn't seem to have touched her.

With a swift, darting motion Louise moved behind them. Out of the corner of her eye Brianna saw her twirl behind Matt, saw the flash of a knife in the moonlight, and she froze. Was this the end?

Oh, God, Matt, I love you. If we just get out of here we'll think of something. I'll never let you go. The words ran through her mind like a litany of hope.

Then she sagged with relief. Matt was still very much alive as Louise swept again out into the center of the dervish, then whirled back to circle around Brianna. She felt the knife cut swiftly through the cords at her wrist, and then Louise was back among the women, her whispered words lingering behind her. "It's all I can do."

"Matt," she whispered hoarsely, "can we get out of here!"

"We're still tied to the stone pillar," he said. "If we try to get loose from that they'll be on us like a cloud of locusts. But we've got a chance, now. Keep alert. Follow my lead."

Keep alert! With the drug turning everything into a dreamscape! But she would try to fight its effects.

Suddenly, as though halted by a giant hand, the women were still. They stood like dark green statues, eyes elevated to the moon as it reached the zenith. They seemed to take a deep, collective breath, then, as though propelled by one burning need, they moved toward the captives.

"Keep your hands behind you!" Matt ordered. "Let them think we're still tied."

"Okay..."

It was all she could do to force the one word between her frozen lips as she watched the advancing horde. Then Alta, her eyes in such deep shadow that they looked like black pits, stopped directly in front of her. Terrified, Brianna couldn't take her eyes away from the tall, gaunt woman. Alta appeared carved from stone herself, ageless, implacable, menacing, as she stared back. There was no recognition in her face as she made a commanding gesture.

Immediately a woman cut the ropes that bound the two captives, and several others grasped their arms. *Don't let them know we're untied.* Matt's words rang in her mind, and Brianna kept her wrists crossed behind her.

Perhaps it was the flickering light; perhaps it was the fact that the women were beyond all rational thought; but it worked. They didn't check the bonds, but pushed them roughly toward the block of stone in the center of the circle.

Brianna thought she had reached the limit of terror, but when she saw the stone, raised from the ground on four blocks of granite, about ten feet long and four feet wide—the stone where she had sat while Alta dictated her harmless little stories—she knew that terror was limitless. Why hadn't she recognized it before for what it was—a sacrificial altar?

As the women placed them side by side on the stone, she managed to twist her head toward Matt. "I think it's about time you came up with whatever you have in mind."

He managed a mirthless grin. "Don't worry; there'll be a slip, a moment when we can make our move."

Alta stood to one side, her arms raised above her as though she were invoking a spirit, and began to speak in a hypnotic, toneless voice.

"Danu, Mother of us all, White Goddess who rides the darkness of the night sky, we await your sign. Your king awaits to cover you with his shadow. The shadow of death that always comes so that you may be reborn in glory."

The chant continued, and Brianna could no longer make out the words. Then she was aware the incantation had ceased, Alta was raising her hand...

"Now!" Matt said.

Before she could respond she heard a low, rumbling sound like a far-off ocean. Matt, halfway off the stone, paused, and Alta, the knife still poised above them in her hand, jerked her head around to see where the sound originated.

Immediately the sound became a loud, ominous roar. Then everything happened so quickly Brianna became completely disoriented. The meadow moved and swelled toward them like ocean waves. A high wind rushed against them. The ground beneath her bucked and jolted.

She couldn't even scream as the mountain that jutted above them rumbled, and a column of flame leaped from its peak into the moon-clad night.

"The volcano!" Matt grabbed her hand and pulled her from the stone slab, but terror and the drug were too much. She couldn't stand; she collapsed.

Then, with a sound like all the fabric in the world tearing, the earth cracked open. Brianna couldn't take her eyes from the sight as a seam started in the far part of the meadow, then moved toward them, widening as it came, until a giant crevasse opened nearly at their feet.

The scene was one of utter confusion; she heard women screaming, saw stones toppling, the roar of the "volcano" behind them penetrated even her numbed awareness.

Matt, with barely a glance around, scooped Brianna from the ground, threw her over his shoulder and began running.

He was panting when they reached the shelter of the trees. Depositing her on her feet, he looked back over his shoulder at what was left of the druid's circle.

After the violence of the earthquake, the aftermath of silence was nearly as ominous. His words rang loudly in the night.

"Can you stand?"

"Yes. Matt, what happened?" She clung to his shoulder, still unsteady on her feet.

"An earthquake," he said briefly. "A big one, and an opportune one."

"But the flame from the mountain?"

"It looks like the old girl woke up. But I don't think it's serious. All I saw was one belch of flame."

Her legs were wobbly but serviceable, and Matt's arm was warm and solid beneath her hand. She took a quivering breath.

"What now?"

"We get out of her as fast as we can," he said. But he made no move to leave. Instead he turned slowly toward her. In the darkness under the sheltering trees she couldn't make out the features of his face, but the pain in his voice sent a tremor all through her body as he pulled her sharply against his chest.

"My God, if I had lost you..." His words faded away into the darkness.

She was keenly aware of his heart thudding against her own, she reveled in the warmth of his body pressed against hers, and in spite of the precarious situation, the devastation around them, she felt secure.

A howl from the open meadow broke the intensity of the moment. Quickly Matt gripped her hand and they plunged deeper into the forest.

"We'd better hurry," he said, his voice grim. "As high as those women are, I don't think a mere earthquake will stop them."

They hardly spoke as they moved swiftly through the forest; Brianna had very little breath left as she tried to match Matt's strides. It wasn't just the fast pace that exhausted her, either. The effects of the drug lingered, making it seem as though she were walking slowly through deep water instead of running as fast as she could.

Matt paused and looked back over his shoulder, and cursed. The women were following, thrashing through the underbrush behind them. Brianna shuddered, knowing how angered they must be at the escape of their prey. Angered and perhaps frightened. Would the goddess punish them for the loss of the sacrifice?

Matt caught the look on her face and saw that she was nearly at the end of her strength. Without a word, he picked her up and dived back into the trees.

Sighing, she put her arms around his neck and lay her head on his broad shoulder. His strong arms held her securely as he moved through the trees with the surety of a mountain lion.

Finally they reached his house, and Matt deposited her gently on the stone steps while he opened the massive door.

"At least it's still standing," she murmured.

He glanced briefly at the log structure. "It would take a pretty good shaker to knock this down. But there's probably some minor damage."

They walked inside and as Matt locked the door, she reached for a light switch, not really surprised when nothing happened. Of course the electricity was out. The moonlight entered in a faint glow, however, and she surveyed the living room. There was indeed some damage: windows broken, shelves overturned, but even so it offered a strong refuge from their pursuers.

On wobbly legs, she walked to a sofa and sank into its comfortable depths. She would sit here until her legs stopped shaking.

"Will they come after us here?"

"I don't know," Matt said, pushing a large cabinet in front of a broken window. "I'm not sure that I know anything anymore."

"We should call the police—or somebody."

Nodding, he walked to the phone, held it to his ear, then replaced it. "The phone lines are out."

He turned to her and gave her a gentle smile. "It may be a long night. How about making us something hot to drink?"

"How?"

"Emergency propane. You'll find the stove works. And Brianna," he said, giving her his familiar wicked grin, "no tea, okay?"

Matt had completed securing the house and lit a roaring fire, when Brianna returned to the living room with a pot of coffee. They sat cross-legged on the rug in front of the flames drinking the hot black liquid.

Glancing at the table, Brianna saw a gun and shuddered. "You do think they'll come here?"

"I don't know," he said. "I certainly don't want to use that gun. Those are my friends out there—or used to be." He ran his free hand gently over her hair, pressing her head onto his shoulder. "But I'm not taking any chances with our safety."

The drug was wearing off at last; she was much more clearheaded, and the lethargy was lifting. She snuggled against Matt; here in his house, with the coffee, the fire, what they had just experienced seemed impossible.

He stroked her arm gently, lovingly. The warmth of his body enveloped her in a lovely cocoon as she felt his heartbeat, took in the aroma of his heated skin. She didn't want to move, didn't want to think. She just wanted to relax in this moment, with no past, no future.

Matt's terse voice brought her out of her reverie.

"Brianna, we have to talk."

"Now?" She shifted her weight to snuggle a little closer.

He bent to place a kiss on the top of her head. "Now. I think I would have told you anyway—couldn't bear the thought of your going away."

"You had a strange way of showing it," she interrupted.

He ignored her words. "But when I realized the danger you were in tonight—that you might be lost to me forever—I knew I could never bear to part from you. I love you, Brianna. I want you to stay here in Hope with me."

He loved her! He'd said it before when they both thought they might never survive the night, but this was different. His words seared through her, and such joy welled up in her heart that she was momentarily speechless.

Matt, misinterpreting her silence, went doggedly on. "I thought a lot about this before tonight—about how we'd live, what we'd do. You know I'm starting a business in Boise, and that's near the university. You could get a job there; we could live here in the summer—"

"Matt, wait," she said breathlessly. "We're going so fast. Are you asking me to marry you?"

"Well, I don't expect you to live with me otherwise. We Stuarts always get married," he said smugly, giving her a squeeze. "Then we get more little Stuarts to keep the logging going."

"Is *that* why you want to marry me? To get more little Stuarts?"

"Don't—don't you want children?" He sounded so forlorn that she almost regretted her teasing.

She'd never thought much about children. Now, having Matt's children seemed the most desirable thing in the world. But her work—she'd worked too long to just throw it away...

"Yes, of course I want children. Someday..."

"I'm not suggesting we get started right now." He tightened his grip. "The reason I want to marry you, darling, is that you are the most beautiful, desirable, wonderful woman I can ever imagine, because you're an intelligent, courageous lady—and because I'm crazy, wild in love with you."

Suddenly a sound came from outside the house and they both froze. She thought she detected the murmur of voices and something scratching against the house. She shuddered; the women must have followed and were lurking outside.

Matt rose swiftly and peered out into the darkness, then came back to her side. "I can't see anything, but I guess we'd better keep a lookout."

"They wouldn't try to break in?"

"Not much chance they could if they tried, but I don't want to take a chance. The craziness and the stuff they've been drinking will have worn off by tomorrow, but maybe we'd better keep our eyes open tonight."

The time for personal conversation was over. As the night wore on, they slept in snatches, and Brianna was glad Matt didn't bring up the subject of marriage again. It wasn't that she didn't love him; she knew she did, with all her heart, but she wasn't at all sure that love was enough. The problem of Matt's protectiveness and her response to it loomed larger than ever.

She thought about the night they had just been through—Matt's insistence that he go with her, the way he carried her bodily from the druid's circle. She couldn't fault it; she had needed him desperately and she had been deeply glad that he had been there.

That was the crux of it. She didn't want to be that dependent on anyone. She had turned everything over to him, relying on his strength, following his guidance. It had felt good and right, and it had been. But she distrusted her reaction. Matt's nature was to take control, order her around, do what he thought was best, and she wasn't at all sure she would have the strength to resist even when she should. She might lose her identity, and Matt might even lose his regard for her.

No, she had to remain her own person and she wasn't sure Matt's strong, virile personality would let her do that. She was almost glad for the interruption that had put off her decision.

When dawn came they took a final look out the window; nothing moved in the delicate gray light, and with a sigh of relief Brianna lay down on the couch for some much-needed sleep.

Matt covered her gently with a blanket, then lay down on the couch opposite her. The last thing she saw before she closed her eyes was his steady loving gaze. Tomorrow...tomorrow she would have a lot of decisions to make.... She fell into a deep, dreamless sleep.

Chapter 16

Matt, already dressed for the day in jeans and a clean flannel shirt, stood beside the couch looking down at Brianna's sleeping face. His heart contracted painfully. She looked so vulnerable lying there with her eyes closed, long lashes brushing her cheeks, delicate lips slightly open, and her hair a tangled mass of gold on the pillow. Vulnerable and incredibly desirable.

He glanced at his watch, then back down at Brianna. It was nearly noon and he had been up several hours, assessing damage and talking to his crew who, one by one had come by to talk to him—apologetic, sheepish, eager to re-establish the old rapport. For them the crisis was over; he knew they were fully aware of everything that had happened and, although they would never speak of it, were trying to make amends.

They also brought him news of the extent of the eruption and the quake; as he had surmised, the damage was localized. The volcano had belched flame several times, then become quiescent, and although the crevasse in the earth remained it was possibly the only lasting result of the earthquake. A few houses had been shaken, windows broken, but that was about it.

Soon geologists and government people would descend on Hope to make their own survey; he didn't look forward to the officials who would swarm over the mountain and make their pronouncements, the media who would wring every ounce of drama they could from the event. Still, for this little isolated moment in time Hope still belonged solely to the people of Hope.

Gently he reached down to pull the blanket up over her bare arms. She was exhausted, poor darling, and probably the lingering effects of the drug also contributed to her deep sleep.

He paused, his heart twisting painfully in his chest as she opened her golden eyes and looked up, a tremulous smile on her face.

"Matt?"

"I'm right here, darling." Where I'd always like to be, he said silently.

She glanced at the sun that was pouring in through the windows, painting gold bars on the rug, and struggled to a sitting position, pushing her hair back from her sleep-softened face.

"My goodness, it must be late. What time is it?"

"Around noon. The power's back on, telephone is working. Why don't you take a shower to wake up, and I'll fix you some breakfast?"

"You look like you've been up a while. Have you had any reports about damage?"

He filled her in quickly on what he had heard, then again suggested she have some coffee. Her eyes were still shadowed with fear, and he wanted to return the situation to normal as soon as possible. Putting his hand gently on her shoulder, he squeezed slightly, achingly aware of the delicacy of her bone structure. "Everything's all right."

She took a long, quivering breath and put her hand over his. "Matt, did it really happen? It all seems like a dream—and yet horribly real at the same time."

"It happened, all right," he said grimly, "but it's over. I don't doubt the Daynew women are feeling about as ridiculous as it's possible to feel."

He took a long look around his familiar living room, thinking how much had changed since they left it the night before. There was the horrifying ritual, of course, providing him a glimpse into the dark depths of the Daynew, a glimpse he had never had before. The enigmatic statements in his great-grandfather's journal were a little more clear; for instance, old Caleb Stuart's statement that if he had to face what the Daynew men faced, he'd be polite, too, now made sense. Matt's lips curved in a wry half smile.

Yet the biggest change, the earth-shattering change, was in his feeling for Brianna. He had loved her before, but last night, faced with the possibility of her death—he hardly thought about his own—he had realized he could not live without her. All that meant anything to him in life was wrapped up in this one lovely, courageous, unique woman. He loved her—fiercely, completely, with every fiber of his being.

He was also very much aware that she had not said she loved him, and had not replied to his proposal. It burned in his gut and he clenched his jaw, his lips thinning to a determined line; he absolutely would not lose her.

But now wasn't the time to reopen the subject. Completely entranced, he watched her stretch like a tawny cat and then reach out with her long legs to slide her feet into her shoes. As soon as she had eaten he would demand an answer. No, he would demand a *favorable* answer!

A few minutes later they sat together at the pine table in the roomy kitchen while Brianna drank coffee and devoured scrambled eggs and toast, and Matt just devoured her with his eyes. In her crisp blouse and fresh jeans, her hair still damp from the shower, she made him ravenous for something other than food.

Impulsively he reached to cover her hand with his, then paused at the sound of the knocker at the front door. Another of his crew, probably, here to make amends.

When he opened the door a quick frown wrinkled his face and he nearly slammed the door shut. Diana, clad in a shirt and jeans instead of the robe he had last seen her in, stood on the step, her gaze fixed unwaveringly on his face.

"What do you want?" He hoped his voice conveyed half of his anger.

"I came to see Brianna."

"I doubt she wants to see you—at least right now. Not unless you have a pretty good explanation—"

"It's all right, Matt. I'll talk to her." Brianna inched around his tall frame that effectively blocked Diana's entrance. "Come in, Diana."

Scowling, Matt unconsciously clenched his fists as Brianna smiled at the visitor. Didn't she realize what had nearly happened to her? How could she treat this visit so coolly?

"No," Diana said, still standing on the step, "I won't come in. Alta wants to see you. Can you come?"

"No, she cannot!" Matt grasped Brianna's arm and pulled her against his side, outrage burning within him at the sheer gall of the woman's request. "You can ask that after what happened last night?"

Diana ignored his outburst. Her gaze caught and held Brianna's eyes in a long, level look. "You will be completely safe, I promise. But she must see you. It's important."

"She's not going," Matt growled.

Still Brianna said nothing as she and the Daynew woman looked deeply into each other's eyes. Some kind of communication passed between them, Matt was sure, but he didn't know what it was. A thin sheen of sweat covered his forehead, and he raised his fist to wipe it off. He didn't know what those women had in mind this time, but he would not allow Brianna to be duped. He had to take care of her, now more than ever when she was so doubly precious to him.

"I don't know..." Brianna said, her eyes still assessing Diana's face as though she could read her intent.

"Please," the woman said. "She must see you. She is ill; she can't come here. But she must talk to you."

As Brianna wavered, fear and anger fought in Matt for supremacy. Didn't she realize how much he loved her? How narrowly she had escaped death last night? To even think of going to see that old witch was crazy. It was—

"All right," Brianna said. "I'll go."

"You will not!" Matt exploded. "I won't let you go. If you don't care about your own safety, I do—"

He broke off as Brianna turned to him with a challenging look. "You won't let me go? It's my decision."

"Brianna," he said desperately, "think about it. I just can't allow it... what if something happened again?"

"It won't," she said calmly. "I trust Diana. She assures me there's no danger."

"That's what they said before."

She paused and looked him straight in the eye. "Matt, I have to go. I have to talk to Alta, finish this thing. I can't just drop it like this."

"Brianna, I don't like to insist, but it's for your own good."

"My own good?" Now there was an angry glint in her eyes. "Matt, I'm an adult. I think I have to be the judge of that."

He started to voice an angry protest, then hesitated, suddenly aware that there was more involved here than whether Brianna went to see Alta. It had somehow become a battle of wills; Brianna was telling him that she was her own person and would make her own decisions.

Could he allow that? Or rather, accept it, when it meant she might get into more trouble than she could handle? Wasn't it his responsibility to protect his woman, guide her, keep her safe? If he didn't, what kind of a man was he?

Her eyes didn't leave his as he wrestled with his need to take care of her, protect her, and yes, he admitted—control her. His internal debate was agonizing. He couldn't afford to lose her; she meant too much to him. Yet as he looked into her steady, golden eyes, he suddenly knew quite clearly that if he imposed his will on her she was lost to him anyway.

He gave a long, shuddering sigh. "Of course it's up to you. Just—be careful, sweetheart."

It was almost worth the gut-wrenching turmoil to see the warm glow leap into her eyes and watch her tremulous smile, and he felt a sudden surge of pride. This was no shrinking violet; she was a courageous, independent woman, and he admired her for those very qualities. Maybe, as she had said to him before, it wasn't necessary to *always* be the strong one.

She darted toward him and kissed him lightly on the lips. "Don't worry, I'll be back soon."

He kept a silent vigil from the doorway until she and Diana disappeared into the line of trees, aware of a hard, cold knot in his gut. She had better come back—and safely—or there would be holy hell to pay. He guaranteed it.

Brianna hesitated at the door to Alta's cottage, a little afraid now that she was actually here. Diana had said little on the trek through the woods, uncharacteristically subdued, and Brianna was silent, too, nearly equally concerned with Alta's request and with Matt's reluctance to let her go.

Perhaps he was right; maybe it was foolhardy to come here alone after what had transpired last night. Yet, in that moment when she and Diana had looked into each other's eyes, she had felt intuitively that she had nothing more to fear from the Daynew women.

But even so, had she been right to disregard Matt's very reasonable concern? She knew she loved him, and even had to admit that his strong drive to guard and protect her was part of what made him the man she so desperately loved. Certainly last night that quality had served them both very well. She hated to think what would have happened if he hadn't insisted on accompanying her, and it was his strength that had enabled them to escape.

So why today had she felt that absolute necessity to assert herself? Perhaps because Matt's possessiveness was just a little too seductive? It would be so easy to relax, float in his love, let him make the hard decisions. It wasn't so much his will to dominate that bothered her as it was her inclination to let him.

Diana moved around her, pushed open the door and then stepped back. Brianna stepped inside and heard the door close softly behind her. A little chill ran down her back; once more she was alone with Alta.

Her eyes surveyed the dim little room, slowly adjusting from the bright glare of the sun. In spite of her brave words, she wasn't entirely certain there was nothing to fear. Her instinct had told her so—but her instinct had occasionally been wrong.

"Come here . . . please."

She jumped at the sound. The voice was so weak that for an instant Brianna didn't realize it was Alta. Then she glanced to the corner of the room where the woman lay in a narrow bed, her head propped up on several pillows.

She gasped again, this time with surprise. It was Alta all right, but an Alta so changed she hardly recognized her. The strong, vital priestess of the Daynew now looked sick and frail and old.

Inching closer, she realized that her first impression was correct. The glow was gone from the woman's skin; it was now an unhealthy gray, the burning eyes were dull, and the hand that clasped Brianna's was surprisingly weak.

"Thank you for coming, dear. I hoped—but I wasn't sure." The words came painfully in little gasps, and Brianna was absurdly sorry. The powerful, autocratic woman Brianna had known was gone, and in her place was a frail old lady.

"You wanted to talk to me," Brianna said softly.

"Yes. I wanted to explain." Alta sighed, and Brianna saw pain and loss in her eyes. "They were right, all those who said the goddess was gone. I know that now. But I truly thought—I was sure you were the goddess."

Brianna tried to interrupt, but the woman raised her hand, and for an instant she was the old imperious Alta.

"No, I must tell you everything. I was so sure. I was sure you knew it, too, but for some reason just weren't admitting that you were she. All the signs were right. The trembling earth, your eyes, you resembled the statue. And you wanted to know all our history. I thought you were preparing us for the time you would go into the earth and rise again."

One look at Alta's face, and she knew the woman was shattered by the knowledge that the goddess had not returned.

"When did you decide I wasn't the goddess?" she whispered.

"The earth opened at the wrong time," Alta sighed. "There was no question about when it should open to receive you. It was clear in all the old stories. First, the king was to die, then the goddess would give herself over to be sacrificed. At that time the ground would open, and you would both descend into the ground."

She turned to Brianna with a disconsolate look. "But the ground opened first. It opened too soon. And I knew then we were wrong. You weren't Danu, who had guided us for so long..."

She turned away and looked unseeingly out the window, and Brianna felt an unaccountable pang of sorrow. The dream was gone. The dream that had sustained Alta through the years, given her strength when others dropped away from the belief and accepted the white man's god, had proved false.

"The other women?" Brianna asked softly. "Did they think I was the goddess, too?"

"Oh, I had to convince them," Alta said. "At first, they didn't believe, but as the signs increased, they did. All but Louise."

"Louise." Brianna felt a burst of gratitude for the woman who had apparently stood alone against the others. If Louise hadn't managed to cut the cords on their wrists, things might have ended differently. "Why didn't she go along with the rest of you?"

"Because of Chad." For a moment the old light flamed in Alta's eyes, and her words were contemptuous. "We weren't sure at first who should be the king. Louise knew it might fall by lot to Chad, and she did everything she could to stop it."

"You finally convinced her," Brianna said softly, remembering Louise's drugged state and the bruises on her arm.

"Not really. Oh, she pretended, but I know now who cut the bonds from your wrists," Alta replied.

"That's why the men tried to scare me away, too," Brianna continued. "They knew one of them might be chosen."

Alta waved a dismissive hand. "The men were cowards." She fell back on the pillow, her face even paler than before. "But it's over now; the new gods have won. The White Goddess, our beloved mother, is no more. She will not come again."

The tone was so bleak that Brianna felt a surge of sympathy. Even though this woman had tried to kill her, she couldn't help feeling sorry for her. Everything she believed in had shattered, and in the process, she was shattered herself. Brianna knew Alta would never be the same. Gone was the autocratic, half-feared elder priestess of the Daynew. Now she was merely a feeble, impotent old woman, whose reason for living had gone with the goddess.

"Will you still tell me stories?" she asked, squeezing the old woman's hand. It felt cold and wrinkled, the bones pushing through the parchmentlike skin.

A faint smile wreathed Alta's face. "If you want me to."

Then the old head slumped and Brianna realized the woman was asleep. She left the cottage, thoughtful and obscurely sad.

But her somber mood didn't last long. Matt was waiting. She lifted her head, shaking off the depression and feeling elation course through her veins as she ran back through the woods. There was something she must do immediately. She hadn't told Matt she loved him, hadn't said she'd marry him, because she hadn't been absolutely sure. She hadn't known whether she could live with his possessiveness. But he had trusted her enough to let her make her own decision. She realized how much strength it had taken for a man like him to let go, to allow her to be her own person, and the knowledge made him unbearably dear.

He was standing at the door. She flew up the steps and into his arms, her breath coming in harsh gasps. His arms closed around her as though he would never let her go, and she hoped he never would.

Finally he held her away a few inches so he could look into her eyes, and she read the depth of his devotion in his clear blue gaze.

"You're all right," he breathed.

"Never better," she managed to gasp.

He swooped her up in his arms and carried her into the living room, depositing her on a couch, then sitting so close to her that their bodies touched from shoulder to thigh. He never loosened his grip, holding her as though she were his salvation.

"You have a question to answer," he said.

"I know—"

He broke in. "I know you think Hope is isolated. And there are probably a lot of things that will be difficult for you. Before you decide, I think there are a lot of things you should consider. Are you going to maintain in your thesis that the Daynew are the lost Tuatha de Danann?"

She looked at him in astonishment. How could she think of that when his lips were only inches away and the hard length of his body burned all along her side? When she had just realized the depth and complexity and solidity of the man she loved?

"The Tuatha de Danann . . . no, I don't think I'll mention my idea in my dissertation. I'm certain myself that's the case, but I have to have so much more documentation.

There's so much more work to be done, so much more to find out..."

"Exactly," he said triumphantly. "And where will you do that work, if not here? You have a lifetime of study ahead of you, don't you agree? You'll—"

"Matt."

"I'm sure you can get a job in the anthropology department at Boise State University, and summers you can complete your work on the Tuatha de Danann, and—"

"Matt, you don't have to convince me. I love you."

He sat absolutely still. Then an expression of such wonder came over his face that she thought her heart would burst with tenderness. He put his hands on her shoulders to hold her away a few inches so he could see for himself the truth in her eyes. Then he crushed her against his chest as he lowered his lips to her eager mouth.

Finally he managed to move away far enough to murmur a soft question. "Then you'll marry me?"

"I wouldn't expect to live with you otherwise," she murmured. "We Royces always get married."

He kissed her again, reverently and thoroughly, and for an endless time nothing existed but her and Matt and their love. She had no idea how long it was before they pulled apart, shaken, but merged in some deep elemental way that she knew would last forever.

Forever. The thought had been niggling around in her mind, and now she mentioned it to Matt.

"You know, one thing still bothers me about what happened. Why did everything about the ceremony seem so familiar? It was almost as though I'd lived it before...."

"The subconscious mind can dredge up a lot of things, and you don't always know the source. You'd read everything about those rituals; they really were familiar to you. And then the drug made you hallucinate, I imagine."

"I suppose that's it." And it probably was. Not racial memory, not reincarnation. All perfectly explainable and understandable.

Yet the costume had seemed familiar *before* she had tasted Alta's drugged tea.

She thrust the thought aside as one of those things she might never know. And didn't need to. She had everything she could possibly want right now, in this life. Why worry about another? She raised her arm to bring Matt's dark head down to meet her seeking lips. Gently she grazed his mouth, ran her lips over his hard jaw, probed the cleft in his chin with her delicate tongue. The slight tremble that ran through his body filled her with exultation and a heady triumph.

"Shall we establish a Stuart tradition, Matt?" she whispered, her breath hot in his ear. "I want to make love to you again, now, right on the rug in front of the fire...."

With a low groan, Matt tightened his grip, and they slid to the floor together.

Matt was nothing if not traditional.

* * * * *

PASSPORT TO ROMANCE SWEEPSTAKES RULES

1. **HOW TO ENTER:** To enter, you must be the age of majority and complete the official entry form, or print your name, address, telephone number and age on a plain piece of paper and mail to: Passport to Romance, P.O. Box 9056, Buffalo, NY 14269-9056. No mechanically reproduced entries accepted.
2. All entries must be received by the CONTEST CLOSING DATE, DECEMBER 31, 1990 TO BE ELIGIBLE.
3. **THE PRIZES:** There will be ten (10) Grand Prizes awarded, each consisting of a choice of a trip for two people from the following list:
   i) London, England (approximate retail value $5,050 U.S.)
   ii) England, Wales and Scotland (approximate retail value $6,400 U.S.)
   iii) Carribean Cruise (approximate retail value $7,300 U.S.)
   iv) Hawaii (approximate retail value $9,550 U.S.)
   v) Greek Island Cruise in the Mediterranean (approximate retail value $12,250 U.S.)
   vi) France (approximate retail value $7,300 U.S.)
4. Any winner may choose to receive any trip or a cash alternative prize of $5,000.00 U.S. in lieu of the trip.
5. **GENERAL RULES:** Odds of winning depend on number of entries received.
6. A random draw will be made by Nielsen Promotion Services, an independent judging organization, on January 29, 1991, in Buffalo, NY, at 11:30 a.m. from all eligible entries received on or before the Contest Closing Date.
7. Any Canadian entrants who are selected must correctly answer a time-limited, mathematical skill-testing question in order to win.
8. Full contest rules may be obtained by sending a stamped, self-addressed envelope to: "Passport to Romance Rules Request", P.O. Box 9998, Saint John, New Brunswick, Canada E2L 4N4.
9. Quebec residents may submit any litigation respecting the conduct and awarding of a prize in this contest to the Régie des loteries et courses du Québec.
10. Payment of taxes other than air and hotel taxes is the sole responsibility of the winner.
11. Void where prohibited by law.

COUPON BOOKLET OFFER TERMS

To receive your Free travel-savings coupon booklets, complete the mail-in Offer Certificate on the preceeding page, including the necessary number of proofs-of-purchase, and mail to: Passport to Romance, P.O. Box 9057, Buffalo, NY 14269-9057. The coupon booklets include savings on travel-related products such as car rentals, hotels, cruises, flowers and restaurants. Some restrictions apply. The offer is available in the United States and Canada. Requests must be postmarked by January 25, 1991. Only proofs-of-purchase from specially marked "Passport to Romance" Harlequin® or Silhouette® books will be accepted. The offer certificate must accompany your request and may not be reproduced in any manner. Offer void where prohibited or restricted by law. LIMIT FOUR COUPON BOOKLETS PER NAME, FAMILY, GROUP, ORGANIZATION OR ADDRESS. Please allow up to 8 weeks after receipt of order for shipment. Enter quickly as quantities are limited. Unfulfilled mail-in offer requests will receive free Harlequin® or Silhouette® books (not previously available in retail stores), in quantities equal to the number of proofs-of-purchase required for Levels One to Four, as applicable.

PR-SWPS

OFFICIAL SWEEPSTAKES ENTRY FORM

Complete and return this Entry Form immediately—the more Entry Forms you submit, the better your chances of winning!

- Entry Forms must be received by **December 31, 1990**
- A random draw will take place on **January 29, 1991**
- Trip must be taken by **December 31, 1991**

3-SIM-2-SW

YES, I want to win a PASSPORT TO ROMANCE vacation for two! I understand the prize includes round-trip air fare, accommodation and a daily spending allowance.

Name______________________________

Address______________________________

City____________ State____________ Zip____________

Telephone Number____________ Age______

Return entries to: **PASSPORT TO ROMANCE**, P.O. Box 9056, Buffalo, NY 14269-9056

COUPON BOOKLET/OFFER CERTIFICATE

Item	LEVEL ONE Booklet 1	LEVEL TWO Booklet 1 & 2	LEVEL THREE Booklet 1, 2 & 3	LEVEL FOUR Booklet 1, 2, 3 & 4
Booklet 1 = \$100+	\$100+	\$100+	\$100+	\$100+
Booklet 2 = \$200+		\$200+	\$200+	\$200+
Booklet 3 = \$300+			\$300+	\$300+
Booklet 4 = \$400+				\$400+
Approximate Total Value of Savings	\$100+	\$300+	\$600+	\$1,000+
# of Proofs of Purchase Required	4	6	12	18
Check One	____	____	____	____

Name______________________________

Address______________________________

City____________ State____________ Zip____________

Return Offer Certificates to: **PASSPORT TO ROMANCE**, P.O. Box 9057, Buffalo, NY 14269-9057

Requests must be postmarked by **January 25, 1991**

ONE PROOF OF PURCHASE

3-SIM-2

To collect your free coupon booklet you must include the necessary number of proofs-of-purchase with a properly completed Offer Certificate

See previous page for details